Butterfly Knife

By

Larry Matthews

A Dave Haggard thriller

Argus Enterprises International, Inc.
New Jersey***North Carolina

Butterfly Knife © 2012 All rights reserved by Larry Matthews.

No part of this book may be reproduced or transmitted in any form or by any means, graphic, electronic, or mechanical, including photocopying, recording, taping, or by any informational storage retrieval system without prior permission in writing from the publisher.

A-Argus Better Book Publishers, LLC

For information:
A-Argus Better Book Publishers, LLC
9001 Ridge Hill Street
Kernersville, North Carolina 27285
www.a-argusbooks.com

ISBN: 978-0-6156706-2-1
ISBN: 06156706-2-8

Book Cover designed by Dubya

Printed in the United States of America

This is a work of fiction. Any similarities to persons living or dead or to actual events is purely coincidental.

Chapter One

It was the feet that kept him awake, not the urine. The stench from the feet was overpowering in the sourness that had fermented on the man. The guy was inches from Dave's nose, just across a trough of sour clothes in the space between the mattresses. Dave Haggard turned over and faced the wall, but it didn't help. The reek of urine came up from his own mattress and he wondered yet again why he thought this would be a good story.

Life On The Street, that's what he wanted to call it. A week with homeless men would give him and his listeners a real understanding of the problem. Washington, D.C., the capital of the free world, the seat of power, the city of monuments and memorials, was also the place where half-insane homeless men begged for change in front of the F.B.I. building and outside Metro stations as over-educated professionals scrambled for a spot on subways so they could get to their jobs at law offices, lobbyists, Beltway Bandits, and other slurpers at the public trough. Shit! Dave Haggard, Ace Reporter, was about to gag on his own story, right here in the shelter. *Why don't they clean the damn mattresses? Who peed here?* He imagined that the others were plotting to steal the few things he had brought with him. His shoe laces were tied to his wrists to prevent them from stealing his shoes.

The man next to him moaned and farted and his eyes opened in a wide stare as he sat up and gazed at Dave. "Are you the word?"

Dave stared back, wondering what the man was talking about. The fellow had not bathed in a very long time, nor had he changed his clothes. Rumor had it that the old guy had maggots crawling around on his skin. The guy was clearly out of his mind. "I'm sorry. What did you say?"

The man leaned closer and looked into Dave's face. "Are you the word?" He was wearing a dirty knit hat and his greasy hair was hanging to his shoulders. His rheumy eyes were red and sad. Something crusty was stuck in his beard. It was hard to tell if he had any teeth.

"No," Dave said.

"Peppers. They call me Peppers. You can tell me your truth." Peppers was about to say something else when a shouting scuffle broke out on the landing outside the door, which had been left open to allow light into the room where eight men were sleeping on the mattresses scattered on the floor of a former Catholic school classroom. Dave heard someone falling down the stairs, or so it seemed, and footsteps running away. Peppers cocked his head but didn't turn around. Another man sat up, looking frightened. The others didn't make a move.

Dave jumped up, careful to take his shoes with him. He walked out onto the landing and saw the priest at the bottom of the stairs, bleeding and trying to speak. Blood was coming from his mouth and he was gasping for air. He was making a moaning, animal-like noise and motioning for Dave to help him. Dave ran down the stairs, bent to the priest, then ran out the front door to find help. Two D.C. cops were driving by, halfway through their shift, hoping for a quiet night. They saw Dave run into the street and wave, pointing to the entrance to the shelter.

"What the hell!" said the driver, pulling to the curb and turning on the patrol car's flashing lights. "What's up?" he asked, thinking that Dave was just another out-of-his-mind drunken bum.

"A guy's been stabbed in the shelter. The priest. He needs help. He might be dying."

The two cops looked at each other. The senior officer, the one riding shotgun, shook his head, thinking of the paperwork that would be involved if a priest in a shelter was stabbed. His first thought, as he opened the car's door, was that he might not get home until noon, eight hours from now.

The officers ran up the stairs, nearly falling on the ice that had built up during the night's cold, and into the vestibule, where two homeless men pointed to the priest, now unconscious. Thirteen minutes later two D.C. Emergency Medical Service members were trying to get Father Phil to breathe again. Father Phil went to his heavenly reward before he arrived at George Washington University Hospital. He had been stabbed ten times; eight of the wounds were in his chest.

Cops filled the building, some in uniform, others in plain clothes. They sealed the exits and tried to herd the homeless men into manageable groups for questioning. It was clear that some of the evening's guests had already gone, driven away by the threat of any contact with the police for any reason. One of the missing was Peppers, a shadowy man under the best of circumstances. He came to the shelter on only the coldest nights. He preferred living under the big bushes near federal buildings, finding a measure of privacy in the tunnel-like warrens between the branches and the stone of the government edifices. But others were gone as well.

By Dave's estimate, about a third of the seventy-odd men in the shelter that night were crazy, another third were unlucky saps whose lives went south and stayed there, and the rest were a mix of criminals on the run, hobos, sociopaths and oddballs of various stripes. More than a few of the men had the shifty eyes of gamblers, swindlers and thieves. Looking around at those who remained to be questioned by the police, Dave saw that the crazy and the unlucky were over-represented, while the shifty had quietly moved on.

One of them was a thin, fit man whose head was covered with a black knit hat. He had used burnt cork to hide his face from glare and notice as he moved down an alley near Connecticut Avenue and into an area that accommodated a small loading dock for one of the buildings that fronted the avenue. A dumpster was set against the wall of the dock and the man used it as a ledge to gain access to an open window. Within seconds, he was inside and the window was shut. Thirty minutes later he walked out onto Connecticut Avenue, just another well-suited businessman getting an early start to his day.

At the same moment, Dave Haggard was answering questions from D.C. Police Captain Daniel O'Neil, a tall, pot-bellied, red haired Irishman who cultivated reporters all over the city if he thought they might one day be useful to him or the department. O'Neil was heading Homicide at the moment and angling for promotion to Inspector. O'Neil worked reporters he thought might be useful and so Dave had been invited for coffee on several occasions in the past. A half-dozen other street reporters in the city had also been subjected to O'Neil's charm and bullshit.

"So, you really are a bum," O'Neil said, laughing at his little joke.

"You guys have been calling us reporters bums for years," Dave replied, looking tired.

"You've been bums for years. Cheer up. You gave your statement to my guys, right?"

"Yeah, I gave it to a couple of guys. Do I need to go downtown?"

"Nah, we're good. I want you to take a ride with me. I got something you might like for your story, whatever you're working on." O'Neil motioned to the door. "Nobody's gettin' any sleep here anyway. Hell, it's almost time to throw you bums out for the day."

Butterfly Knife

O'Neil drove a standard-issue police sedan, a black four-door, rear-wheel drive behemoth with black wheels. The car might as well have had a neon sign blinking "COP". He liked it that way. He was the kind of cop who liked people to know he was around and he cultivated a get-out-of-my-way attitude that he found helpful in street investigations. That he coached his son's Little League team and was an usher at his church in southern Maryland was not widely known to the people he routinely intimidated.

"So, what the hell are you doing sleeping in a place like that?" O'Neil asked.

"I'm researching a story about homelessness in Washington. I have a couple of stations interested in a series of reports about it." Dave worked for a company called Now News, which sold Washington-based stories to radio and television stations across the country. There were dozens of such operations in Washington, most of them one-man or one-woman offices. Now News was staffed by fifty people, most of them young and available cheap. Some were part time and a few were stringers who worked for peanuts. Dave was Now News's ace investigative reporter, mostly aiming at official misdeeds, but occasionally going after gritty street stuff.

"Who gives a shit about street bums?"

"Well, as it turns out, people in Chicago, St. Louis and Seattle think it's a good story. Here we are in our Nation's Capital, handing out quarters to beggars within sight of the Capitol and the White House. Maybe it makes people in Chicago feel better to know that misfortune isn't theirs alone." Dave was trying to be wry and failing at it.

"We got another misfortune for you to look at. Father Phil ain't the only one who got wacked tonight." O'Neil liked to use words like "wacked". He thought it gave him a tough guy image. He drove into an alley off Connecticut Avenue near Dupont Circle where the lights of police cars were making crazy images on the walls of the adjoining office buildings. He pulled up behind a dumpster and motioned for Dave to get out. "We got another priest meeting his maker."

The alley was slick with ice that had formed after the sun went down and the melted snow refroze. It was hard to walk in spots and Dave braced himself against a wall, nearly tripping on a dead rat that lay squashed on the concrete. A man's body was covered by a black plastic tarp but his hands were visible and his body was propped against a building as if he were taking a nap sitting down. Several officers milled around, rubbing their hands together. A police photographer was leaving.

O'Neil talked to a detective who had been smoking in a small alcove, both men motioning to the body and drawing diagrams in the air. Dave wished he had a heavier coat. He also wished he hadn't given up smoking. O'Neil walked over to Dave and shook his head. "Same thing as the other one. Multiple stab wounds. Somebody really wanted this guy to suffer and die. What do you think? Some kind of Catholic thing?"

Dave was surprised that O'Neil would ask him about the crimes. "I'm not a detective. I don't know how you guys solve these things."

O'Neil laughed. "Shit, neither do I, that's why I'm askin' you. Hell, let's get warm. I'll drive you downtown and we can talk there. You want to take a look before we go?"

"What's to look at?"

"See for yourself."

Dave walked over to the body and looked at it. He felt a strange sense of not caring that the man had been alive when the sun went down but would be on a slab when the sun came up. He looked up and took in the details of the alley, grabbing his notebook to jot down the layout of the buildings. A man was standing on P Street, at the end of the alley, looking in. It took Dave a minute to recognize Peppers, who was rubbing his hands together and nodding his head. Dave began walking toward Peppers but the man screamed "Are you the word?" and ran away.

Chapter Two

Homicide was working out of the Fourth District headquarters on Georgia Avenue. It was an ugly building put up during a period in which the city of Washington was seen as the crime capital of America, a doped up, shoot-em-up, gang infested haven for people of color who had nothing but contempt for their white masters. Or so the narrative went. During this period the people who make such decisions designed government buildings to make serious statements about the power of the folks in charge. These buildings were not designed to evoke feelings of faith in government. They were built to evoke feelings of fear. Big, ugly, functional, concrete. In future years no one would thank the powers-that-were for erecting them. The Fourth District Headquarters stood out among the early Twentieth Century buildings along Georgia Avenue for its ugliness and size. And, of course, for the police buzzing in and out at all hours.

Homicide had been moved around from one site to another for years as police buildings were renovated or space was needed for yet another anti-crime initiative. Space at police headquarters on Indiana Avenue near the federal courthouse was always at a premium and given the politics that swirled around the crime issue, and where funding was blowing at any given moment, office space was perishable. And so Homicide was currently on the second floor at 4D, as it was known in the department.

This place could use some paint, Dave thought, *and some new furniture.* The government-grade wooden desk chairs were listing to one side and the linoleum-topped desks were scratched and stained. Wanted posters were tacked to the walls along with department directives and union notices. The ceiling was water-stained and a patch of tile was missing where the ceiling met the outer wall. A window was open because the building's heating system was unbalanced and Homicide and adjoining offices were oppressive, despite the outside cold.

"Welcome to our little corner of paradise," O'Neil said, motioning for Dave to take a seat next to his desk, piled high with forms, newspapers, and old paper coffee cups.

"What a shit hole," Dave said, wiping what appeared to be bread crumbs from the chair.

"Maybe you could do a story about it."

"What can you tell me about the priests?"

"I'm assuming you know Father Phil. He's well known in the homeless community as a guy who likes to buck the system. He got the Archdiocese to open up the old school as a shelter during the winter months. Certain people, I won't mention their names but you can guess, weren't happy about that. The building is on Rhode Island Avenue downtown next door to some high priced real estate and there are those who think the Church would do better to make some money on the place than fill it up with street people. Certain Catholic higher ups and business people, if you get my drift. But you know all that." O'Neil paused to see how Dave was reacting to what he had said. He had enough experience to be able to read people by observing how they behaved during the silences that followed an exchange of information. He wanted Dave to say something. "Did Father Phil know you were a reporter?"

"Yeah. He and a couple of other guys there. I didn't want to spread it around. You never know. But, yeah, he got me a spot in the shelter and agreed to do a recorded interview when I wrapped up the story."

"How'd you find him?"

"Like everybody else. He's in the papers, on television, radio. He's kind of the homeless guy's priest. I called him and we worked it out. He was happy to get some publicity for the shelter. Not this kind, you know, but what he thought I'd report."

"You ever see a dead guy before?"

"I've been a street reporter for a long time, Captain. So, yeah, I've seen dead people."

"So let's play investigator. I'll show you mine if you show me yours. Tell me how you think this went down."

"Somebody in the shelter was pissed off at Father Phil and killed him."

"That's it?"

"What else is there?"

"Motive, opportunity, maybe more than that."

"Okay, what's yours?"

"You could be right. Maybe it was just some crazy guy with a knife. But why did he pick Father Phil? Why not some other homeless guy or somebody on the street? It could be a simple argument gone bad or it could be some kind of hit, a real murder and not some nutcase. And there's the other priest. Same kind of stabbing. Maybe even the same knife." He again studied Dave. "Did you hear anything that might have predicted this? Anybody say anything bad about Father Phil or the Church? Any homeless guys make some suggestion? Anything like that?"

"Nah. Most of them didn't make much sense, to tell you the truth. Some of the others just grumbled about everything or wished they could get some drugs in the shelter. I didn't hear anybody say they'd like to hurt Father Phil or anyone else. Tell me about this other priest."

"We're still nailing down his ID but we think he's a professor at Catholic University. I can't tell you why we think that right now. You can say we're investigating whether the stabbings were linked. We don't have any suspects. We're pursuing leads. You know—the standard press release stuff. PIO will put something out later today. The Archdiocese will issue a statement and maybe close the shelter. You can take that for what it's worth."

"It'll be all over the morning news. I'll have to file something. How about a quick taped interview? Tell me what you just said. It'll give me something I can use."

"Can't do it. Taped stuff has to come from the Chief or the PIO. I'll make you a deal. Let's keep in touch. If you come up with something, call me. I'll let you know what I can. You'll be at the head of the line."

In other words, O'Neil was offering himself as a source in exchange for Dave's notes. It was a devil's deal, one that street reporters often make but hate anyway because it makes them feel like whores. "I'll call you later today."

"Don't call until after five. I need to get some paperwork out of the way and go home to get some sleep. You need a ride?"

"Yeah. I live on Massachusetts near Seventeenth."

They listened to the radio on the way to Dave's building. A reporter for the all-news station was on live, speculating that a street person had gone berserk and killed the city's most beloved homeless advocate. He had soundbites of homeless men stating that the killer should burn in Hell.

Six blocks away, in a fancy hotel just off K Street, a well-suited, fit man sat on a king-sized bed and flicked open a butterfly knife with a speed that made it impossible to see his wrist move or the blade appear out of the handle. The knife had been purchased in the Philippines two years earlier. With a six-inch blade, it was unusually large, but the user found it helpful in his work. A butterfly knife has a split handle that counter-rotates around the blade and in the hands of an expert can be faster than the finest Italian switchblade. In the closed position, the handle covered the blade. The knife in the hands of this man was all steel and well oiled. The blade could cut a floating piece of paper. He could open it with either hand. The man was a priest. He used the knife in place of beads as he said his Rosary, one opening for each prayer. When he was finished, he crossed himself and put the knife into a concealed pocket in his suit jacket, removed all of his clothes, and went to sleep.

Chapter Three

The Philadelphia House was at the edge of Embassy Row on Massachusetts Avenue Northwest, on a block that contained a world-class think tank and a renowned university foreign policy graduate school. A half dozen apartment buildings lined the block, most having been built in the early Twentieth Century and converted to condominiums in the eighties. It was an international block, with the sounds of many languages floating above the sidewalk and into the lobbies of the apartment buildings and centers of higher thinking.

Dave lived in a five-hundred square foot efficiency in the back of the Philadelphia House, overlooking an alley that came in from Seventeenth Street. His primary view was the building's garage, loading dock and service entrance. He lived on the third floor. It was a twelve-story building and, if he had been so inclined, he could have spent his evenings observing others in the nine stories above him in the apartments that looped around to form a kind of courtyard over the roof of the garage. His fellow residents were not always careful to close their blinds. He was not a peeping Tom but he had, on occasion, seen things best left private.

He used his electronic pass to enter the lobby and checked with the desk to see if he had any messages or mail. All of the staff at the desk were male and all were from Cameroon and so spoke French as well as English. They were universally polite and helpful and could be counted upon for small favors. Each was well-tipped at Christmas.

The young man on duty was wearing a blue blazer with a crisp opened collared white shirt. "We missed you. Have you been away?"

"No, just working on a story. Anything for me?"

The man went to a wall of small boxes and found Dave's apartment number. "Yes. You have two items." He handed Dave a letter and a small package wrapped in brown paper. "You look tired. I think you need some rest." The man smiled and his teeth were like bright lights against his very black skin. Each of the Cameroonians had impeccable manners. They all went to Howard University.

"Long night. Thanks." Dave walked to his apartment, opened the door, and flopped onto his bed. He intended to reflect on the night's events and put together a report he could file but he fell asleep as his thoughts drifted from the shelter to his conversation with O'Neil. His cell-phone woke him up an hour later with its 'dobro riff' ringtone, a telltale sign of his East Tennessee upbringing. It took him a minute to dig the phone out of his small backpack. It was his boss.

"You ever think you might want to file a goddam story?" Sid Slackey was old school. He had humped a tape recorder through the jungles of Vietnam and had even jumped with the 82nd in Panama, the only journalist to have talked his way into a parachute in the invasion that toppled Manuel Noriega, a head of state who was also a drug lord. Now he was running Now News as a kind of drill-sergeant-slash-editor. "Let me see if I get this right. You're working on a goddam enterprise piece at shelter when the priest who got you a bed gets killed. Then you sit on it all night so you can get some sleep. Is that about it?" Sid was pissed.

"Yeah, ah, look. I'm working on some angles. So far this is just a local crime story. I don't think any of our stations are interested in a local D.C. stabbing."

"Is that right? Maybe you haven't turned on the morning shows. The national ones. It's all over the national news. Did I mention that it's a national story? Did you think to call the desk? You got any tape?" Audio recording was all digital now but Sid still referred to it as tape.

Butterfly Knife

"No, not yet."

"Jesus Christ! We've got a three o'clock feed going out to all the stations and I need you to file. We can get by without sending anything out this morning since it just happened and we like to tell ourselves that it's better to be right than first, but we can't let the whole day go by without being all over this. Now News! Get it? Now!"

"Look, I've been up all night and I need to get a couple of hours' sleep. I have a police source who'll probably have something for me late this afternoon, so maybe I can have something after that." Dave leaned back into his pillow and rubbed his eyes.

"Not good enough. I need you to put together a background piece on the priest and the homeless issue in D.C. We can top it with the latest from the cops or whatever else comes up during the day. Call the desk when you've got it and come in to record it. Then you can get your beauty rest. I know you're tired and I'm sure your story will be great, but we can't sit on this. Shit, Dave, this is your fucking story." Sid hung up.

Dave made a cup of coffee at his small espresso machine and sat down at his dining table, which also doubled as his desk, and opened his laptop. "Father Phil was a beloved figure on the streets of Washington. Not the Washington of power figures and lobbyists, but the Washington of the down and out…" He had no sound bites so he kept it to two minutes, a minimum time for what the news types called a "think piece". His office was a few blocks away on P Street where he recorded it and he was back in his apartment ninety minutes later.

He was about to sink back into his bed when he noticed the items from the front desk and decided to open them before he went to sleep. The letter was a rejection from a magazine in response to a short story he had written. The package was wrapped and tied with a twine, so he used a kitchen knife to open it. It was a cardboard box, the kind used to contain inexpensive jewelry. Inside was a Rosary of simple black beads. There was a small tag attached to it. It read: Father Phil. Dave spread the brown wrapping paper on the table, looking for a name or a return address. There was nothing except for the block letters that addressed the package to him. He called the desk to ask when it had been delivered and the young man said he didn't know. It was some time during the night. Was this Father Phil's Rosary? Was someone playing a joke? He closed the box.

He lay back and tried to work through his next move when he dozed off, unable to fend off the sleep that had escaped him the previous twenty-four hours.

The Dobro riff woke him up at five. It was O'Neil.

"You got anything for me?" The cop got to the point without any pleasantries.

"I could ask you the same thing." Dave had trouble shaking off the sleep.

"I'm a block away from your place. Meet me out front."

The black sedan pulled into the drive in front of Philadelphia House two minutes later and O'Neil honked his horn as Dave hurried down the corridor, wishing he had time for coffee. The rush hour traffic on Massachusetts Avenue was heavy and the usual backup to Dupont Circle had drivers pounding their steering wheels. A few well-heeled deep thinkers from next door gazed at the commuters as though they were vermin to be avoided. A gay couple walked in front of the car as O'Neil pulled out, flashing his lights and waving his badge. The couple sashayed as if to tease the cop. "You gotta give 'em credit. They got balls," O'Neil said.

Chapter Four

It was a black and white dusk. The sky was overcast in a kind of gunmetal way and the buildings were silhouettes illuminated by the lights in the windows. Small patches of icy snow were tucked against the curbs. It was not the kind of day to lighten one's mood.

"You ever think about moving to Florida?" O'Neil looked up at the sky.

"Isn't that what all cops think about? Moving to Florida?" Dave watched the people on the sidewalks. The foreigners were dressed to the nines, even in the cold. The Americans, or the people who appeared to be Americans, were dressed like students in jeans and overstuffed jackets. The gay men wore scarves.

"Cops think about the day when they don't have to deal with shitbags every day. But Florida would be nice. Fishing and sitting in the sun. No dead priests washing up on the beach."

"Speaking of dead priests, any news?"

"You first." O'Neil gave Dave his most insincere smile.

"I got a package. A rosary with a tag that said 'Father Phil'. It was waiting for me when I got back to my place this morning."

"Did you think it might have been a good thing to call me?" O'Neil had put on his cop face.

"I thought it was a good thing to get some sleep."

"Have you been handling this Rosary, saying your prayers with it?"

"Just when I took it out of the box. I put it back when I saw the tag. I have it with me. Now you."

"We don't have anybody we're looking for right now. We're checking to see if Father Phil had some personal issues, maybe a boyfriend or some things he didn't want anybody else to know about. Whoever did him was pissed. A crime of passion, I'd say. Lots of stab wounds."

"How about the other priest?"

"He's a professor at Catholic. His name is Father Eduardo Pollis. His students called him Father Ed. He taught philosophy and theology. Forty-seven years old. Born in Newton, Massachusetts. He was considered very conservative on church issues, especially women and gays. We're still working on a timeline for how and why he ended up dead in an alley. Other than the stab wounds, we don't have a direct connection to Father Phil's murder."

"Sounds like a press release. What do you have that you haven't given to every other reporter in the city?"

"None of this stuff is on the press release, except for the connection to Catholic."

"I need more than the usual 'police are investigating' crap. You have an ideas on the killer?"

"Just between us girls, yeah. We have a person of interest. There've been similar killings in San Francisco, Chicago and New York. Cops there think it's one guy who's got some kind of religious weirdness involving knives and priests. We're waiting for sketches and possible background info. You can't use any of that right now. Maybe soon." He pulled the car into a spot at 4D. "C'mon up and bring the Rosary. I'll give you something you can use."

4D was busy. A desk sergeant was being harangued by an elderly couple about a street robbery on Georgia Avenue, three handcuffed teenagers were sulking against a wall, a middle-aged man with a bloody nose was waving his arms and announcing that he was not drunk. A crusty-looking black man with leaves in his hair was nodding off as an arresting officer tried to fill out some paperwork.

Butterfly Knife

"Welcome to the work of the people of your Nation's Capital," O'Neil said, waving his arm at the scene on the first floor. He led the way up the back stairs to Homicide. He slipped off his overcoat and suit jacket and sat on the corner of his desk. "Pull up a chair."

Dave sat in an old wooden desk chair that listed to one side and made a creaking sound like a cat being tortured. "How long you guys gonna be here in this dump?"

"We serve at the pleasure of the chief," O'Neil said. "We will be informed of our new digs in due time." He raised his eyebrows as another detective snickered.

"How many cases are you working on right now?" Dave wanted to know how much time the cops could give to the priests' killings.

"Depends how you define it. It's safe to say the events of last night are a top priority right now. You can take that any way you like. May I see the Rosary?" He pulled a pair of medical gloves out of a box in his desk and put them on.

Dave handed it over and watched O'Neil as he opened the box and examined its contents. He handed everything to another detective, who left the room. "Did you touch it?"

"Yes, I took it out of the box and looked at it."

"We'll need to get your prints."

"So, what do you have for me?"

"Do you know anything about the Rosary?"

"Catholics do it. That's about it."

"It's a prayer ritual. For many Catholics it's a mystical meditation and devotion. There are mysteries to meditate upon, twenty of them. There are joyful mysteries, luminous mysteries, glorious mysteries, and sorrowful mysteries. People who say the Rosary meditate on a different set of mysteries every day. These are spiritual mysteries, not the detective kind. We think our knife man might be working on a Rosary thing."

"Why's that?"

"Can't tell you right now. It's only a theory. You can't use that but you can say that we believe we might be looking for a psychotic religious fanatic. How's that?"

"Can I get you on tape?"

O'Neil looked at his fingernails for a long minute. "I'll have to moderate what I say, but, yeah."

Dave took out his recorder and got a two minute interview, most of which was boilerplate press release stuff about how the police were working on leads and asking for the public's help in bringing the perpetrator to justice, the usual bullshit. But O'Neil did make a twenty-second statement to the effect that police were working on a theory that a form of religious fanaticism might be behind the killings. He would not confirm on tape that the murders in D.C. might be tied to such killings in other cities.

Chapter Five

The man responsible for the carnage had been born forty years earlier in Pawtucket, Rhode Island to a Presbyterian minister named Joshua Welsh who believed that all human feelings were a weakness and a French Canadian mother named Blanche, whose mystical Catholicism and French temperament accounted for virtually all of the emotion in the marriage. Their lone offspring was named Darius because his mother read in a magazine that the name meant "good and kingly". His father didn't think names had any meaning, so it was not a concern to him. And so Darius Welsh became the apple of his mother's eye and the object of scorn from his father, who saw the boy as nothing more than a squalling interruption of his composition of sermons, which nearly every member of the flock believed were boring to an extreme.

Darius spent his childhood under the guidance of his mother, who secretly practiced Old World Catholicism in Latin, and his grandmother, a woman who spent her days experiencing visions of the Virgin Mary and who believed that suffering was the highest form of human existence. Darius came to believe that the world was divided between men like his father, cold and disconnected from God, and his mother and grandmother, emotional and spiritual with a raw and sometimes painful connection to Heaven.

He went to seminary at the age of twelve and devoted himself to an unsuccessful attempt at purging his earthly passions, by a self-imposed punishment if necessary. He became a Jesuit and worked for a time as a parish priest in a prosperous area of Connecticut, spending his days listening to the spiritual whining of the comfortable, developing a loathing for all they represented. His evenings were spent in flagellation, whipping himself for his own sinfulness and weakness, a punishment that almost always gave him a shameful release. He became a devoted follower of the Virgin Mary and he believed she appeared to him with messages of love and understanding. It encouraged him to even more extreme forms of worship. He believed he was a mission for Her and he would do anything She asked.

And so, on this day, his back was bloody from fresh wounds and scarred from old ones. The whip, its knotted cords soaked with blood and skin, lay limp over his shoulders. He was losing blood and it troubled him that he could not go on. He worried that he would lose consciousness and be unable to defend himself should they come for him. He concentrated on his breathing, in and out. The pain was exquisite. He felt at one with Christ, who suffered in such a way. Another of the Sorrowful Mysteries. First, Jesus sweats water and blood on the night before his passion. The man could not make himself sweat blood, but he could make others offer such a mystery and he had. Priests, all of them. Ten Hail Marys, each with its own thrust of the knife. *Hail Mary, full of grace.* The priests had died in a glorious mystery. Now he, in this act, was living in the second mystery of sorrow, The Scourging at the Pillar.

When he was able, he would move on to the third mystery. He had marked the chosen one who would be crowned with thorns. He must act soon. They were coming, he knew. They would try to stop him. He glanced behind him and saw the blood pooling on the plastic sheet he had placed upon the bed. He was light headed. He picked up the knife and began his prayers, flicking open the handle to expose the gleaming blade. *I believe in God, the Father Almighty, Creator of Heaven and earth...* The blade was his bead, his concentration, in his Novena of pain and death.

As he bled and prayed, another man sat on a hotel bed four hundred miles north, in the gritty former mill town of Lowell, Massachusetts. He was on the phone.

"You got a lead?"

He paused, listening to the man on the other end of the call explain that this time two priests had been killed.

"Washington? How the hell did he get to Washington? I thought we had eyeballs on him!".

The man on the other end talked for several minutes. The fellow on the bed grew angrier and jumped up, pacing. "We gotta stop him, goddam it! I'm going down there and I'll call you again and I want you tell me where he is. Got that? Jesus, how damned hard can it be to find this guy? He's driving a rare fuckin' car! How many of these things are on the road? Goddam it!"

He packed his small bag and climbed into the ten year old sedan he had picked up from a rent-a-wreck outfit in Lawrence. It was a car that would not be noticed. He headed south, pulled into a truck stop, stomped the cell phone into pieces and threw it into a trash can. He would buy another one in Washington.

His name was Peter Malone and he was a member of The Warriors of Mary, a band of eye-rolling fanatics who believed that they were chosen by The Virgin Mary herself to keep the true faith and protect those who serve it. Malone was tracking one of their own who had gone rogue. *It wasn't supposed to be like this.* He fumed as he drove south on I-95 and he pounded the steering wheel of the car when he was stuck in a traffic backup on the George Washington Bridge. He tried to make up the time in New Jersey but he was pulled over by a cop who clocked him on radar at eighty-three miles per hour. He managed to get away with only a warning ticket. The cop appeared uninterested in the middle-aged man with thin hair and a paunch who looked scared because he had been pulled over in a speed trap. The cop himself was middle-aged and felt sorry for the guy in the old car. He was more interested in the young Spanish punks who had the attitudes and the fancy rims and, he suspected, drugs in their cars. So he quickly filled out the ticket and told the man to watch his speed.

Malone kept up with traffic past Philadelphia and Wilmington and was stuck in slow traffic near Baltimore, but he kept moving, stopping only for gas and fast food at the service facilities along the highway. He did not turn on the radio and he did not pray. He stared at the road ahead and tried to form an image of the man he was chasing dead on the floor of a church, prostrate before a statue of the Virgin, eyes open, arms spread, a leather Rosary around his neck. The image made him happy.

I-95 proper empties onto the Capital Beltway in Maryland, directing travelers south across the Woodrow Wilson Bridge into Virginia to a maze known as the Springfield Interchange and an escape from the Beltway to points as far away as southern Florida. But this man had no interest in those places. He exited the Beltway at I-295, a short freeway into the District of Columbia. He drove the car to Constitution Avenue at Fourteenth Street and stared at the Washington Monument, illuminated by the powerful lights that ignited the patriotic spirit of those who gazed upon the capital's landmarks after the sun went down.

Malone was a veteran of the last days of the Vietnam era and his patriotism was mixed with the cynicism that was left in the wake of the war. What he felt as he gazed upon the obelisk was sorrow for what he believed were the lost ideals of his country. He believed that the Virgin Herself had a hand in the nation's affairs and that she had been ignored and thus the nation was in peril. His twisted logic had produced a belief that he was on a mission to save his country. He saluted the monument and drove up Fourteenth Street until he found a tourist hotel near Thomas Circle. He checked in and went to his room to cleanse himself.

Chapter Six

The car Malone was chasing was under a custom-fitted cover and could not have been seen in any event because it was backed into a small space behind a large utility fan in the far corner of the bottom level of parking garage. The garage was accessed from an alley off K Street, near Vermont Avenue, a short walk from the White House. The garage was a by-the-month facility whose primary customers were the well-heeled who could afford exorbitant monthly fees to see that their expensive machines were pampered while their owners slaved in the wood-paneled offices of those who bought and sold influence in Washington.

The workers who looked after these top-tier nameplates were, for the most part, immigrants whose green cards were suspect. They were familiar with the ways of men in expensive suits, and so they were polite and deferential to the swells who dropped off their rides every morning and picked them up every evening. They were also open to the exchange of cash for off-the-books space in an out-of-the-way spot for a few days. And so the red 1959 MGA roadster was safely tucked away where a casual observer would not see it and come over to take a look at the classic British car.

One of these men, a Colombian named Silvio Estavedo, fancied himself a car buff and spent a good portion of each day admiring the Bentleys and BMWs that were squeezed into the tiers of the parking garage. Estavedo had never seen a classic English roadster. The MG was very small by current standards and he wondered why anyone would want to drive something like that. He took the liberty of removing the cover. He admired its condition and ran his hand over the curves of the fenders, looking for flaws in the restoration. He found none. The shiny red paint was smooth, with no runs or rough spots. The wire wheels glistened. The interior smelled of quality leather. The car was better condition than it had been when it left the showroom decades ago. Estavedo was surprised to see that the car had no door handles and was accessed by a cord on the inside of the door next to the driver. He opened the door and sat in the driver's bucket seat, gazing at the strange controls. The car had a choke and a starter button. There was no radio. He tried to imagine what it had been like to drive such a car through the countryside in the days when it was new.

He closed his eyes and moved the steering wheel, seeing rolling green hills on a bright sunny day in the country. He dreamed that one day he would own a car that would turn heads and that those who admired his car would know that he had become a man of importance like the men who drove the machines that occupied these spaces each day. For now, alas, his days were spent moving the cars of others for a few hundred dollars a month and a bunk bed in a basement in the suburbs. He took a deep breath and opened the door of the MG. He did not see the man who was standing behind a pillar. The man had come to check on his car. It was an hour before anyone noticed that Estavedo was missing or that the small English car was gone.

O'Neil arrived at the park an hour after the body was discovered under some bushes at the base of one of the few Elm trees still standing in Washington. The body had been found by a homeless man who lived in the bushes. The man was not of sound mind and had flagged down a patrol car to report that a burglar had broken into his home. The burglar, he stated to the officers, had no head.

O'Neil got out of his car and saw the dome of the U.S. Capitol three blocks away. He had an odd thought that the victim may have died while he was looking at the seat of the government. He pulled his coat closed against the night cold and walked past the yellow crime scene tape that kept the curious away from the area where officers were taking pictures and looking for evidence. A uniformed officer waved O'Neil to a knot of officers who were huddled at the edge of the bushes.

"We got a body but we ain't got a head," the officer said. He was a thin black man with rimless glasses and a sincere, intense expression on his face. "They're checking the dumpsters."

This part of Pennsylvania Avenue was east of the Capitol and was not along the more famous section that ran west from the Capitol to the White House. This section of the avenue was residential with small storefronts of restaurants and shops. Young white professionals were competing for space with older, black residents who had lived in the area for decades and the neighborhood had a mix of bodegas, coin operated laundries, cutting edge vegan restaurants and bars.

O'Neil looked down the block and wondered how many dumpsters and trash cans would have to be searched and whether any of them contained the head of the man in the bushes. "Yeah, okay. Where are my guys?"

The officer pointed to three men in trench coats who were working their way through the bushes around the body, which was stomach down on some large roots at the base of the tree. The man's hands were tied together and bound to his belt at the small of his back. O'Neil bent down and duck-walked to the body.

"Hey, Captain! Check the hands." The voice came from a detective named Carlisle DuBose, a fourth generation Washingtonian whose family came north when they were freed after Lee's surrender. DuBose was a part time minister in his church and saw the hand of God in the motives of even the most craven criminals. "It is not for us to judge," he was fond is saying, to which O'Neil would laugh and say, "Yes, it is!"

O'Neil moved closer to the body and saw that the dead man's hands had been pierced through the palms, most likely while they were pressed together. The man's shirt was bloody and cut in the shape of a cross.

"We got a mess here," DuBose said, "I see the hand of Satan himself."

"Or somebody acting on his behalf," O'Neil said, bracing himself against the tree as he stood. "What did you find?"

"We're still looking. No weapons or anything obvious. The guy's got some knife wounds but there's no way to know if they killed him or if he died when his head left his body. He appears to be a Hispanic. No ID. Hard to say how old. Not many people used the park today because it's cold, so that might help us. We got a wagon coming to take this guy to the morgue. Maybe we'll find his head around here. By the way, there's a TV truck waiting for a statement from somebody and that reporter Dave Haggard is waiting to talk to you."

"Tell the TV people the PIO will be here to say something if they think it's newsworthy and tell Dave to meet me at my car."

Dave was at the curb, trying to figure out how to use his phone as a recorder when O'Neil walked up. "See this thing? It can do anything a tape recorder can do and I can record an entire story on it, edit it, and file it right from here." He held up the phone.

"Do you know how to do that?" O'Neil looked at the phone like it was a snake.

"No, not yet. I have two days to learn or they'll send me to some guy who'll work with me. That's not why I'm here. Anything new on the priests?"

"Nah, not yet. We think we have a few leads about this and that. I'll let you know."

"This and that?"

"Nothing hard yet. I'm working this one right now. Guy got his head cut off."

"Jesus! Local guy?"

"We don't have an ID on him yet. Wagon's coming and the examiner will take a look at him."

"Got time for a cup of coffee?" Dave motioned to a chain coffee shop across the street.

O'Neil raised his eyebrows and nodded. The two men were silent as they crossed Pennsylvania Avenue and stood in a short line for coffee. They found a small table that had not been cleaned of the previous occupants' cups and napkins. Dave shoved them aside.

"I've been talking to a couple of street reporters in Chicago about the priest killings there. Two of them, like here. Some cops there think it's a serial killer who's gone over the edge for some kind of Catholic nutcase group. Maybe even a church goon squad. You know anything about that?"

"The church has goon squads?" O'Neil laughed with his mouth but not his eyes. "We're hearing the same thing. Just between us girls, we're looking at a group called the Warriors of Mary, some kind of fringe Catholic thing. A source at the FBI says they've heard that something strange is going on but they don't know what it is right now. You can't use any of that."

"They're killing priests?"

"We don't know if it's them or somebody like them. Some of their members are law enforcement types who like their faith a little on the strong side and they pass things on to other cops and like that. It's all very quiet right now. So tell me more about your friends in Chicago."

Dave took a sip of his coffee and wondered how much he should share with O'Neil. He decided that nothing much was on the table at the moment. "You know, street reporter stuff. They get stuff from their cops just like I get stuff from you." He smiled.

"And?"

"These called me when they heard about the killings here. The Church is powerful in Chicago and it's a bigger story there, so they're looking for sidebars and tie-ins to their own murders. We talked back and forth and they said their dead priests are like ours, popular guys who were stabbed multiple times. One guy said they're looking into a Rosary angle because the stab wounds match the prayers in parts of the Rosary. What a sick bastard!"

"Are any of these theories backed by something besides somebody's opinion in a bar?" O'Neil leaned forward and put on his cop face.

"Just passing it along is all. You guys have any theories of your own?"

"We've heard the Rosary theory. We're hoping our friends in the Warriors of Mary can help us out with that one. Or, maybe it's just some sicko who likes to kill priests. I gotta go. The wagon's here to pick up the headless guy. Keep in touch." O'Neil left and stopped traffic by waving his badge at oncoming cars on Pennsylvania Avenue.

Dave picked up his phone and pressed playback on his voice memos. There was the clear voice of Captain O'Neil. Well, it works, he thought, as he stepped into the cold night air. He walked east to a Metro stop and was moving to the escalator when a man stepped in front of his, waving a finger in his face.

"Are you the word?" It was Peppers, wearing a ragged coat with newspapers stuffed into it.

"Do you remember me?" Dave asked. "I was at the shelter when Father Phil was killed."

"Are you the word?"

"What does that mean?"

"I heard the man say it. I heard him say Father Phil would die when he got the word. Are you the word?"

"Who was the man?"

"He looked like you. He wasn't one of us. You're not one of us, either. Are you the word?"

"Have you talked to the police?"

"I don't talk to them. Police are trouble. Here." Peppers handed a book to Dave and ran down a side street and into the dark. Dave stood and watched him disappear until all that was left was the odor of the man. He looked at the book. "The Power of the Novena." It was hardly more than a pamphlet with an imitation leather cover. It fit into the palm of his hand. The pages were stuck together with still-gooey blood.

Chapter Seven

The people who make the news business function, such as it does, are not street reporters trolling bars and alleys for leads or the political reporters who spend their idle time imagining that is it they, not the elected ones, who determine the fate of the nation. Nor is it the screaming news directors or executives who flatter themselves into believing they are the thinkers of the big thought, journalism-wise. The people who make the news business function are a breed apart. They are the assignment managers, line editors, and "desk assistants" who form the background to the daily work of reporting the news.

They don't look like other people. They tend to be pasty, soft, pale people who appear to be one with their office chairs. They have the appearance of men and women who never see the sun or spend time away from the phones, which they work in much the way at conductor works an orchestra. They have developed immunities to other people's egos, which is a basic survival mechanism in a world of me-first reporters and I-know-what's-right bosses.

Gabriel Santoro was such a person. He was thirty-one years old and had a journalism degree from the University of Maryland, a new miles north in College Park. Gabriel was raised in Silver Spring in a family of Italian Americans. Both of his grandparents were born in southern Italy. His father worked for the General Accounting Office and his mother was a teacher. His mother's brother was believed to have something to do with the Mafia in New York. Gabriel had no known bad habits. He didn't smoke and he drank only the occasional glass of wine or can of beer. He was married to a sweet young woman whose life was devoted to the study and teaching of art. He worked fourteen hours a day. He was known as a patient man who could put up with great displays of ego, temper, and other common elements in newsrooms. He made Now News function.

Gabriel was at his desk, staring at his computer screen and on the phone when Dave walked in. Gabriel waved at Dave and beckoned him over. "So, what've you got on the priest thing?"

"Who knows?" Dave was having a down moment.

"Well, I need you to file something. Sid's in a mood, if you know what I mean. Stations are calling and some are pissed off that we're not on top of this. Chicago is thinking of sending their own guys down to tie our killings in with theirs. San Francisco is threatening to find someone else to file on it, although that's pretty stupid given that this is your story, which gets us back to the need for you to file." Gabriel could make demands without making people angry and he was doing it now to Dave. He had a wide, open smile over his friendly eyes and a soft voice that reflected his experience with hysterical people facing deadlines. "I'll get you into a studio in ten minutes if you can make it. Chicago wants to do a q-and-a with you, so you don't even have to write anything right this minute. By the way, you got any tape?"

Dave rubbed his face and wished he still smoked. "Here's the deal…" He spent the next ten minutes explaining what he knew and what he had been told by O'Neil. He ended his briefing by producing the bloody Novena book. "This street guy Peppers gave this to me and ran away. You tell me what I can file." Dave needed guidance and he knew Sid would demand that he use everything, including his surreptitious recording of O'Neil in the coffee shop. That would slam the door on any future access to the Captain and possibly to the entire D.C. Police Department.

"Did you tell O'Neil about this?"

"No, I just got back. I haven't even looked at."

"You know me. I'm not much of a rule breaker. You need to turn this over to the police without getting more fingerprints on it. Can you open it? It looks kind of stuck shut.?

Dave tried to insert a pencil under the cover to lift it up but the sticky blood caused some of the pages to bind and he worried that it would tear, so he gave up. He used his phone to take some pictures of it, front and back. The warmth of the newsroom caused the blood's odor to bloom and Gabriel pulled away. "That thing's going to grow some maggots pretty soon. Let's get it out of here." he returned to his phone and pressed a speed dial button. "Chicago," he said, waiting for the other end to pick up. "Hey, Frank, I got Dave here for the q-and-a on the priest killings. Hang on." He motioned for Dave to go into a studio to record a chat with a reporter for the Chicago station.

Q-and-a's are a cheap and easy way for broadcast journalists to file. A reporter makes himself available to be interviewed by someone else, say an anchorwoman, and simply answer questions about the story. No writing is required for this type of filing, just a notebook with some jottings and the ability to memorize a few simple facts. It's done every day on television and radio. Scripted and produced pieces can be added to the mix later.

Dave was in no mood to banter back and forth with whomever the Chicago station had put on the line, but he knew it was expected. He went into the studio and sat down at a small desk over which was hung a microphone suspended by a flexible metal boom. There was a multi-button telephone on the desk and a computer screen and keyboard. Directly beneath the mic was a stand to hold copy, of which Dave had none at the moment.

He pressed the blinking button on the phone. "Dave Haggard here."

There was a slight pause and a woman came on the line, sounding as though she were on speakerphone. "Carol will be right with you Dave. We're bringing you up on the line so you'll be on the mic. It might be a couple of minutes. Thanks for doing this."

"Yeah, sure." The line went quiet. He was on hold. He tried to organize his thoughts about what to say and what to leave out. He would stick to the basic facts and mention the similarities between the D.C. murders and those in other cities, including Chicago. He would include the possibility of a religious motive, although police had no firm suspects or groups at the moment, at least they had not publicly made any statements connecting the murders to any specific person or group. He'd allow himself to ramble over these points for a couple of minutes and hope that Carol, whoever she was, would be satisfied with that and let him get on with his own work. He was satisfied that he had it under control. To pass the time he placed his phone on the desk and played back his conversation with O'Neil. The cop's reference to the Warriors of Mary and statement that some of the members were police officers who were offering what could be leads startled him. The implication had not come to him during his conversation in the coffee shop. He played it again and noted the harsh edge to O'Neil's voice when he told Dave he could not use the information.

Dave wondered why O'Neil would bring it up if he didn't want the information to find daylight. He would transcribe the conversation and hold the information until he had something else to back it up. The phone line came to life.

"Dave, put on your headphones and give us a level." He leaned into the mic and gave his name and a few lines from a racy couplet he had memorized in his youth. He heard a voice in the headphones telling him the level was good.

"Hi Dave, this is Carol. We're ready on our end and we're rolling. Actually, we've been rolling, so we already have the tape. We just need the guy's name. I assume he's a cop."

Dave looked down at his phone, which has been positioned in front of the microphone. "You can't use that. It's a confidential source. I was just reviewing it. It's all on background."

"Give me a break! This is good stuff, Dave. We're already on the Warriors of Mary and the cop angle is great. We're going with it if we can track it down."

"This is all background. There's nothing to back it up. It was just a conversation in a coffee shop. It might be bullshit. I have to ask you to spike this for now." Dave was breathing hard and feeling that he had lost control of the O'Neil angle because of his own stupid mistake. Rule number one in broadcasting is the mic is always on.

A male voice came through his headphones that sounded as though it was in the back of the room. "Hi Dave, it's Andrew. I run the shop up here. We'll hold the tape for now but we won't hold the information. We're already working it on our end. I've talked to Sid and he's on board. Nice job digging this up but it's no good if you sit on it. We'd like you to put something together and file. You and Sid can work out the package. We'll pass on the q-and-a for now to give you some time."

"Dave, it's Carol. We're closing down now and we'll talk soon."

The line went dead and the phone light went dark. Sid walked in and leaned against the sound tiling on the wall. "We need to talk about this. Come into my office. This place is bugged." It was an old joke.

Chapter Eight

It was cold and dawn was hours away. The sky was clear and stars were visible above the city lights. Father Darius's back was aching from the punishment he had imposed on it. He had parked the car in the public garage at Union Station and walked to the far corner where he had left it after he had disposed of the man he believed to have been a Mexican. The garage was only a few blocks from the park where the headless man had been discovered. He had placed the man's head under row house porch on C Street, next to an old basket that had been left there. It would be months before it was discovered.

He sat in the bucket seat, leaning forward to avoid the pain that was the result of his self-imposed penance. He pulled out the choke, pressed the gas pedal to the floor and pushed the start button. The engine came to life, sputtering and emitting a small cloud of smoke through the tailpipe. When the engine had settled down, he pushed the choke halfway back into the dashboard and waited until the machine had warmed itself to its full performance. He pushed the choke all the way in and backed out of the space and slowly drove down onto Massachusetts Avenue. He drove to Pennsylvania Avenue and then to Constitution, which he took past the Washington Monument and down to the Roosevelt Bridge and into Virginia, glancing at the Kennedy Center reflected in the water below.

He took the George Washington Parkway north, with the Potomac on his right. He kept to the speed limit to avoid problems with the U.S. Park Police, who waited in hiding for drunks and speeders coming up from D.C. The

MG had no windup windows and the side curtains he had inserted into the tops of the doors bowed away from the car at speed, so the cold night air rushed into the car, causing his hands to shake on the wheel.

He was carrying a Washington state driver's license identifying him as Walter Williams, a resident of a working class neighborhood of Seattle. The photo was of a nondescript man of middle age, no facial hair, thinning hair, blank, white face. An average person could not pick him out of a crowd of average middle aged white men. That was the point. The photo looked something like him but, in fact, it was not him. He had obtained the license through unofficial channels. He turned off at Route 123 and drove to an address in Mclean.

Peter Malone bought a prepaid cell phone at a store on 14th Street. The owners were Koreans who crammed the small store with food, beer and wine, Korean kitch, tobacco products, rolling papers, condoms, phones, pre-paid phone cards and assorted backroom items such as brass knuckles and K-bar knives. The Koreans glared at each customer as though he or she had come into the store to murder the proprietors. It was assumed that there was a shotgun behind the counter. The neighborhood had gentrified in recent years and the threat of crime had dropped to a point where the likelihood of a robbery was about as great as it would have been had the store been located in prosperous Bethesda across the line in Maryland, but the owners remained vigilant. Malone noted the security cameras and was satisfied that his face could not be identified under his fedora.

He liked the place. He wandered the cluttered aisles and appreciated the small Washington Monuments and "Nation's Capital" tee-shirts next to garish hats bearing the flag of the Republic of Korea. It reminded him of the bodegas in his own city where he had worked the streets, first as a patrolman, later as a detective. He liked street life and the possibility of crime and its many fingers. He allowed himself a moment of nostalgia. He smiled at the Korean man behind the counter, who was eyeing him with suspicion. "How's it goin'?"

"You pay now!"

He gave the man cash, keeping his face away from the cameras in the ceiling. He went to the car and cut the phone out of its plastic wrapping and went through the process of activating it. He had five-hundred minutes of time on it. That should be sufficient. If he needed more, he would destroy the phone and buy another one at different store. He pulled away from the curb and drove a zig-zag route for fifteen minutes, coming to a stop on P Street near Dupont Circle. He sat in the car watching the neighborhood, trying to get a feel for it and who might be sitting in a window unable to sleep and killing time by idly watching the street. A lesbian couple walked past the car, glared at him, and kissed passionately. They were hoping to shock him. He would not have been shocked if they performed a sex act with a goat. He was past shocking for almost any reason. Any reason aside from betrayal.

The lesbians moved on, huddled together in the cold night air. Malone saw no one else on the street or peering from windows. He dialed a number. The man on the other end spoke for two minutes and ended the call. Malone drove to the Philadelphia House on Massachusetts Avenue, parked the car at a meter, and got out to take mental notes of the neighborhood. There were very few people on the street, not even barflies who had closed the joints on 17th Street. Malone was quick to note the security people who were watching the diplomatic addresses. They looked like security goons anywhere, trying to appear as normal as possible while remaining in a small area, armed and dangerous to anyone who had ideas of attack on the nations whose flags hung over the doors of Embassy Row. A few Uniformed Secret Service vehicles were conspicuous under street lights to offer a measure of reassurance that the United States was watching over the diplomats who were guests in this country.

Malone thought the scene looked a bit tidy for his taste. He liked his streets scenes a bit rougher, with junkies, hustlers and whores in the doorways. Philadelphia House was like the other buildings in the neighborhood, gentile in an early twentieth century way. He had an odd thought about whether anyone actually got laid in a place like that or whether they all just sat around reading books that no one else understood.

Inside, Dave was not reading, he was asleep. He had called O'Neil to arrange to meet him in the morning and hand over the Novena book but the cop didn't answer, so he left a vague message and turned in for the night. The small noises outside were drowned out by the hum of the furnace fan. Only the whoop of a police car responding to a street crime interrupted his sleep, but he was soon dreaming again. Sirens were part of the sound of the city and very few people paid any attention to them.

Malone was back in his car before the patrol car sped by. It was unfortunate that the young man had come upon him in the alley behind the Philadelphia House. The fellow seemed to be waiting for someone and was facing 17th Street when Malone was upon him. It was quick. The guy probably felt nothing but a moment of panic. Malone could not take a chance that he would be seen and recognized. *What was he doing on the street at this hour, anyway?* Malone wondered. *No time for sentiments. Poor guy shit his pants. Happens.* In these moments Malone felt his emotions draining away and he felt nothing at all for other human beings. It bothered him. It's what drove him into the arms of The Virgin. He believed that she would heal him of this coldness and bring him into the Eternal Light. He sat in his car and allowed tears to flow down his cheeks. Maybe they would bring him some peace about himself. He reached into his jacket pocket and held the beads to his chest. He crossed himself and began. "I believe in God, the Father Almighty, Creator of Heaven and earth; and in Jesus Christ…"

He took his time, reciting The Apostle's Creed and each Our Father, Hail Mary and Glory Be slowly, allowed each word in the prayers to roll over his tongue quietly as he lost himself in what believed was his cleansing. When he had finished the Rosary he said a short prayer for the young man he had strangled. Dawn was turning the city sky gray as he opened his eyes. Early walkers and joggers were out on the sidewalk and he could see the shops near Dupont Circle coming to life. He had an urge for coffee and a croissant but he dared not leave his spot. It was one of the few parking spaces on Massachusetts Avenue where he could park during rush hour.

By seven o'clock the sidewalk had become crowded with men and women going to the jobs their high priced educations had given them. They would spend their day pouring over arcane facts and numbers about trade or policy. They would feel good about themselves and their contribution to the well-being of the world. They were unaware that darker forces were at play at the edges.

A police sedan pulled into the drive in front of the Philadelphia House. Malone recognized it immediately, even though it was unmarked. The man inside had cop written all over him from a block away. Malone assumed the man was Captain O'Neil, commander of Homicide. He had been briefed about O'Neil's link to Dave Haggard and was not surprised when Dave walked through the door and climbed into O'Neil's car. He watched as the two men talked, then drove away. He followed the car into the heavy morning traffic on Massachusetts, over to 14th Street, up to Military Road, and to 4D on Georgia. Malone knew he was following someone who would notice a tail, so he kept back and even ran on parallel streets for a few blocks. He was satisfied that O'Neil did not pick him up.

He found a space near 4D and waited. It began to snow heavy, wet flakes that coated the streets and caused gridlock in the rush hour. He debated whether to turn on his wipers and risk being seen or to allow the snow to build up, blocking his view of the street. He couldn't risk being seen. Watching a building full of detectives was risky enough without advertising himself, so he sat and watched the snow build up on his windshield. He was cold and he craved strong, hot coffee. He watched women coming and going from a hair salon and idly allowed himself a fantasy about them.

Inside, O'Neil was staring at the Novena book, which Dave had given him wrapped in a paper napkin. "Tell me again where you got this?" Dave related his encounter with Peppers across the street from the headless man in the park. "I gotta tell you, nothing about you adds up right now. You're there when Father Phil gets killed. Then somebody sends you his Rosary. Then this homeless guy Peppers happens to hand you this book, all bloody and sticky. Hey, Brice, this make any sense to you?" O'Neil nodded to a detective who was sitting at a nearby desk, watching O'Neil and Dave.

"Hey, Captain, I'm just a worker ant here. Shit happens, you know. What can I say?"

O'Neil let out a dramatic sigh. "That's why I have you guys in the unit. Geniuses, one and all."

"Okay, like with the Rosary, did you get your fingerprints all over this?"

"Some, just when he gave it to me."

"We'll let the lab guys look it over. Okay, you showed me yours, now I'll show you mine. Do you remember how I told you that what we discussed at the coffee shop was confidential and not for public consumption?"

"Yeah, of course."

"Well, either you broke our deal or somebody in Chicago has very good hearing because the cops angle in the Warriors of Mary is all over the news there. You know anything about that?"

"How'd you hear that?" Dave knew he would have to deal with it sooner or later but he didn't think it would be this soon.

"It was on the fucking news. Cops in Chicago talked to other cops. Did you do this?"

"Okay, here's what happened..." Dave tried to explain how he had come to record his conversation with O'Neil and how he had played it back in the studio while the station in Chicago listened and recorded it. The more he spoke the stupider he sounded and the more implausible the story became. His face grew red as he attempted to justify what was a breach of the near-holy pact that reporters make with sources. He reached the point where even he felt as though he were listening to an idiot try to explain something that could not be justified. He felt like a five year old trying to explain why he had mud on his Sunday clothes. In the end, he gave up. "Stupid mistake," he said, looking O'Neil in the eye.

"No shit," O'Neil said, allowing the moment to slip into silence. No one spoke for several minutes. Finally, Dave broke the quiet. "What can I do?"

Chapter Nine

Sid was pissed off, there was no getting around it, even though that is exactly what Dave was trying to do. Sid was banging his fist on his desk as he glared at Dave and his face was red. He was breathing hard and there were sweat marks under his arms. "Has it occurred to you that you're letting this damned story get away from you?"

Dave sat down on the small sofa that occupied a spot across from Sid's desk. He looked at his hands while Sid worked himself into what his staff referred to as "one of his moods". Finally, Sid sat down and stared at his desk. "So, let's review the bidding." Sid was a weak bridge player who used card jargon to season his rants. "You're doin' a story about homeless people when a priest gets killed right in front of you. You get some information from the head of homicide. You decide to go home and get some sleep before you file on this story, even though you know the cops think there's a serial killer out there who's most likely a religious nutbag.

Then, just to make it interesting, somebody sends you the dead priest's Rosary, which you finger a little bit and hand over to your friend the police captain. Then, you get tape, against your deal with this guy, about how other cops and this Warriors of Mary group may be tied up in hunting down this sick fuck killer. Then, to put a cherry on top of this wonderful saga, some homeless guy hands you a bloody book, which you then hand over to the captain. Finally, you do a bullshit q-and-a with Chicago and they, accidentally, you say, hear the above mentioned recording and use it, scooping the shit out of us, meaning you. Does that about sum it up so far?" Sid was in full bloom rage.

Butterfly Knife

"May I say something?" Dave was convinced he was about to be fired.

"Oh, by all means, say something." Sid sat back, pulled out his bottom drawer and used it as a foot stool. "I'm all ears."

"O'Neil is playing me. He gives me things and takes them back. He drives me around, shows me a body or two, and feeds me something he says I can't use, then he wants something in return. The priests killings appear to be part of something bigger but I can't tell you what it is right now. And I'm freaked out by the Rosary and the book. I think somebody's watching me."

"You think?"

"Here's how it looks to me. Somebody, one guy, probably, is out there with a knife saying his prayers as he cuts up priests. I need to look at why these particular priests are being singled out. This guy is part of the Warriors of Mary in some way. They have something to do with police. These guys are more interested in getting to him as a priest killer than in bringing him in to face charges. If that's the case, they're after him to kill him. Either that, or I'm full of shit and I'm nowhere outside the press releases we're getting from Indiana Avenue."

"Well, you need to get on that angle but you need to get your cop friends to find out who's sending you these presents. They know where you live. Why do you think this guy Peppers gave the book to you? You think he's just nuts or did somebody tell him to find you?"

"Who knows?" Dave was nervous and he tried to keep his fear from showing.

"I need you to file three stories before you leave the building. We need to get back on top of this thing. Give me something in the two to three minute range on all of what we know or what you've been told by sources. Then I need two others in the minute range, one on Warriors of Mary and cop angle, the other on the Rosary and the book. Use whatever tape you can but I want everything we have on the air. We'll get clearance on every station on the system and my guess is somebody out there will call you with something after they hear what you've got. And I want updates on this every damned day. If Captain O'Neil keeps jerking you around you can drop him as a source. My guess is he needs you more than you need him right now. Whoever's doing this is making contact with you, not him. Now go." Sid waved at the door.

Gabriel was on the phone, as usual, using his polite voice to persuade the person on the other end to consent to a recorded interview. It sometimes required reassurance that the interviewee would "sound great" and would contribute to the story. Most people want to be on the radio or television but they worry that they won't sound or look good, so a dose of reassurance and ego massage can get them to consent. Once the interview is over these same people will phone everyone they know to announce their forthcoming airtime. In this case, it was a local attorney who was happy to lend her talents and knowledge to a story about problems in the mortgage business. "Okay, I'm going to put you on hold. The next person you talk to will be Elena. She'll be asking you a few questions for air. Thank you again ." He put the line on hold and pressed a button. "Elena, your phoner's ready on line two."

"Elena?" Dave's shocked expression amused Gabriel.

"Guess who's back."

"What's she doing here? I thought she moved to New York."

"New York didn't work out, I suppose. Maybe she just missed D.C." Gabriel was trying to hide his smile. He and everyone else in the room had wondered how long it would take for Dave to notice she was back.

"I'm so screwed. Things didn't exactly end well." In fact, things with Elena had ended in a shouting match over her decision to leave Washington. Dave had known where her buttons were and he pushed them all, reducing her first to tears and then to rage. His black eye had been an office joke for days.

"Too much information, my boy. Whatever went on with you two is your business, not mine. I hear you'll be filing a few stories for us today."

Dave went to a computer station and logged in. He pulled up the wires to kill some time while he got his thoughts together and was reading a story about a budget bill in Congress when his top-of-the-line message signal beeped. It was an in-house system of communicating between computers. This one had Elena's name. "Fuck you!" it said.

"Welcome back," he responded.

"Eat shit!"

"You know they monitor these messages," he replied.

"Fuck you!"

The fact that she swore like a man had always attracted him. He smiled at her messages and thought about provoking her to send more but he thought better of it and closed out her line. He opened a blank page on his computer and began to type the first of the stories he would file. He was a fast writer and within thirty minutes he had written all three reports. He did not use any sound because he had decided to call O'Neil "a source with knowledge of the investigation", which allowed him to use the information he had on the tape without, technically, violating his agreement with the captain. He chose to ignore the implications of the Chicago station's use of the recording.

Elena was at a computer station editing the interview she had conducted with the lawyer. She wore headphones and ignored him when he walked past her to a booth to record his pieces. He was finished half an hour later, his pieces placed into the appropriate audio file for producers to access for the feeds to stations across the country. He had cut and edited in a few custom closes that used station call letters for the bigger outlets in cities like Chicago. Smaller stations would make do with the generic close, "Dave Haggard, Washington." These reports would also be up on the Now News website.

She was waiting for him when he left the booth. He opened the door and looked into her face and it took his breath away. Her black hair fell to her shoulders, her brilliant brown eyes glared at him. Her perfect skin was the color of copper and her Mayan heritage had given her a warrior goddess's bearing. She stood like a stone in the door. Every face in the newsroom was turned their way.

"Hi," he said, feeling like a seventh grader at a dance.

"You prick," she whispered.

"You're giving me a hard on," he said, hoping it was a joke.

"You know where to stick it. Not one call? Not one goddam email? I'm in fucking New York and you don't even say hi, how's it going up there?"

"You told me to fuck myself when you left! You said I was worse than dog shit and you never wanted to see me again."

"You're an asshole, you know that." She turned to face the others in the room. "I want to make an announcement. Dave Haggard is an asshole." She turned back to him. "We had a fight. You were supposed to come after me. What about that do you not get?"

He looked at the faces looking back at him. "Okay, she's right. I'm an asshole." He leaned over and whispered, "Can we talk about this someplace else?"

"Not yet." She walked to her computer, sat down, and put on her earphones.

He was supposed to go after her? Dave was confused in the way a six year old wonders why his parents are yelling at him. He thought he should say something but he had no idea what that might be, so he offered a weak smile to the faces looking up at him, grabbed his coat and left the newsroom. He went to a coffee shop and sat down, watching the well-dressed and busy professionals hurry by, wrapped against the cold. He and Elena had dated for nearly a year before the dustup over New York. She wanted something permanent and he wanted to be able to spend his time as he wished, chasing street stories and staying out all night. He had to admit to himself that she was the grownup in their relationship but that didn't really change anything. He also had to admit that he loved her. Did he love her more than he loved the street? Was he ever going to grow up?

Chapter Ten

Dave liked to think of himself as one of the grizzled, rumpled, ink-stained wretches who lived the lives of the heroes in the great books about the news business or even detective stories. He had known quite a few of those guys. They actually wore the dirty trench coats and ill-fitting seer sucker suits of legend. They smoked too much and drank too much and, sadly, they sank into a semi-functional state of journalistic limbo in which they did nothing more than collect press releases, suck up a few free drinks, and wait for the end. But in their prime they were caped crusaders who exposed wrongdoings, championed the downtrodden, and brought down the corrupt power mongers who preyed upon the weak. At least that was the narrative that drifted into the conversations they had with each other in their soft and boozy moments at the press club. At other times they told each other it was all bullshit.

Dave was thirty-three years old. How much longer could he do it? He didn't know. He didn't want to end up as a sad drunk in a bar full of reporters but he had to admit to himself that he didn't know what else he could do to make a living. It was not as though he had a real skill. He didn't want to end up like Sid, either, yelling at people like him and trying to wrestle a news day out of his staff. He knew Sid spent a good part of his time arguing with stations about one story or another or, as today, about Dave. Elena made him feel small in his life. She forced him to think about a life that was larger and warmer. He was empty when she left. Now she was back. He didn't know if he could handle it. Right now he had a story to work.

The city of Washington had placed benches between the sidewalk and the curb under the romantic idea that the well-heeled professionals who worked in nearby offices would rub shoulders with wide-eyed tourists on balmy days, each admiring the wonders of their nation's capital. In reality, especially in winter, the benches were daytime haunts for homeless men and women, who wrapped themselves in whatever they could find to comfort them as they held out cups to the office workers who hurried by. "Change? Spare change?" Some of the pedestrians tossed a few coins into the cups and others offered insults or no acknowledgement.

Benches near heating grates or Metro vents were prized because of the warmth that they offered, however briefly. Peppers was asleep on a bench directly across the street from the coffee shop where Dave was feeling sorry for himself. The bench was close to a Metro vent and when the trains came through the tunnel beneath the vent, a rush of warm air would be expelled. It was midday so the trains were on twelve minute schedules. Peppers had learned to open his blanket when he heard the distant rumble of an oncoming train and to trap some of the warm air that came his way. He imagined that God Himself sent him the warm air that comforted him. He spent his days in a rainbow of hallucinations. He no longer bothered to try to separate real from unreal. He slept the sleep of a child. He was immune to the disgust he generated. It took him a few minutes to come around when Dave shook him. "Peppers! Wake up! Peppers! It's me, Dave Haggard!"

A distinguished man in an expensive overcoat and polished shoes stopped to watch Dave shaking Peppers. "Leave him alone, for God's sake! Can't you see the man is sleeping?"

"He's a friend of mine," Dave said, not bothering to look up.

"I'm sure," said the man, waving an arm at Peppers. "You must go to the same tailor."

Peppers opened his eyes and sat up. "Are you the word?"

"I need to talk to you. Can I buy you something to eat?"

Peppers smiled his toothless grin and sat up, gathering two plastic bags that contained his worldly possessions. "We can to Berbers. They let me sit upstairs."

Berbers was a fast food joint on L Street that was a throwback to the days before the swell's moved into the downtown area in their new office buildings. It was in a building that was the product of the hope that came to the city with Franklin Roosevelt in the thirties and had a grandeur and sense of purpose that the glass boxes that now defined the area did not. It had the look of a building someone cared about when it was designed and built. The new boxes had the look of something thrown together in an afternoon, something to stack boxes on top of each other.

Berbers occupied a corner space that contained two floors accessed from the sidewalk. If the place wasn't crowded homeless people were allowed to sit upstairs in the back as long as they bought coffee once an hour. If the smell was too bad, all bets were off. Peppers tested the limits of Berber's management, but on this day the place was nearly empty because of the snow, so Peppers and Dave were not given much notice as they climbed the stairs. They found a table in the back near the bathrooms and Dave went to get food for Peppers. He was gone less than five minutes. The young girl behind the counter smiled at him and made a comment about the weather. He paid for the burger and fries and asked for a bottled water. The girl seemed to be flirting with him but he was still thinking about Elena and Peppers and the information he could get from him, so he took the paper bag and the water and waved goodbye to the girl, who looked sad.

Dave was tired. He felt like he was in over his head with the dead priests story and in even deeper with Elena. He had a how-did-this-happen moment as he climbed the stairs, moving like an old man. He watched his feet as he moved from step to step and nearly walked into the wall at the landing to turn for the second floor. He looked up when he had reached the top stair and started to walk to the back when he saw that Peppers was not at the table. His plastic bags had been torn open and the pitiful contents were scattered on the floor. Filthy shirts, plastic cups, a baseball hat, matches, cardboard and mismatched gloves. He assumed that Peppers had experienced a panic attack that had sent him into his bags looking for something. Dave placed the food on the table and went into the men's room to get Peppers.

"Peppers! You in there?" There was no answer, only the hollow sound of Dave's voice bouncing off the tile. "Hey, Peppers! I got your lunch." There was no response. He assumed that Peppers was on the toilet, so he went back to the table and to wait for him. Ten minutes went by and Peppers did not come out. Dave went back to the door and opened it. "Hey, man, your lunch is getting cold." Silence. Dave walked into the restroom past the partition that prevented diners from seeing someone on the toilet. He saw Peppers feet under the toilet door. "You okay?" Silence.

The door was not locked. It opened when Dave pushed it. Peppers was sitting on the toilet with his pants up and one of his scarves pulled tight around his neck. His eyes were half open but he was not breathing. Dave stared at him for a full minute; his reporter's eye was taking in the details. Peppers' tongue was sticking out. His head was at an odd angle. Dave touched his neck and felt no pulse. He placed the back of his hand under Peppers' nose and felt no breath. He dialed 911.

Malone was in a sandwich shop across the street when the first patrol car arrived, skidding on the wet snow that had not yet been plowed. The patrol car was left in the street, blocking whatever traffic was trying to negotiate the snow, as the officers got out. They were both wearing earmuffs and gloves and their shoes were covered in rubber galoshes that were unfastened. Dave knocked on the upstairs window and waved them up. Less than a minute later a second patrol car arrived and two more officers were at the scene. One of them stationed himself at the door to prevent anyone from entering or leaving Berbers. An EMS truck arrived and two men wearing D.C.F.D. jackets got out, grabbed a medical kit, and ran inside. Malone watched it unfold like an exercise at the police academy. Soon, a detective car was on the scene. Before Malone's coffee had turned cold, L Street outside Berber's was swarming with cops, fire department vehicles, and news trucks.

Malone could see Dave talking with detectives, one of whom was Captain O'Neil. It was time for him to leave. A District snowplow was stuck in traffic at Connecticut Avenue as frustrated city drivers sat in the backup caused by the weather and what a local traffic reporter called "a police action" on L Street. Two Hispanic men with snow shovels were trying to clear the sidewalk as Malone walked east and he stopped to allow them to clear the area in front of him. He glanced back and saw that Dave and O'Neil were sitting by the window and O'Neil was pointing a finger at the reporter. Malone moved on. He found his car and placed a call.

O'Neil was sprawled over two chairs, warming his hands on his coffee cup. "Why is it that nobody can drive in the snow around here? Look at that mess. I'll bet you five dollars that cars are already abandoned on the Beltway and the stores are sold out of toilet paper and bread."

Dave knew that O'Neil was just in the preliminaries of what would become an interrogation. "I guess that means that when it snows around here folks just sit on the toilet and eat bread until it's over."

O'Neil chuckled but his eyes held no merriment. "That's a nice thought. You think the big guy over at the White House is on the throne right now?"

"So, let's talk about Peppers. What do you think is going on?"

"That's what I was going to ask you. Tell me again how you knew this guy?"

"He was in the shelter when Father Phil was killed. He was sleeping next to me. Not sleeping, actually, since he seemed kind of zoned out most of the time. He kept asking me if I was the word. He gave me the book. I saw him on a bench and offered to buy him something to eat. We came here. He went to the bathroom. Then he was dead. That's about it."

O'Neil never believed that anything was "about it", so he pressed Dave. "Well, see, you're being played here, you know that. It's not normal when people keep getting killed around one guy, especially when that guy gets deliveries of things from the people being murdered. I need you to think about everyone you came into contact with since you got this idea to do a story about homeless people. How did you make that happen? Who did you talk to? I know we've gone over this before but we need to go over it again." He stared at Dave with a passive face but his eyes bore into the reporter.

Dave was dealing with some questions of his own. The first was what the hell is going on?

Chapter Eleven

It is a myth that classic British roadsters drive poorly in snow. The two-thousand pound rear-wheel drive car can do well if the snow is only a few inches deep. Its clearance is six inches. Weight on the rear wheels can improve the car's ability to negotiate snowy streets. So it was with the red MGA being driven by the man whose license identified him as Walter Williams of Seattle. His real name Darius Welsh, SJ. There was nothing in his possession that would identify him by that name. He had removed the spare tire to make room for a wrapped package weighing just over two hundred pounds. Inside was a living man, bound and gagged. Pressed onto his head was a coiled crown of wire to which were attached a number of two inch razor spikes, each with a barb that made them exceedingly difficult to remove. The man was bleeding at an alarming rate and the driver was worried that his sacrifice to The Virgin would die before he could deliver him to the spot he had chosen.

Only one lane of Route 123 through Mclean was plowed in each direction and abandoned cars littered the roadway. It was late so traffic was light but the going was slow. The small roadster was in the hands of a skilled driver, so the icy road was not a danger. The southbound lanes of the George Washington Parkway were almost clear after road crews had done their work to prepare the road for morning commuters. The Roosevelt Bridge was snow-covered but Constitution Avenue was clear. A D.C. police officer sitting in a cruiser near the Museum of Natural History noticed the car and gave the driver a thumbs up. The cop turned to his partner and said, "I'd hate to be in a stinkin' accident in a thing like that."

The MG proceeded down Constitution to Pennsylvania and New Jersey Avenues, then turned left on North Capitol Street at the main post office. Plows were still clearing the main roads but there was very little traffic as the car proceeded north to Michigan Avenue, where it turned east. There, on the left, was the largest Roman Catholic Church in North America, the Shrine of the Immaculate Conception, a basilica dedicated to the Virgin Mary. Its Romanesque-Byzantine dome and tower rise over Catholic University and nearby neighborhoods. It is the center of worship for the veneration of Mary in the United States and, according to the Church, for the entire continent.

The small car turned left into a parking lot and the driver got out and knelt in worship on the icy blacktop as he gazed up at the blue-tiled dome. "It is all for you," he whispered. The basilica was quiet. There was no one about and magnificent structure rose from the white of the recent snow as a profound statement of faith and Father Daruis began to sob. He allowed himself a moment of torment to ponder the sins of the world. "We are here to suffer!" he shouted into the cold night air.

He rose and went to the MG and opened the small trunk. His package was leaking blood. He gently removed the man known as Monsignor Jose de Palma of the Diocese of Arlington, whose special ministry was to the Hispanics who had no papers to work in this country. These men, women, and children had a special affinity for The Madonna and in his twisted logic Father Darius believed that Monsignor de Palma was deserving of special suffering because of his love for them.

Monsignor de Palma was only vaguely aware of what was happening to him. His loss of blood had weakened him and he had trouble breathing through the thick butcher's paper that was tied to his face and body. He felt himself being lifted out of the car but could not determine whether he was being carried up or down. He tasted blood. He felt no pain. He could not remember what he had been doing before this moment.

Father Darius carried Monsignor de Palma up a small set of stairs and across a paved area to a spot against the basilica, where he propped his package against the outer wall. He opened the butterfly knife and cut the twine that held the paper to the priest. The Monsignor was bleeding profusely and his head and neck were crimson and shiny in the light from lamps that illuminated the area. To Father Darius the monsignor was a holy sight, an example of suffering for The Virgin. He believed that the priest was only moments away from his heavenly reward and he was grateful that he had been chosen to give this gift to the Monsignor as he had given the gift to the others. God Himself would make final judgments on us all but He had chosen those who would act here on Earth.

Father Darius was delirious with joy and the effects of his own suffering. He bent to look into the Monsignor's face and to gaze into his eyes at the moment of death, hoping to see even a small glimpse of Heaven as the soul departed. The knife did its work and the man watched as the soul of Jose de Palma left the bloody body that had been its home for forty-three years. He saw no sign of heaven as life left the priest. Disappointed, he wiped the knife on the priest's sweater and walked back to his car. He went to his room to pray.

The body of Monsignor de Palma was found by a priest who was on his way into the basilica to prepare for early Mass. He was walking near the parking lot when he saw something that looked like a pile of red clothing standing out from the snow against the building. Upon investigation he vomited on the ground and dialed 911. A squad car arrived within five minutes, followed almost immediately by a D.C.F.D. medical team, whose members saw immediately that they could do nothing for the victim. The scene was secured to await the arrival of detectives.

O'Neil was cutting apples for his son when the phone rang. It was his morning to fix lunch for the boy and take him to school. His wife, a nurse, had worked the overnight and exhausted. He let his cell phone ring while he bagged the apple slices and placed them and a small container of peanut butter into an insulated canvas lunch bag, along with a cheese sandwich and a juice box. He zipped the bag closed and handed it to the boy, then he checked the phone and saw that Sergeant Meyer, who had overnight duty on the squad, had left a message.

"Captain, we got a situation with a priest. Call me."

O'Neil knew that Meyer would not have called on a routine murder in a rowhouse in Northeast or a drive-by in Anacostia. Those cases would have been handed by the duty squad. The key word in Meyer's message was "priest". He drove the boy to school and dropped him off near the multi-purpose room, where kids hung out before the opening bell. It took him an hour and a half to get to the Shrine because, in a process as mysterious as life itself, traffic in the Washington area becomes a nightmare at the merest hint of snow, even if roads are plowed to the pavement. The weak winter sun was well up when O'Neil arrived to gaze upon the stiff body of Monsignor de Palma, now fully photographed and examined and waiting for O'Neil's permission to move it.

Waiting with the other reporters was Dave Haggard, bundled against the cold in an overstuffed jacket recently purchased from a mail-order New England outdoor store. Dave was dictating something into his smart-phone when O'Neil waved him over. "How long you been here?"

"I got a call from the desk at Now News about an hour ago. These guys were here when I got here. Some of the TV people have been doing live shots. The Archdiocese hasn't issued a statement yet. Is it true that the guy was wearing a crown of thorns?"

"Just between us girls, yes. Pretty sick stuff. And he was also cut up with appears to have been the same type of knife. It looks like he was alive for awhile with the crown. It's actually a kind of barbed wire that uses razors shaped like barbs. His head is cut up pretty bad. Keep that on background until the PIO gives you the usual bullshit then come to me and I'll fill in the blanks anonymously. You know the drill. Now, what do you have for me?"

"Nothing new. No new deliveries. You get any information on Peppers?"

"He was a veteran. Real name was Andrew Krieger from someplace in Pennsylvania. His prints came up on that database and he might have worked for the FBI at some point. We're not getting much help from them. I think they're looking at him first to see if there's anything they don't want to share with us. He could have been an informant or something else. It might not mean anything. I'll keep you posted." O'Neil was looking at Dave to gauge his reaction. "You're not recording this, are you?"

Dave looked at his phone and saw that the record program was on. "Nah, I was just making some notes to myself."

"I'm just gonna tell you in a nice way that if I hear this conversation on the air in any way, even in Chicago, I'll make sure you never get so much as a press release from downtown on any police story. We clear?"

"Yeah, no problem. You get any history on Peppers? Like how he became homeless?"

"Who knows with these guys? Like I say, we're working some other angles. And we got this situation here. Pretty sick stuff."

"Has an FBI profiler looked at this guy?"

"Just the usual stuff these guys come up with. We already know he's a religious nut who's got a knife and Mary thing. Probably a self-flagellator. Likes to whip himself or stick pins in his eyes. Who knows? For all we know he'll crucify somebody next. Indiana Avenue is up my ass on this because we're getting a lot of media heat. Maybe you could mention something about how we're working some leads and we think we'll bring this guy in soon."

"Are you?"

"Yeah, sure." O'Neil chucked his mirthless noise. He walked away as two men from the coroner's office took de Palma's body to the morgue for an autopsy that would find that the Monsignor had died of multiple stab wounds to the chest. It would also find that the priest's blood volume was critically low at the time of death. There were seventy-three arrow shape razor barbs in his head.

Chapter Twelve

Dave stared at the computer screen and felt nothing for the copy he had written. It was boiler plate stuff that everybody else was filing about the latest priest killing. Who, what, where, yakety yak, no suspects, police intensifying investigation, gruesome killing. The copy that stared back at him was nothing more than another layer of the background noise of daily journalism, another item that blew through like another leaf in the fall, leaving no impression. Such stories were forgotten even before they were finished. Who remembers last week's murder? Yesterday's?

In such moments he believed he was wasting each day he spent doing this work, but the moments didn't last. The truth was he liked working the streets. He would have walked away from the whole thing if he had been stuck covering the quicksand that was Capitol Hill, where the currency of the day was deception and hypocrisy. When he was a cub reporter on the Hill an old hand walked away from a committee hearing at which very powerful members had grilled very powerful business leaders, putting an arm over Dave's shoulders. "Just remember, kid, every word is bullshit. Once you get that, you'll be fine up here." And so it was.

He looked again at his copy. He stared at the ceiling and thought about all of the elements of the story that were missing. It was not just another local crime story. Three priests. Some weird religious group. Killings in other cities. Who was watching him? Why were items linked to the crimes delivered to him? That was an angle that had not made it to air, yet. O'Neil had demanded that no mention be made of the Rosary or the book and Sid had complied.

But all embargoes have an end date and the news business is dynamic, so it was only a matter of time before another reporter got wind of the evidence that had been in Dave's hands.

He inserted a plug into his phone jack and pressed the playback to listen to his surreptitious recording of O'Neil at the Shrine. Peppers was really Andrew Krieger. He had some kind of FBI connection. The profilers had determined that the killer of the priests was probably a self-flagellator. He was willing to impose pain upon himself, so, of course, he had no trouble imposing it upon others. He probably felt he was doing a good deed, a holy act. Dave listened several times and decided that O'Neil had given him a great deal of information, whether or not he knew he was being recorded.

He changed his copy to include a reference to FBI profilers, went into a studio to record it, and left. There was a note in the pocket of his coat. It was from Elena. "You're a piece of shit," it said, in her bold cursive handwriting. Under the word "shit" she had drawn a small heart. He looked around the newsroom but she was not at a work station. Her face appeared in the small window on a studio door. She gave him the finger and smiled. He thought she was beautiful.

He went to his apartment and laid out all of his notes. He wrote a long story that contained all that he had been told, including speculation, just to see how it went together. He had a source at the FBI who had proven to be semi-reliable in the past and he gave him a call. The man was an agent in the Washington field office and he gave Dave the creeps. His name was Milford "Bud" Ossening and he had the manner of a street hustler, an easy smile and a soft voice that contained no assurance of truth. He took to heart the Supreme Court's ruling that law enforcement officers could lie to everyone about everything, and so he did. He also understood that well-placed leaks and assistance to reporters could reap benefits down the road, and so he offered occasional tidbits to people like Dave Haggard. He duly reported all contact with reporters to his superiors.

After a few preliminaries about the weather, Dave asked Ossening about Andrew Krieger. "He apparently did some work for you guys. Anything you can find out for me?"

"We don't talk about our sources of information."

"So, he was an informer for you guys?"

"I didn't say that. I said we don't talk about our sources just like you don't talk about yours." Ossening's manner was friendly and to Dave it sounded like the product of training at Quantico.

"How about unofficially? I'm looking into some information that he did some work for you. He was the street guy who was killed in the fast food joint. You probably saw it in the paper."

Ossening's snicker had no warmth. "Yeah, I heard about it. It's a local murder. We don't have anything to do with the investigation."

"You guys working on the priests killings?"

"I think I saw something about that in the paper."

"Profile the killer?"

"You'll have to get that from Public Affairs."

"Anything you can tell me?"

"Dave, I can't give you any information about ongoing FBI investigations. I can say that we are involved in interstate crimes and, technically, D.C. is FBI territory, although we try to stay out of the business of local departments. We cooperate when asked."

"Have you been asked?"

"Officially, I can't comment. Unofficially, we talk back and forth about a lot of cases."

"Captain O'Neil says you're not cooperating about Krieger and his background with you."

"He tell you that?"

"It's come to my attention."

"They'll get what they need."

"Who decides what they need?"

"Like I said, we talk back and forth."

"Well, I'd like to say something about how the FBI is trying to solve these murders. There's a lot of interest in these priests and some of the good fathers are worrying if they're next."

"Serial killers are a specialty item, Dave."

"So I can say you're looking for a serial killer?"

"You can say what you want. It seems to me that the facts as known speak for themselves. You can say a source at the FBI confirms the Bureau is working with local departments to track down killer or killers involved in these heinous crimes."

"Killers?"

"Take it for what it's worth, Dave."

The line went dead. Dave wrote the word "killers" on a legal pad and circled it. It made sense, but only if there was a conspiracy. The knife wielder appeared to be one person, at least from the evidence that the police were sharing. How to explain the deliveries to Dave and the selection of victims and the logistics of what was happening were other questions. He called O'Neil. "How about coffee in the morning?"

Chapter Thirteen

Elena walked east on Massachusetts Avenue, down from Dupont Circle, stepping around icy spots on the sidewalk. Two European men, who were in town for a meeting at a think tank, watched her and clucked their tongues. She was wearing knee-high, spike-heels boots, a tight, short skirt, and a full-length coat buttoned to the waist, allowing the men a flash of leg as she walked. Unseen by the men was a see-through blouse, under which was a black lace bra. She was on her way to an unannounced visit to Dave's apartment, the purpose of which was to drive him crazy with desire and leave.

To a casual observer she was just another stylish young woman in a world class city. To Malone she was a gift. He gathered weaknesses like so many acorns in a squirrel's nest, to be used as necessary. Elena was one of Dave's weaknesses and Malone was happy she was back in the nest. He had been tracking her and his task became easy when she gave up her adventure in New York, so now all he had to do was sit and wait. She looked good, he mused, as he watched her. He envied Dave. At least for the time being.

Another pair of eyes was watching Elena approach the Philadelphia House. Father Darius was standing at the window of a four-story building that bore the flag of a Baltic nation. The building was part of a trade mission and he was there claiming to be an agent for a medium-sized U.S. firm wishing to do business overseas. It was mere fortune that put him at the window as Elena walked into the lobby of Philadelphia House. He had hoped for no more than a glimpse of Dave. He had planned to savor a small moment of allowing himself a fantasy to be played out in coming days. Elena was the Madonna he could barely bring himself to imagine.

The young man who called himself Richard was working behind the desk when Elena buzzed the door. He smiled as he recognized her and pressed the small button under the desk to release the lock. She looked radiant and her skin was glowing from the cold air. Richard was overwhelmed by her beauty. "It's nice to see you again," he said. "We haven't seen you in awhile. You have been missed." His accent was a mix of African and French and gave him an elegant, formal air.

"You're as handsome as ever," she replied, offering a dazzling smile. "Is the ace reporter in?"

"I believe he is, yes. Shall I tell him you're coming?"

"Oh no! I want him to be surprised. Do you have any mail I can bring up?"

Richard went to the mailboxes and retrieved a small package. "Just this."

Elena took the elevator and her hands were shaking as she walked to Dave's door, took a deep breath and knocked. There was no answer, so she knocked again. Dave was sleeping in a chair and the sound from the door was incorporated into a dream he was having in which he was running down an alley, trying to catch a man who looked like Peppers. The knocking became pounding and Dave woke up, imagining that the apartment was on fire. He ran to the door and opened it, breathing hard. For a moment he thought he was still dreaming. He stared at Elena and his eyes began to tear.

"Aren't you going to say hello?" She walked past him and into the apartment.

"Elena?"

"Are you okay?"

"Yeah, yeah, I was sleeping." He stood at the open door and watched her take off her coat. She was dazzling in a way that made him light headed.

"Can we talk?" Her voice was like music.

He closed the door and rubbed his face. "Can I get you some coffee?"

She sat down and said nothing. He went to the kitchen and made two cups of espresso and tried to get his thoughts together. Were they going to fight? Make up? The moment clearly was hers to define. He put the cups on the table and sat across from her. "What are you doing here?"

"What am I doing here? You should be at my door begging me to take you back. Instead, I'm here, waiting for you to make it up to me." She crossed her arms and glared at him. "Well?"

"What can I say?"

She slapped the table with both hands. "What can you say? What can you say? You shit! You can say you're sorry! You can say you'll do whatever it takes to get me back!"She stood up and walked to the window. The light made her blouse transparent and he could see the lace bra and her perfect body. He wanted her but his emotions were shut down. His brain did not offer him any solution. He was mute.

She turned to face him with tears in her eyes. "You better say something."

He sat like a man in shame and looked at the floor. He loved her but he was powerless to say it. He didn't know what saying it would mean, so the words would not come out. It was the same story, told again. She frightened him and he felt as though he would lose himself and all that he had become if he gave himself over to her. She was strong and he was weak. He imagined himself as a pathetic dog following her around, waiting for table scraps of life. She overwhelmed him and he felt ashamed.

She walked to him and slapped his face, then she picked up her coat the walked out. He heard her footsteps down the hall and her weeping was loud enough to carry nearly to the lobby. He sat in his chair and admitted to himself that he had to find the strength to get up and make a move with his life. He had never felt this way about a woman and his helplessness troubled him as much as his feelings about Elena. He made another cup of coffee. He saw that she had a left a package on the table, a small, wrapped box. The wrapping looked familiar. He opened it and found a small, arrow-shaped razor wrapped in gauze. Blood covered most of it. There was no note.

In the lobby, a nondescript middle-aged man sat reading the Washington Post. He had told Richard at the desk that he was there to meet a real estate agent about one of the units available for rent. He could have been one of a thousand guys on the street at that moment, which was the point. Richard would have a hard time offering a detailed description to anyone asking about the man. "You know, he was middle aged, white guy, suit. I don't remember anything else."

The man watched Elena storm by dabbing her eyes. He made a show of looking at his watch before he stood up and waved to Richard. "I guess she's not going to show up." He walked out behind Elena and watched her turn west to Dupont Circle. Another pair of eyes watched from a window across the street. Father Darius smiled. He knew who was coming for him and it made him happy. He exited the building into an alley that took him to 18th Street. He walked south to a small parking garage where he retrieved the MG and drove across the Potomac into Virginia. He wanted to pray, rest, and eat a good meal.

Chapter Fourteen

Sid was scared and it showed. He leaned forward on his desk and his face was twisted with concern. "I don't know what's going on here but it's more than we can handle. I think we should both meet with your guy O'Neil." He pointed to the bloody arrowhead razor. "This changes everything. I think you need to get out of town and I think you need protection."

Dave was in no mood to argue. He was shaken and his mind was addled by the reality of his situation. He was a central character in whatever was going on and it was not lost on him that he was the mouse in a world dominated by murderous cats. He was the object of amusement. He could be consumed in the drama on a whim. "Yeah, you're right. I need to file on this and go somewhere safe."

Sid was ahead of him. "We're done holding this. File four or five pieces for the can on the stuff you've been sent and we'll top them with updated material that comes in. You know what to do. I'll call O'Neil and tell him what we're doing and get him down here if he'll come. Otherwise, we'll go up to 4D. Maybe we can get him or somebody else from the police to go on tape."

"Good luck with that. I think he's playing with us. I'll get on it." Dave walked into the newsroom and sat at a computer, logged in, and stared at the screen. His computer beeped with a top-of-line message. It was from Gabriel. "You okay?"

He sent back, "I'm filing some pieces. Have you talked to Sid?"

"File and get the hell out of here."

Other staffers were looking at Dave with the expressions usually reserved for traffic accidents or heart attacks; pity and shock. Word had spread through the newsroom that Dave had been sent items linked to the murders of the priests. The story would go national and now Dave was a subject, not a reporter. Such line-crossing had killed more than one journalism career, whether or not the reporter in question was responsible. And his colleagues knew that he had to go into hiding for his own protection. That in itself was news.

He stared at the screen for several minutes, not writing a word. His heart was beating and it occurred to him that his strongest feeling was about the story, not himself. He didn't want to leave the story to someone else to report, he wanted it for himself. He wondered if he was going over the edge when he weighed the benefits of remaining in Washington to report on whatever happened next against the dangers he faced if he did that. He was excited by the danger. He was brought back to Earth by a mental image of himself bleeding to death in an alley or in his own apartment. Is it worth a story? Part of him answered yes. Another part imagined his funeral as colleagues and competitors gathered in small knots talking about his career. What would they say? He knew that many of them would say he had been stupid. It was not that the priest murders story would go unreported. His greatest regret was that it would go unreported by him. He could hear the last line of the story about the priests killings. "And reporter Dave Haggard came out of hiding." It embarrassed him.

His top-of-line beep broke into his daydream. It was from Elena. "Why didn't you tell me?"

"Sorry."

"I'm so sorry I was mean."

"We can talk about this later. I have to file."

He wrote four pieces about the rosary, the book, and the bloody razor arrowhead and how they had been delivered to him following the grisly killings. He kept his stories to the materials and left out anything that could be updated by events or a police department press release. His copy tied each item to a specific murder. He left out any mention of whether the police lab had linked them, leaving that to the wrap-around copy the newscaster would be given. He went into a studio to record the pieces and saw that Sid and O'Neil were waiting for him Sid's office when he came out.

O'Neil had a smile on his face. "I think I should call you Goat. When Africans want to catch a lion they tie a goat to a tree and wait. Maybe we could do that with you." He put his arm around Dave. "I have a place for you to go. You'll be okay there."

Sid wasn't smiling. "The good captain has agreed to a short Q and A. Elena will handle it and we'll get someone else to wrap it. We're putting a special together that the stations can carry." So-call "specials" were good for business, whether the broadcaster was public or private. Stations liked them because they were easy to hype and funders or sponsors liked them because they were believed to add gravitas to a news operation. He sat back and used his bottom drawer as a footstool. "There's a place in Virginia where you can go until this cools off. Captain O'Neil has a friend who has a place where you can stay. We'll keep you up to date on what's happening and maybe you'll be able to file something, depending."

"On?" Dave let the question hang in the air.

"Whether something happens." Sid looked uncomfortable.

O'Neil seemed to be amused by whatever was taking place between Dave and Sid. His eyes were merry as he watched the discomfort both men felt. "Dave, do you know where Sperryville is out in Rappahannock County?"

"Sort of."

"We have a friend out there who has a place on about five-hundred acres. He can put you up for awhile. You can go for long walks." O'Neil added a small laugh. "I'm gonna send one of my guys to your place while you pack your things. I'd take enough for a few days if I were you."

Rappahannock County, Virginia is known for a world-class restaurant in the county seat, Washington, known as "Little Washington", and the Shenandoah National Park, on the county's western border. The town of Washington is named for the teenage surveyor who laid it out in the summer of 1749. The population of Rappahannock County is less today than it was in the 1830s, despite its proximity to Washington, D.C. and the well-heeled swells who could afford weekend homes there. This is the result of the county's revulsion at the growth of nearby counties, where strip malls and townhouses crowded out farms and scenery. Rappahannock County has no strip malls, no fast food outlets, no stop lights and none of the other trappings of modern day growth. Its severely restrictive building policies ensure that the place looks pretty much as it did a hundred years ago, with breathtaking vistas of the Blue Ridge and its valleys. Small vineyards, inns, farms, and hamlets dot the landscape.

Visitors from the nation's capital drive to Warrenton, an outer suburb, and head west on Route 211. Soon the suburban ugliness disappears and the rolling hills of the Piedmont butt against the Blue Ridge. Dave and a detective named Jefferson were in an SUV that had been confiscated from a drug dealer in D.C. It was a luxury vehicle and Jefferson liked the feel of it, which he mentioned every few miles. He blasted the vehicle's sound system at a high volume, swaying to Reggae tunes and slapping the steering wheel. As the winter sun was setting over the mountains, Jefferson pulled onto a blacktop side road that took them to an open farm gate over which was a sign that said, "Spring Farm, est. 1831." A gravel drive took them past a dozen cattle huddled against the cold, across a wooden bridge that spanned a bubbling stream, and up into a forest that hugged the mountainside. The drive was just over a mile and it ended in the yard of a modern stone house that looked down over the valley. One wall of the house was glass and Dave could see a grand piano near the window and a stuffed black bear standing and snarling near the keyboard.

An older man, stout and vigorous, opened the door. "Welcome to Spring Farm!" His face was consumed with the smile and his large hands were wide with the welcome. "C'mon in. It's cold out there."

Jefferson greeted the man like an old friend. Dave grabbed his bag and stepped inside. "Hello, I'm Frank." The man appeared to be in his 60s, had thinning white hair and the air of a fellow who spent a lot of time outdoors. "Boy, you guys must be tired. Let me get you something." Frank was very friendly, sort of like a salesman, Dave thought. Frank led the men up a twisting flight of stairs to a large room that faced the valley below. The silhouette of the Blue Ridge was punctuated by the lights of the hamlet of Sperryville to the west and by isolated farms tucked into the valleys and hillsides.

"Hell of a view, isn't it?" Frank said. "I built this place myself. It took me years to put together the property." He went to a small bamboo bar and poured bourbon into three highball glasses, which he passed to Dave and Jefferson. "Here's to peace and quiet."

Dave looked out at the night and wondered what was going to unfold in the days ahead. He sipped the bourbon and glanced around the room, which encompassed a living/dining area, a large kitchen, and a book-lined den along the far wall. He went to the stuffed black bear near the piano and was amazed at how tall it was. The animal had been stuffed at its full height, front paws extended in aggression, a snarl on its lifeless face.

"I call him Bob. Bob the Bear." Frank poured another glass of bourbon. "Watch this." He walked to the bear and placed the glass into its right paw. "I had the taxidermist fix it so Bob and I could have a drink together." He laughed and toasted the Bob the Bear. "I shot him right there on the deck. He came up and tried to get at some dinner I had out. Got him with a 30.06 modified Springfield right in the throat. I figured if he wanted in, I'd let him stay right there next to the piano. Helen used to play it. She passed away a couple of years ago, so poor Bob doesn't have anybody to play for him anymore."

Bob stood in the room, holding his drink, staring out through his glass eyes at the man who shot him. Dave gazed at Frank's round, smiling face and wondered if the man was out of his mind or simply a country eccentric.

"So, Dave, this is where you'll be staying for awhile," Jefferson said. "Not here, exactly, but in a small guest house Frank has up the hill a little way. There's no phone there but you can use your cell and, believe it or not, there's WiFi, so you can surf the Internet and check your email. Do not tell anyone where you are but you can say you're well and safe. There is some fine hiking up here and Frank has a decent library, so you'll have something to read. You'll need to keep your head down until we can sort things out."

Frank's smiling face was red from the bourbon and he nodded as Jefferson spoke. "You'll like it here. It's a world away from what you're used to."

"Not exactly. I'm from East Tennessee, so I'm comfortable in woods and mountains." What he didn't say was that he left Tennessee to get away from all that.

The guest house was a two-room structure about a hundred yards from the main house. There was a small living room with a wood stove set into a fireplace and a Pullman kitchen, and an adjacent bedroom with a king-sized bed. A full bath was off the bedroom. Dave settled in and started a fire, more for the comfort than the warmth. On a whim he called Elena and left a message on her voicemail that he was safe.

Back at the main house Jefferson and Frank were having a phone conversation of another kind.

Chapter Fifteen

Elena lived in a third-floor walkup on Columbia Road in the Adams Morgan section of Washington, a neighborhood of shops, restaurants and bars representing the two dozen Latin American nations whose people resided in the blocks branching out from Columbia Road and 18th Street Northwest. Anglos, Africans, American Blacks, Asians and Native Americans created a kind of world soup on the streets as pedestrians walked through a cloud of international music blasting from the nightspots and bodegas.

The young people on the streets tended to be edgier than their buttoned-down contemporaries in Georgetown or their suited-up fellows along K Street. Adams Morgan had attitude and world culture, not to mention the food and the languages. It was positioned between the upscale gay culture of Dupont Circle and the gentrifying U Street corridor, where white people were grabbing up the row houses that had recently housed working class African Americans who had held the neighborhood together for decades.

Elena liked the diversity of her neighborhood, even as she complained about the noise that rose up like a thick fog from the streets on weekend nights as drunken bar patrons shouted at cops, who shouted back and handcuffed revelers whose enthusiasm for their good times overflowed into spitting and fighting at all hours. It was quieter during the cold weather, but it would never be described as peaceful. But it had energy.

She got off the bus a half block from her apartment and walked fast through the cold night air. Two men from El

Salvador noticed her and shouted an obscene invitation, which she ignored. Salsa music came from a speaker outside a Latin American market and she saw several people inside picking through the winter produce. The woman who owned the store was behind the register and waved to her.

She hurried on, thinking about Dave and wondering why she bothered with him. She knew why. She loved him and it infuriated her. She climbed the stairs to her apartment, ignoring the murals that depicted an ideal life in a fantasy Latin country. She smelled the cooking from the apartments near hers and she regretted that her dinner would be leftover Chinese.

She opened her door and turned on the light, closing and locking the door and hanging her coat on a brass hook on the wall. She poured herself a glass of red wine and placed her dinner in the microwave. She glanced at her phone and saw that the message light was blinking. She took a deep breath and a swallow of the wine, sat down, and pressed the button.

The first message was from Sid telling her he had changed her schedule because Dave was away. She was due in for the early morning feed and was expected to produce at least two Washington pieces for the stations. She had to be back at work in six hours. The second was from Dave telling her that he was safe. She played it again. There was no "I miss you" or "I wish you were here". She drank the rest of the wine and felt sorry for herself. She ate her leftover dinner and turned out the light.

Outside, standing next to his car, Malone saw that the apartment had gone dark. He went back to his room. He pondered his next move and prayed that he would have the strength to do what had to be done. He sat in the darkness and pondered the great questions between life and death, God and Satan, man and woman. He considered the man he was chasing and wondered what he was doing at that hour.

Father Darius was in a small room at a bed and breakfast in the Virginia countryside, also sitting on a bed, pondering the same great questions. He was experiencing a pain he believed to be exquisite, a sacrifice to Her, The Virgin, to whom all fealty was due. He was bleeding from the discipline and the knotted assembly of leather spiked with small tacks. He saw himself as a spiritual disciple of those who scourged the flesh in ancient days and the blood that fell upon the plastic sheet on the bed was a modest price to pay for the eternity of Her in Heaven. He experienced a sexual release and said a Rosary, hoping for expiation for his sin.

Elena slept and dreamt of Dave, seeing him as a man running from evil. In the dream, his face was passive. Evil was hard to see in the dream, just an idea, really, chasing him as she watched, unable to intervene. She was sweating when the alarm went off at four o'clock, and breathing hard. She pressed the button to silence it but heard a police siren outside her window racing toward Columbia Road and in her confusion she pounded the alarm again. She showered and dressed and took a cab to Now News, arriving just after four-thirty.

The newsroom smelled of old coffee and the stale odor that came from the jackets of those who secretly smoked in the stairway. The coffee had been made hours earlier and was thick and bitter, so she made a fresh pot. The overnight desk assistant, a pasty young woman named Megan, had a permanent stricken look that gave her the appearance of someone who has just heard bad news. In fact, she always looked like that, even after Sid promoted her from a part time, weekend job. Megan had been reading the wires and nothing much had caught her attention, something she shared with Elena.

"Have you heard from Dave?" she asked, looking quite stricken and concerned.

"He's fine," Elena said, logging in to a work station.

"I hope no one kills him," Megan said, offering a slight smile.

Elena was shocked and upset. "Yeah, me too." She did not look Megan in the eye.

Elena's cell phone rang and she pulled it from her purse and saw that Dave was calling. "Elena here," she said.

"Hey, it's me."

"I'll have to call you back." She got up and went to the ladies bathroom. Her fingers were trembling as she pressed the button labeled "Dave". He picked up after one ring. "I had to go to a private place," she said. "I don't want everybody to know I'm talking to you."

"Are you working?" He asked.

"Yeah, I just got here. Sid called me in to work on some projects because we're short-handed. How are you?"

"I miss you."

"Now you say that! You're in fucking hiding and you tell me you miss me!"

"Yeah."

"Where are you?"

"I'm not supposed to tell anyone. I'm in Virginia at some mountain place. One of Captain O'Neil's men drove me out here. Maybe you can visit."

She was scared, that much she knew, but was it for him or herself? "Is is okay for you to have visitors?"

"I don't know why not. It's not like you'll tell anyone. I think Sid already knows."

"I'll ask him. Then we can talk about it." She looked around to see if anyone was listening. "Are you all right?"

"Aside from the fact that I'm in hiding, yeah, I suppose so."

"What are you going to do with your time?"

"Try to figure this out. I've never been in this spot before." There was a sound in the background and Elena heard him respond to another person. "I've got to go. I'll call you later."

She stared at the phone and put it into the pocket of her jeans and went back to her work station, wondering whether he was in danger.

Dave answered the door and saw a smiling Frank blowing on his hands. "I hope you like early breakfast because it's ready in the house. Did I hear you talking to someone?"

"Yeah, someone at work. I'll get my coat." He followed Frank down a path that looked like an old logging road. It was not plowed and the thawing and freezing of the snow had made it icy.

"Watch your step," Frank said. "You don't want to fall here or you can slide down the mountain."

It was hard to see what was on the other side of the road. Frank had laid some logs alongside the edge where the road gave way to the mountainside. The logs were rotting and in places they were nearly gone. The road appeared to have been cut with a bulldozer following a line from Frank's house to the cabin. The sky was growing gray with the light of the coming day as the two men walked into the house.

"I make a mean egg casserole," Frank said. "I got bacon and biscuits to go with it and some strong coffee. Let's dig in."

Dave sat at the table and gazed past Bob the Bear at the gray valley below and into the shadow of the mountains beyond. He missed Elena. Even more, he missed working the street.

Chapter Sixteen

Frank was eager to show off his place and he hurried to clear the table and left the dishes in the sink. "It's pretty light out so let's us take a little ride." His bright salesman's face was as eager as a boy's. He grabbed his coat and told Dave to meet him at his truck, a beat up old Ford pickup with four-wheel drive. He had installed chains on all four wheels to help him get up and down the mountain paths.

The terrain was rough and beautiful. "I got my own bulldozer and cut these roads myself," Frank said, waving his arm in front of him as he steered the truck around large rocks and downed trees. "See that pond? I put that in about ten years ago. It's got some nice bass in it and some big old catfish that clean up the bottom."

"Pretty nice job," Dave said, not really knowing what a nice job was in pond making. It was ice covered and nearly black in the gray light under the leafless trees. "Can you skate on it?"

"Only if you don't mind getting wet. The ice around here is never thick enough to skate on. I've seen deer try it and fall in. One drowned a couple of years ago." Frank jerked the wheel to avoid a tree that had fallen near the pond. "Damn! Just missed that one!"

Frank drove to the top of the mountain and parked near a rocky outcrop that towered over the valley. "Come on. Look at this."

He and Dave walked to the rock and looked down over the fields below where Frank's cattle were huddled and grazing on a mound of hay he had opened for them. "You come here in the summer and I've got bees for honey. Damn bears get at 'em now and then, but they leave me enough to give away at Christmas. You be careful up here.

Butterfly Knife

It's a long way down." He pointed at the lip of the rock. "Pretty slick there near the edge."

"How long have you had this place." Dave asked.

"Oh, long time. I started putting it together over twenty years ago. Nobody wanted the mountain land because it's hard to farm, so this part was cheap. The fields down below were expensive."

"What kind of work do you do?"

Frank's face hardened and he looked at Dave. "Well, it's hard to say. You might say I'm in the security business. We'll leave it at that."

"As in police?"

"As in it's not something we'll talk about. Now, let's go down to see the girls." He motioned to the cattle. "So, what are you planning to do to kill time while you're up here?"

"I don't know. I'd like to work the story over the phone and maybe have my girlfriend come to visit." It had been awhile since he had called Elena his girlfriend and he was not sure she would agree that she was.

"So long as you don't tell everyone where you are. You're ass deep in something, you know." Frank drove down the mountain, sliding on icy spots, and trying to stay clear of the edges of the road that could tip them down into the valley, assuming they weren't stopped by the trees on the way down. He was stone-faced as he drove, shifting gears and controlling the truck, and he left Dave in silence and white knuckles. The mountain gave way to the fields and Frank pulled up next to a small silo next to which several cattle were eating hay that had been left for them. "I want to show you something," he said, climbing out of the truck.

Dave followed him into the silo and saw what appeared to be some kind of control center with computers and communications gear in racks around a circular desk. "This is what the military would call a classified installation." Frank waved his hand around the room. "We kind of keep track of things here. This is not an official government operation, if you get my drift, but we work closely with certain people under certain circumstances, one of which this is. You are not authorized to describe this in any way in your reporting. Understood?"

Dave nodded before he considered what he was agreeing to. He gaped at the equipment. The computer screens were alive with what appeared to be audio tracks, the same kind of tracks the computers at Now News displayed when recordings were being made and edited. The lines were moving, an indication that recordings were underway. "What is this place?"

"We can target certain individuals and monitor them, where they are and where they're going, and what they're saying and who they're saying it to. That's what you're seeing. We're monitoring some of the people who we think might be involved in whatever is going on with you and killer or killers of the priests. I wanted to show you this to let you know that you're not alone and we're not just sitting around sucking our thumbs."

"You guys have any more of these around the farm?"

"If you need to know, you will. I need to tell you that the penalties for revealing information about this place without authorization can be severe, so I need your word that you won't be reporting this or telling your girlfriend or your boss what you're looking at here."

"You have it." Dave wondered whether it was a promise he could keep. He walked over to one of the screens. "Can we turn the sound up on this?"

"So you can listen? No. It's probably just jabber anyway. Have you ever listened in on a phone call? It's all 'Hey, what's up? Nothin'. How about you? Nothin'.' I brought you here to let you know we've got a handle on this. The rest us up to us."

"Okay, two questions. Who's us? And do you guys know who's killing the priests?"

"We think we know who might be involved and who we are is best left alone for right now."

"So you know who you're hiding me from?"

"We know who to watch out for and we think you're safe here."

"Let me ask the obvious question. Why don't you just go get them?"

"Things aren't quite that simple." Frank attempted a laugh but it fell flat. "Enough of this. Let's go to town and get some lunch."

Sperryville is a village that contains a few antique stores to interest the weekenders who come for the views or to hike Old Rag Mountain. One of the stores claims to make antiques daily. There's a small post office and a couple of cafes. At one end of the main street is a store that sells kitch, "genuine country" items, and thousands of things that no one in their right mind would buy unless they were out for a Sunday drive in a picturesque setting; small figures of stuffed animals, tiny moccasins, glass apples and the like.

Frank drove down the main street like a fellow running for mayor, pointing out the sites, as scarce as they were, with a pride that belied his true interest in Rappahannock County. He pulled into a spot in front of a café whose sign was faded but Dave made out the word "Homemade" on it. There was a counter on the right and some Formica-topped tables on the left. The far wall was lined with well-worn wooden booths. Old Coca Cola signs and license plates from the fifties were attached to the walls.

"Get the grilled cheese and the soup," Frank said, taking a seat at the counter. "It's just like grandma made if she worked in a place like this." He waved to a stout older woman behind the counter. "They don't have any sushi and they don't have any vegan stuff. Meat and potatoes. Meatloaf on Wednesdays complete with mashed potatoes and gravy and canned green beans. Nothing better." He displayed his wide salesman's smile.

The woman approached with two glasses of ice water. "Hey, Frank. Soup today is vegetable and the pie is apple. We're out of the cake."

"Soup and grilled cheese for me. Coffee." He turned to Dave.

"Me, too." Dave was in no mood to read the menu. "Ice tea."

"See these folks? They're the best on earth. They work hard, they pay their bills, they don't cause trouble. It's people like this that people like me work to protect. You guys in the media need to spend more time reporting on real folks, not the shitbirds that turn up in the paper."

"I'm sure you've heard it before, but we report on the shitbirds because we assume that they're the exception, not the norm. We assume that everybody else is what you call real people. So, in reality, we're optimists." It was an old argument that even reporters were sick of but something had to be said and that was a go-to response to the question of why the news media don't spend much time on what's good and lots of time on what's bad.

"Well, now you have a real exception, don't you? Somebody wants to *except* you right into an early grave. Hell, one of them might be in here having lunch, looking like a yokel in a tractor hat." Frank winked at Dave.

"That's why you're here with me," Dave said. "You're my protector."

"Hell, it might be me."

The soup and sandwiches were placed in front of them and the woman left the check under Frank's plate. "Take it to the front when you're ready," she said.

Dave looked at the others in the café and wondered about their lives. He had a habit of creating fantasies about strangers, speculating about their private lives. He was taken with the idea that the plainest, most normal-looking people could be leading exciting or even sordid private lives. A stout middle-aged woman wearing an old-fashioned hat sat across from an older man wearing a tractor company hat on the back of his head. Neither spoke as they ate. Dave wondered about their sex life and whether they had even engaged in anything debased or perverted. Perhaps they spent their evenings murdering strangers or engaging in ancient sexual rituals. He had a friends, an older couple newly married, who had confessed to him that they had a taste for pagan sexual practices involving animal skins and crystal pyramids. They also grew marijuana in their basement, so they would not be classified as law abiding citizens in any event. But they had professional-level jobs and wore upper middle-class clothing, so no one would suspect them of anything abnormal. Maybe it was the same with the couple eating the soup of the day. He doubted it.

He scanned the room for potential mass murderers who were capable of torturing and stabbing priests but all he saw were country people and a few suburbanites out for a day of antiquing. He was surprised at how many people had braved the weather, although it was warming and the roads were clear.

"Ready?" Frank stood up and grabbed the check.
"Sure."
Frank paid at the front after leaving a five dollar tip, something that would be noted by the waitress, who usually counted tips in change. The two men climbed into Frank's pickup and headed back up the mountain.

"Looks like it's warming up," Frank said, honking at the cattle that were standing in the creek. "There's some good walking if you're interested in that kind of thing. For me, it helps clear the mind. Just make sure you don't get lost. I'll leave you at the cabin and come up when dinner's ready around seven."

Dave left his shoes by the door and flopped onto the bed, lost for the afternoon. He didn't particularly feel like going for a walk in the woods. He felt like working the streets as a reporter and he wondered what was happening back in the newsroom. He called Sid, who picked up after one ring.

"How's life?"

"Boring. Have you ever been left in the woods?"

"Not since I was a baby and was raised by wolves. How's the company?"

"Weird and interesting in ways I can't talk about, if you get my meaning."

"I talked to O'Neil about visitors and he says it's okay if we're all discrete, whatever that's supposed to mean. I thought discrete meant you didn't get caught fooling around on your wife."

"I talked to Elena this morning about it. Okay if she comes down?"

"Yeah, she mentioned it, that's why I called O'Neil. She knows she can't tell anyone. We'll be the only ones who know. I'll be coming down myself in a day or two. How are things between you two?"

"Hell if I know. Stay tuned."

"Let me give you a word of advice. Nobody needs any drama right now. The last thing we all want to face is a freak-out over a lovers' quarrel. Don't invite her down there if you're gonna send her back up here throwing things around and hollering that you're a dick. People don't think clearly when they're hysterical."

"I know. Any word on the reason I'm here?"

"O'Neil is up to something but he won't say what it is. Our station in Chicago is looking into some links and the reporter there is working some leads. You being in hiding is the big story right now, even bigger than the murders. I think some of your competitors are hoping you'll be next. Eat the wounded, that's our motto."

"Want me to file?"

"Damn right. See what you can work up. Maybe a think piece about your situation or a backgrounder about how you got into the story or, how about this?, a think piece about Father Phil and how his murder has changed the narrative about homelessness, dropping in some stuff about your angle." A think piece was reporter commentary that added feeling or even opinion to the facts of a story to flesh it out and give it context. Hardened street reporters thought of them as another way to pick lint out of navels and resisted them. Dave was not of that opinion.

"Let me see what I can work up. Maybe I can do daily things to give me something to do."

"Let's see how it goes. By the way, Elena's gone home. I have her working mornings. She won't be off for a few days, so don't be tempted to get her to call in sick or anything, no matter how much you would like to, ah, enjoy her charms."

"You have a dirty mind."

"And you're alone in a cabin. Get to work and call Gabriel when you're ready to file. I'll tell him to edit it for content so we can keep the loop small." The line went dead.

Dave opened his laptop and was surprised to see that Frank had an open WiFi network, so he checked the sites of the newspapers he read, the wires, and Now News, which had his photo prominently displayed on its home page. He even managed to log in to his account and wrote a think piece about being part of a story. Then he took a nap, promising himself that he would call Elena when he woke up.

Chapter Seventeen

Malone was satisfied with himself. Once again his instincts had been true. He had guessed that O'Neil would send Dave to the Virginia farm and he had been correct. He nearly jumped up when Dave and Frank walked into the diner, not expecting to see them so soon. He had been sitting with the woman, the one from the store, when the two had come through the door after getting out of Frank's truck. The woman had been a stroke of luck, a chance meeting of two people who shared a table in a crowded café. Malone had been worried that Frank would recognize him but that had not happened. Frank had warned him to lie low for awhile but he had ignored the advice. His worn farmer's coat and hat and his decision to sit with his back to the door had kept Frank's eyes on other things. He caught Dave looking at him and the woman but there was no spark of recognition in his eyes and Malone thought Dave must have been thinking of something else.

The task was clear. The trap was set. It was time to wait. He found a bed and breakfast near Skyline Drive and settled in with his thoughts. He made a call to bring the man on the other end up to speed on events and took a shower, then he slept.

The MG was parked behind the inn in a small spot that was hidden from view in the shadow of a holly tree that had been allowed to grow into what amounted to a large bush. Late model cars and SUVs were too large to use the space but old roadster was not much wider than a high-end riding mower and could be tucked in without effort. Father Darius was a guest at the inn under an assumed name and was observed to be a well-educated, well-dressed person of not much interest, certainly not a type to take attention away from the obviously wealthy peacocks who made the inn a destination to impress their arm candy, the fabulously beautiful Seven Sisters grads who found their way to the rich and powerful in Washington, eighty miles away.

Even on a winter weeknight the restaurant was full, although several of the expensive rooms upstairs were available. All would be occupied on the weekend. Certain influential foodies thought of it as the best restaurant in America and to those who cared about such things, the trip from D.C. was well worth it. For many, the ride was made easier in the back of a limousine. It was not unusual to see a cabinet officer or a Senator dining there. Father Darius knew how to blend in as wall paper in such a place. After all, he had been parish priest in a wealthy community and knew the social codes.

He sat by himself at a small table set aside for the rare lone diner. It was in a small nook in a corner near a window that looked out at the garden and the holly tree where his car was parked. He liked it here. He had always seen himself as someone who appreciated the finer things in life and the idea of the very best excited him. He saw himself as the very best at what he did and, in his mind, he assumed that everyone else in the dining room would appreciate his personal quality if they could know what he did, which, of course, they could not, given the state of things. He lamented that as he consumed an exquisite first course of a local cheese, greens, and a root vegetable puree he could not identify.

They were coming, he knew. They might already be here. Or nearby. They were stupid to think he wouldn't know about the farm. The young woman would be coming; he felt it. He would enjoy the meal and the evening of chamber music near the fire and leave the mundane details to tomorrow.

Frank's evening was less elegant. He had a few drinks with Dave and was relieved when the reporter walked back to the cabin to brood. Frank had things to do. He had seen Malone in the café and he was not bothered by the man's disregard of his advice to lie low. In truth, he was satisfied that things were going as planned, but he did not know the whereabouts of others and it disturbed him. He went to his laptop and opened a program that would allow him to analyze the audio traffic that had been picked up during the day. It gave him the location of the cell phones that had been monitored. A key target was missing and Frank assumed that his phone had been ditched for a new one, a pre-paid device that was a wild card at the moment.

He sat back and pondered the situation, taking small sips of his expensive bourbon. He liked Dave but he had no respect for the general news media. He believed that they cherry-picked facts and created stories to meet their needs. In that regard he was no different than most law enforcement and security professionals. He had a problem with using Dave as bait. But events had not gone as he had hoped and for that he was sorry. He opened a desk drawer and took out a manila folder in which was contained a photograph of a handsome Italian-American man. He had dark hair, intense eyes, and a cocky smile. Andrew. His partner for seventeen years. A man who could be counted upon in a difficult situation. What a waste. It was a bad idea to send him undercover. It was Andrew who had chosen the street name Peppers. He looked at the photograph. *This one is for you,* he vowed.

Elena was trying to sleep but going to bed early was never something she sought. She was a natural night person and the demands of working early morning shifts in a newsroom did little more than make her tired and cranky. She tossed, seeking a comfortable position that would bring sleep, but her thoughts turned to Dave. He had called just as she crawled under the covers and told her again that he missed her and wanted her to visit him. She promised only to think about it. Being with Dave felt both right and wrong and left her troubled and the threat on his life and his need to hide out in the mountains did nothing to make her feel better about their relationship, what there was of it. Still, he seemed sincere, so she would see how she felt in a few days when she got a break at Now News.

Dave was near panic in the cabin on the mountain. He knew he was in over his head and was part of something he didn't understand, but he had no idea what it was or what to do about it. He sat at his laptop and wrote long pieces about the murders and what might be behind them, but none of the stories would ever be aired. He was just filling time to occupy his mind. He would call Sid tomorrow for a heart-to-heart talk about what the hell was going on.

Captain O'Neil was a happy man. He sat and watched television with his family, content in the knowledge that a trap had been set and it was only a matter of time, a short time, before it was sprung. He and his son watched the Wizards lose another game, this time to Phoenix, and acknowledged that another season was going down the drain.

Sid was at home with his third glass of expensive tequila. He was sitting in an old overstuffed chair whose arms were worn shiny and whose seat was sagged. He was listening to Beethoven's Symphony #4, considered a troubled creation by some music critics, a kind of bastard work between the more honored symphonies #3 and #5. Sid himself was troubled and the alcohol was not bringing him peace nor was the music. He felt like a man who had wandered into danger but had no idea of its scope or source.

"Something's not right!" he said out loud to himself. "Goddam it!" He felt it as surely as he would feel a knife in his back. Things didn't add up. He had been a reporter for decades and smelled bullshit even in tiny amounts and this had the stink of a major pile. But where? He was convinced that Captain O'Neil knew much more than he had let on and he regretted agreeing to let O'Neil chose where Dave would hide because O'Neil had control. Sid thought about calling a friend, a source, at the Justice Department to see if he could arrange another safe spot for Dave but he didn't know what he would say to the man. He knew he couldn't just say he didn't trust the D.C. Police Department without offering a reason and I've got a feeling wouldn't be good enough.

It was late but he didn't care. He called O'Neil, who answered after a single ring. "We need to meet in the morning," Sid said, without waiting for O'Neil to say anything.

O'Neil could tell that Sid had been drinking. "I can be at your office at ten."

"Fine." Sid hung up. He poured himself another drink and closed his eyes, hoping clarity would come to him. It did not.

Chapter Eighteen

It was nearly seven before the daylight was noticeable through the window. Dave lay in the bed, staring at the thin curtain, wondering what the day would bring, if anything. He had not slept well and had, in fact, imagined that a bear was trying to get into to the cabin in the night. He spent a few anxious moments wishing he had a gun before it occurred to him that the black bears in the mountains were hibernating during the winter and were no threat. He reasoned that the wind must have pushed branches from the pine tree against the house. Still, it had not comforted him. He wished he had a cigarette, then he wished he had a joint and some sweet wine. He occupied his mind by listing his vices and weaknesses, trying to organize them by their self-destructive capacities. In his heart, his deepest desire was to be a cub street reporter who indulged himself in anything he felt like, chasing fire engines and bank robbers, drug dealers and whores, street bums and the insane. He was a sucker for adrenaline. He wished he had the guts to be one of those guys who parachute off of cliffs and high buildings.

He rubbed his face and considered showering and shaving, but then what? A walk in the woods? The world was going about its merry way, with its schemes and plots, while he sat on a mountaintop and saw no joy in his day. He heard footsteps outside and banging on the door.

"Dave? It's Frank. I got breakfast damn near ready. Come on down to the house." There was a pause. "Dave?"

"Yeah, Frank. Give me a couple of minutes and I'll be right down." He pulled his legs over the side of the bed and shook his head. At least it would give him something to do for an hour or so. Fifteen minutes later he was sitting at Frank's table, eating eggs and bacon and drinking excellent coffee.

"Anything you'd like to do?" Frank asked, sitting back with an amused look on his face.

"What're my options?"

"When's your gal coming down?"

"Not for a few days, if she comes. She's working. She might be down when she gets a day off."

"Can't she get a day off? I'd think your boss would go easy on her, given the circumstances."

"The news business goes on and we're short-handed with me away. It's kind of like police work. Somebody has to be there."

"Sometimes I think the world would be better off with less police work, but that's just my opinion. I'm going into Warrenton to do some shopping but I think you should stay here. I'll only be gone a couple of hours. Feel free to make yourself at home. I wouldn't leave the farm if I were you. Just a precaution." Frank appeared to be trying to put a twinkle in his eye but it wasn't working and he had a demented look for a moment before he broke into a grin.

"Let me ask you a stupid question. Are there any bears out this time of year?"

"You see a bear?"

"No, but I thought I heard something last night and I thought it was a bear but then I remembered that they hibernate this time of year." Dave displayed a shy smile.

"As cold as it's been, they're in their dens now. They don't actually hibernate. They go into a torpor and if something bothers them they can wake up and be real nasty, but if you leave them alone, they'll just sort of sleep until its get warmer and there's something to eat. I don't think you had one outside the cabin. It was probably something else that the wind moved. If you see one outside this time of year he's probably in a bad mood, so I'd leave him alone. Ain't that right, Bob?" Frank raised his coffee mug to the stuffed Bob the Bear.

The sun was warm by the time Frank drove his truck down the mountain to his shopping in Warrenton, the nearest community with a decent supermarket. It was a half-hour drive each way, but Warrenton was another world, an edge suburb of McMansions, townhouses, mini "estates," car dealers, strip malls, and chain restaurants. It was an easy place to blend in and not be noticed. Khakis, a sweater, and a good quality leather jacket put Frank in the ranks of the other older men who sat in a chain bookstore coffee shop, chatting.

Dave decided to go exploring and stepped onto the road that Frank had carved into the mountain and headed up. He walked past the pond, now half-covered with thin, slushy ice. A pair of ducks paddled on the far side near the shore where the trees grew thick against the mountainside. The melting snow trickled into the pond, which was fed by a small stream that burbled over rocks on the far end where the water was clear of ice. Frank had placed two large pipes into the berm that dammed the stream, allowing the stream to continue its way down the mountain after the desired pond level had been achieved.

He stepped onto the berm and gazed into the water, looking for fish or anything that lived there. He gazed up at the trees at a crow that had landed a hundred feet away, cawing and making a racket. He recalled his youth in East Tennessee when a crow in a tree was considered a target for any boy with a .22 rifle. Crows are smart and seem to know when someone aims at them, so they're hard to hit. At least that's what Dave believed, even as he fantasized about shooting this one. He had been a good shot as a boy and could hit a starling on a branch at a good distance, but he wasn't as good as his best friend Willis, who could pick up a running squirrel at a hundred yards. Willis's family saw squirrels as food and both of the boys in the family were expected to put something on the table.

The sunshine felt good on his face and he walked up to the top of the mountain and found himself at the cliff where Frank had taken him. He sat on the rock ledge and gazed down on the valley. Frank's cattle were grazing, as usual. A few pickups and cars moved along the paved road. A farmer on a tractor was moving a wheel of hay in a distant field. The tree-covered hills in the county had once been clear-cut and apple and pear orchards had been tended on them by slaves and later by small farmers. The orchards had disappeared along with those who tended them and the woods returned, maples and oaks and dogwoods and sumacs. Creation of Shenandoah National Park had removed many of the farm families from the area and drought and economics many others. Left behind was a treasure of nature and a snapshot of how things used to be.

Dave smelled the air and admitted to himself that he felt most at home in a place like this. He felt peaceful and settled. He also admitted that he had a weakness for the smell of a city street and its diesel smoke, fermenting garbage, crowds and odd people. He wondered if he could afford a weekend cabin in the mountains, a place where he could go to ground himself after a week on the streets. He chuckled out loud at the absurdity of it.

In those moments while Dave pondered the grandeur of the mountains, Sid and Captain O'Neil were sizing each other up across a small conference table in Sid's office. Each man had a hand wrapped around a cup of coffee and each wondered what the other was hiding. Sid believed that O'Neil was holding the better cards and he was correct in that assessment. Sid, in fact, didn't have much. He had played his best hand by turning over the items that had been delivered to Dave after the killings and was now pinning his hopes on something new and important coming over the transom, possibly from the member station in Chicago. With Dave on ice, his ace reporter was out of commission and in no position to add anything to what was already known. The fact that Dave's life was in danger was not at the front of Sid's thinking at that moment.

O'Neil was aware that Sid didn't trust him but he knew enough about human nature to feel in control of his relationship with Sid. There was no way Sid could know what was going on unless someone told him, which was unlikely, given how things were playing out. "What can I do for you?" he asked.

"What's going on?"

"What do you mean?"

"There's more going on here than you've let on. I'm not asking you to give me an interview we can use on the air but if there's more to this than I know I think you should come clean. It's my guy who's in danger here."

"He's in good hands." O'Neil softened his voice.

"Do you think the guy who killed the priests plans to kill him?"

O'Neil decided to reveal another card. "There may be more than one person involved in those killings."

Sid was quiet for a moment. Dave had told him about the F.B.I. source's hints at more than one killer, so he was not surprised by O'Neil's statement. "Do you know who they are?"

"We have some leads."

"That's not what I asked."

"We are confident we will arrest those who are involved in this."

"So where does Dave fit in?"

"We're still putting that together." O'Neil was becoming uncomfortable.

"You're using him as the goat aren't you? You're got him out as bait."

"As I said, he's safe. He's with people who know how to protect him and he's in a place where he can be isolated. He's in good hands. I hear he wants his girlfriend to visit and we have no problem with that as long as it's kept under wraps and nobody decides to make a public story out of it."

"Do you think it's wise for her or me, for that matter, to see him?"

"Like I said, keep it quiet and be discreet. You don't have to wear a disguise or anything. Just don't put out a memo that you're off to see Dave in hiding and directions where to find you."

"Okay. We need to move and advance the story here. Can we get a quick interview on tape about how you're confident this thing will end? As you've heard, every media outlet in this city is on this all day and we need something from our end or we'll look like we're behind our own story."

O'Neil knew this was coming and he had already prepared a statement so general in nature that there would be no real news in it, but it would be "fresh" tape for Now News. They could tout it to their audience and he would not make himself available to other news outlets, so Sid would have something that could be called cooperation.

Elena took him to a studio where she asked him several questions which he answered in the news-speak that contains no news, sort of like junk food contains no nutrients, but offers a food-like experience. Twenty minutes later, as O'Neil was sitting in traffic on L Street, Now News offered its stations a "special report" with "exclusive" information about the threat against Dave Haggard and the investigation into the serial murders of Catholic priests.

Within an hour other news organizations had jumped on it and O'Neil's non-news was being analyzed on cable television channels as "the latest developments in the unbelievable story of journalist Dave Haggard." Sid sat at his desk watching the television coverage and had what he told Elena was an "out of news" experience, "something like an out of body experience only worse."

He called O'Neil. "How do I get to this place where you have Dave?"

O'Neil gave him directions and Frank's phone number, suggesting that he call ahead. The number was the land line in Frank's house, not his cell phone, and it went unanswered. Frank never bothered with voicemail. Sid got his car out of the parking garage where the attendant had assumed it would be all day, so it was up against a wall on a lower level and several other cars had to be moved to free it. Half an hour later he was on Constitution Avenue, heading for the Roosevelt Bridge where he picked up Interstate 66 and drove west to Route 29, which took him to Warrenton, where he turned onto Route 211 to Rappahannock County. The winter sun was low in the sky when he pulled up to the sign for Spring Farm and turned onto a dirt and gravel drive that took him over the creek and up into the woods.

Dave was waiting at the door to Frank's house when Sid pulled in. Sid was wearing his usual cheap suit, bargain basement white shirt, and a tie given on a long-ago holiday. He was a walking example of another era, a time when reporters wore suits that were suitable for fist fights and dirty alleys. Dave looked like an ad for an outdoor magazine.

"Nice view," Sid said, gazing down into the valley.

"Yeah, if you like trees and hay. How was the drive?"

"Anything to drink around here?"

"Frank should be back soon. He'll have something. Come up to the cabin and we can talk."

The two men walked up the dirt and slush road in silence. Unknown to them their short journey was captured by a small tree-mounted camera that Frank had activated hours earlier. It was motion sensitive and would go to sleep thirty seconds after the men entered the cabin. An audio bug in the cabin was voice-activated and what Dave and Sid did and said would be captured in a digital file to be reviewed at a later time.

Sid walked in and looked around. He had two reactions. The first was that the cabin was a nice place to spend a night on a weekend in the country. The second was that he would go crazy spending more than one night in the place. He walked over to a small table and sat in one of two chairs that had been placed there. He took out a reporter's notebook and a mechanical pencil and wrote the words "Are we bugged?"

Dave had wondered the same thing but it had not been an issue because the only person who had been up to the cabin was Frank who, presumably, would have been the man who bugged the place. He shrugged.

Sid wrote "Let's go for a walk" and said out loud, "I'd like to see the view from higher up. Can we walk up there?"

Frank's tree camera could not capture the men on the other side of the cabin, so their conversation would be private. Frank was an expert at analyzing audio recordings and voice patterns, so, when he got around to reviewing the recording, he would know that the monitoring was no secret. He could tell by the tone in Sid's voice that the man was suspicious.

"So, tell me about this guy Frank," Sid said, feeling water soaking his wingtips.

"Hard to say. He's no jolly old farmer. He's part of some kind of organization that's involved in tracking the priest killers. I think they're looking for more than one guy. There's a CIA-type monitoring center in a silo at the base of the mountain. He took me there to show it to me and made me promise to keep quiet about it. I took that to mean he wanted me to tell somebody, probably you. They're listening in on calls and maybe other things. He says he's in the security business, whatever that means. I don't know what his connection is to O'Neil. These guys seem to know who they're after."

Sid was not surprised that the "farm" was a front for something else and he felt better knowing that there was a monitoring station on the place if only because it justified his paranoia about bugs in the cabin. "I think we're ass deep in something here but I don't know what it is. My guess is you being up here is more than a way to protect you from the bad guys. I think they're using you for bait. I know it sounds like some spy novel thing but my guess is they want to lure the bad guys out here."

"Frank's got a lot of guns around." Dave was trying to make himself feel better.

"Aside from your tour of the silo, anything else odd happen?"

"No. We went to lunch at a place in Sperryville. Not very exciting. Since then I've been up here. Frank went to Warrenton to do some shopping."

"Did you see anyone in the diner who looked suspicious?"

"Now you are sounding like a dime novel. How would I know what someone suspicious looks like? They all looked like farmers or people from D.C. out on a day trip."

It was getting dark and there were no lights on the mountain. Sid was cold and his feet were wet. "Let's go back. Maybe Frank will have some hospitality for us."

Frank was sitting at his desk when the two men knocked on his door. He closed his laptop and put a smile on his face as he welcomed Sid to the mountain. "Well, come on in! I'm Frank and my guess is you could use a little something to warm you up." He was wearing his best salesman's face. He led the men into the living area and gave Sid the story of Bob the Bear, even placing a drink in Bob's paw.

"Damn! This is good bourbon," Sid said. "Do you mind if I take off my shoes? They're wet."

"Hell, no. Put them over there by the fire and let them dry out while you enjoy your drink." Frank was beaming like a school boy.

"How'd the shopping go? Get what you need?" Dave asked, wondering what Frank had really been doing in Warrenton, if that's where he went.

"Great. I got everything I went for." Frank took a deep pull on his bourbon.

"So, how's my boy?" Sid glanced at Dave, who felt uncomfortable at the suggestion that he was Sid's son.

"He's behaving himself. I think he'll feel better when he gets settled in."

"I had a little chat with Captain O'Neil today. I think there's more to this than what we're being told and I'd appreciate it if you could bring me up to date."

"What'd O'Neil tell you?" Frank's smile was forced.

"Depends how you look at it, I suppose, but it's my feeling that Dave here is bait and you all are waiting for someone, maybe more than one someone, to come after him."

"Why would you think that?"

"Just a feeling. What is this place, really?"

"It's what it looks like. A farm in the mountains."

"Where you have electronic monitoring devices?"

Frank looked at Dave. "I thought that was confidential."

"I share things with my boss. I agreed not to do a story about it but my safety is at risk here."

"We're looking after your safety, Dave. We are in the security business, Sid, and I'll leave it at that."

"Is Dave safe here?"

"We'll do our best, which is very good."

"And will you brief us on what's happening in a timely manner?"

"That's not my pay grade. Think of me as a caretaker."

"Who makes that decision?"

"He's not here. That's all I can say. Maybe O'Neil can help you out." He stood up and walked to the window that looked out at the Blue Ridge. "Why don't you stay the night. I have some spare rooms that will be quite comfortable. You can enjoy more of this fine booze of mine and get a good night's sleep."

"I'll take you up on that but I think I'll bunk with Dave." Sid sat back at gazed at the fire, allowing himself to relax. He loved a good story and this was turning into a doozy.

Chapter Nineteen

Father Darius had slept well. His wounds, no longer fresh, had scabbed over and allowed him a measure of comfort. New ones would be inflicted in due course, but that did not concern him at this moment. A fine meal and a half-bottle of excellent wine had afforded him the sleep of a child, free of the concerns that worried the sleep of the less holy. His room faced east and its two finely-decorated windows had kept the sun at bay until it was well into the sky. Even the winter angle of the sun could not hide its brilliance on this day and he felt its warmth upon his face as he climbed from his slumber.

He rolled onto his knees and grabbed his Rosary for his morning devotions, offering the discomfort of his bladder as a sacrifice to Her. He was in such a state of completeness that he repeated the Rosary before his morning ablutions. After he had dressed, he looked out the window at a cloudless sky and decided it was a grand time to go for a drive. He would stop for breakfast at a place the desk had recommended and then enjoy the mountains.

He ate in a small restaurant that had once been a gas station and the island where the pumps had stood was still there with its chipped curb and fading sign. The building was rather shabby, he thought, but the place had a good reputation among the foodies who were devoted to this area of Virginia. Inside, the place was nearly full even on a weekday morning. A fresh-faced young woman in black shirt and pants greeted him, waving a menu as she led him to a table near a fireplace where a log burned and crackled. The old wood floor creaked as he walked on it and men in formal riding attire looked down at him from horse country prints on the walls. He liked the feel of the place.

He ordered Eggs Benedict, applewood-smoked bacon, and jalapeno biscuits, along with a small pot of Italian roast coffee and fresh-squeezed orange juice. His good cheer made him hungry. It was not often that he allowed his appetite a free rein and he was thin from years of self-denial. On this day he felt as though the Virgin Herself wanted him to eat.

The sun was higher when he left the restaurant and he decided to put down the top of the MG and to endure the winter air which stung even though it was warm for the time of year. He buttoned his overcoat and placed a wool golf cap on his head. He drove west on Route 211 past Sperryville and into the park until he found an entrance to Skyline Drive, then he headed south along the spine of the range, breathing the clear mountain air and feeling exultant. On another day he would have felt ashamed at his sheer happiness, but not today.

He drove for several hours, waving at other drivers who wondered to themselves or their significant others why the man in the MG had his top down in the middle of winter. He laughed at them. *What did they know? Nothing, that's what.* At least that what he told himself when he saw their faces bundled in their warm cars. He began to sing Ave Maria, his voice loud but lost in the wind. "Ave Maria, gratia plena...Maria gratia plena..." It had been his grandmother's favorite and so it was his. She had sung it to him as a boy after the two of them had knelt before the statue of Her, where the candle was glowing inside a red glass container. Often she had cried as she sang and he had comforted her. He was only a boy but he venerated both his grandmother and the Virgin. She had taught him the Rosary. It was her beads that offered him the comfort of the Rosary even now, years after the accident.

Tears rolled into the wind as he sang and remembered her. He had been told to control his rage and to channel it into his faith. "Offer it up," they said. It was a priest who killed her, a drunken priest. A Jesuit, no less! How can he let that go? His good cheer evaporated as he wept and remembered her, the good one who venerated the Virgin with him. His only comfort had been the sure faith that his grandmother was now and would forever be in the arms of the Virgin Mary, sitting next to God, waiting for him.

He pulled over at an overlook to pull himself together. He got out of the roadster and looked down at the farms in the valley and thought of what he was about to do and it gave him joy. He took the butterfly knife from his coat and flipped it open, testing its action in the cold air. He knelt under a tree and said a Rosary with it, keeping the image of his grandmother in his mind as he prayed. "It is nearly done," he whispered.

A U.S. Park Service Ranger saw the MG parked at the overlook and noticed that its top was down. His name was Roger Etter and he had an MGA of his own in his garage in Front Royal. It was partially restored and was far from a condition where it could be driven, but he admired others that ran, so he pulled into the small parking area to have a look at the car. Etter saw that the car appeared to be in mint condition. Its seats could have come directly from a showroom and the outside paint was perfect. He walked around the car, checking the chrome and wire wheels. He looked around for the driver but saw no one, at first. He yelled, "Hello?" but got no response.

It occurred to him at the driver may have come here to jump. It had happened in the past. He looked over the side of the overlook and saw nothing that caused concern. Etter assumed that the driver had pulled over and gone for a walk in the forest or had gone off to relieve himself. In the corner of his eye he saw something in the woods and went to investigate. There was a man on his knees, masturbating while fondling a knife. He seemed to be praying but it was hard to understand his words. The man was crying and swaying back and forth.

Etter stepped closer to the man and was about to say something to him when the man saw him and jumped up, running and waving the knife. Etter had no time to defend himself. Before he could grab his radio to call for help Father Darius was on him, severing his vocal cords. Seconds later Etter was bleeding out in the woods he had spent his working life protecting. He was thirty-three years old, married to a kindergarten teacher, and had two small boys. He was in the Virginia National Guard and had served in Iraq as a military policeman. He was a volunteer firefighter and a leader of a home Bible study group at his church. He coached Little League baseball and youth soccer. He was the kind of young man communities pray for. In Front Royal, he was as good at it got when it came to young men. His body would be found the next morning and his community would go into shock for days. Father Darius had no feelings at all for Roger Etter. He was nothing more than a threat that had to be eliminated.

The MG was driven back to the inn where Father Darius was registered as Walter Williams, where it was parked behind the holly tree. It had been observed passing through Sperryville by Malone, who was smoking a cigarette on a metal bench in the yard of an antique shop when he looked up and saw what he believed to be the man he was chasing. He saw the car heading east on Route 211 and he ran to his own vehicle and caught up with the small red car within a mile. Father Darius was driving very slowly, enjoying the late afternoon sun as it faded into a winter night. Malone settled back a good distance. It was not hard to follow a small red car with its top down during the middle of winter. He watched as it was hidden behind the holly and he used a long lens to take pictures of the man who walked away from it and into the inn. He felt like a hunter bagging a deer. It was almost too easy.

Chapter Twenty

Murders are rare in the Shenandoah National Park, but they occur. Usually, it's a hiker on the Appalachian Trail who is found dead under mysterious circumstances. Because it is federal property, the F.B.I. will be brought in to sort through the evidence and drive the investigation. The murder of Roger Etter was different. He was a Ranger, for one thing. He was a local pillar of the community for another. Etter was a man who was loved and admired by his entire town and his death sent his family, friends and neighbors into shock.

The Shenandoah Valley is place and a state of mind. It is the low area between the Blue Ridge Mountains and the Appalachians. It was the scene of horrendous suffering during the Civil War, with its towns changing hands dozens of times. Its fertile land fed the people of the East and its music fed the souls of mountain folks. To many who call it home it's a magical place embraced by the mountains to the east and west. It is a Christian place where churches are taken seriously and faith is a gift that must be nurtured day by day. It is a conservative area that produced the Christian Right, a powerful political force that sets the agenda for millions of Americans who embrace what they believe to be basic American values based upon the slogan In God We Trust.

Roger Etter was a devoted follower of all of it and he displayed his faith with deeds and devotion. When his body was brought to a funeral home after the autopsy hundreds of his fellow citizens lined the road, weeping, and more than a few vowed vengeance. His autopsy had been expedited by the F.B.I. and had taken place in a laboratory in Washington, then it was brought home. It had all taken a day and a half. Television stations as far away as Washington covered the procession live.

Malone sat in his room and watched it, smiling. He knew the name and location of the killer. Roger Etter's life was of no concern to Malone. If asked he would have expressed sorrow over a senseless death. In his private thoughts he had already placed Etter into the place where all of the other senseless deaths he had seen and been a part of, a place where the dead are forgotten.

Father Darius was watching the live coverage from a bar in Warrenton, a place that advertized all-you-can-eat pizza at a low price. He was wearing jeans and a cotton jacket in hopes of fitting in with the dads, moms and kids in the place. He felt out of place and to anyone who paid attention he was, but no one was paying attention to the man who sat at the bar and watched the TV screen.
"Hell of a thing, ain't it," said the bartender, shaking her head. "Probably some psycho hiking the trail. They need cops up there or something."
"Yeah, hell of a thing. You hear if they have any leads?"
"Not that they're saying. Hell, they're still looking for whoever killed those hikers two or three years ago. Probably long gone to Georgia by now." Georgia is the southern end of the Appalachian Trail.

He had ordered a draft beer as part of his effort to look like everyone else but his taste ran to higher fare and he could barely swallow what he classified as swill. He had only managed to down a quarter of the beer and he knew he would never get the rest down, so he left the glass on the bar as he gazed at the screen.
People were lining the streets of Front Royal, waving flags and tearfully reaching out to the hearse as it passed by. He thought it was silly and couldn't understand why so

many people cared about Roger Etter. To this man, Etter did not have the sense to leave him alone. Why mourn a man like that?

"That your little red car out front?" the bartender asked.

"Yes, it is."

"Kind of cold to be driving something like that ain't it."

"Not if you dress right." He was in no mood to talk about the car.

"That thing have a heater?"

"Yes, it does and it works fine if the top is up and the side curtains are installed."

"You have a normal car?"

The man bristled at the word normal. He had been told all his life that he was not normal and took offense. "Just what is a normal car?" he snapped.

"Well, you know, a car like everybody else drives." The bartender was beginning to worry about the man and backed away. "I didn't mean anything by it; just making conversation, you being alone and all."

"No offense taken." He glanced again at the screen and put some money on the bar. "Good day."

He was upset and in turmoil and breathing hard. *Normal! What was that supposed to mean? Normal car, normal thoughts, normal, normal.* He was sick of it. *What is normal, anyway? Does she think she is normal? What kind of life is that, serving drinks to people whose kids are stuffing themselves with all-you-can-eat pizza?* A Fauquier County Sheriff's car drove by and deputy at the wheel stared at the MG and then at the man. He issued a small wave and drove off when the light turned green. *Hicks,* Father Darius thought, *people too backward to accept that a classic roadster was not something to stare at.*

Malone was having a better moment. He was elated. He didn't believe in luck but when it appeared that luck had indeed come his way he accepted it. He settled in with a bottle of medium-grade bourbon purchased at a state liquor in Warrenton and allowed both the booze and the satisfaction to wash over him.

Captain O'Neil was facing a much more difficult moment. He had the autopsy results from Roger Etter and they were unsettling. The pathologist, who specialized in certain crimes, had said that the knife that was used in the killing of Etters was of the same type used in the murders of the priests. That did not mean it was the same weapon, but it was the same type. In O'Neil's mind, and in the opinion of the F.B.I. agents who read the report, it was the same killer. That meant that the man was sniffing around the farm, waiting for a moment of his choosing to the make his move.

O'Neil's dilemma was whether to tell Dave or to allow things to play out. After all, using Dave as bait was the plan. How was O'Neil to know it would play out so soon? If he didn't tell Dave and word got back to him from other sources, which it well might, he would have a problem controlling Dave and who knows what that might bring? He'd sleep on it.

F.B.I. Special Agent Milford "Bud" Ossening saw an opportunity he could not resist. He read the report on the autopsy of Roger Etter and believed, along with everyone else who read it, that the person who killed the park ranger was the same person who had murdered at least two priests in Washington. The theory was that the killer was psychotic and was acting out a religious issue probably left over from his childhood. So how did Etter fit in? The folks at Quantico were working on it. Ossening was privy to more than the autopsy report. He was part of a task force that was tracking the Warriors of Mary and they had uncovered

Butterfly Knife

disturbing information about a secret law enforcement connection to the group, a so-called Posse Maria, whose members took it upon themselves to perform extra-legal activities on behalf of what they believed to be their calling from The Virgin.

The task force was tracking a half-dozen law officers, including O'Neil and Malone, and knew all about the farm and where Dave was hiding even before O'Neil's delayed information had arrived at the Bureau. He doubted that O'Neil would tell Dave or his boss about the killer being nearby. He placed a call.

"Dave Haggard here." The voice was thin and Ossening assumed that Dave was stressed and bored.

"Dave, Bud Ossening. Have I called at a bad time?" It was a line that always perked up the person on the other end. Such a question was assumed to be the introduction to something important.

"No, actually I have all the time in the world. What's up?"

"Have you heard about the U.S. Park Ranger who was killed not far from you a couple of days ago? A guy named Etter."

"Yeah, it's all over the news. He seems to have been quite the guy."

"That's what I understand. That's not why I'm calling. What I'm about to tell you must remain confidential. You cannot share it with anyone and you most certainly may not use my name as a source nor may you use the information as a news item. Are we clear on that?" Ossening in no way believed that Dave would keep the information to himself but he wanted to go over the usual ground rules anyway just to say he had.

"Okay, sure. What's up?"

"The special examiner performed the autopsy on Etter because he was a high profile guy and a federal employee, so the guy knows what he's doing. The pathologist is not some country hick. This guy knows his way around a corpse, so we have a high degree of confidence in what he says." Ossening paused as though he was thinking about his next words.

"What'd he say?" Dave was half listening, wondering what this had to do with him.

"He says the guy who stabbed Etter is the same guy who killed the priests." Ossening let that sink in, knowing that what he had said was a stretch from the autopsy report, which had merely stated that death was from the same type of knife as the priest killings.

Dave was silent. His mind was running over a list of questions. How did they know? Did that mean the killer was from Virginia? Then it hit him. "He's out here, isn't he? He knows where I am."

"I would think so, yes." Ossening let the hook sink.

"Why haven't I heard from O'Neil on this?"

"That's not my area. As I said, this is not to be shared. You need to find another way to confront him on this if you plan to do that."

"Do you think I'm safe here?"

"I assume O'Neil knows what he's doing and I know you're not alone. From what I hear, Frank's a good man."

"What do you think I should do?"

"Keep your head down. I gotta go. Remember our deal." The line went dead.

Chapter Twenty-One

Sid was watching Elena as she pounded out a story about a budget fight on Capitol Hill. She sat at a work station, earphones pressed against her head, editing an interview from a subcommittee chairman who was the only member of Congress who was available when Now News needed audio for the four o'clock feed. He was worried about her. She had been even more volatile than usual these past few days and the staff was jittery, as though a wild cat was loose in the newsroom. He knew why she was nervous. He knew more than he should have about her relationship with Dave, mostly because neither she nor Dave had ever tried to hide the explosiveness of their on-again-off-again romance. He thought the cat comparison was apt. She was the cat and Dave was the dog. She was the beauty and Dave was the beast, a feral, slobbering newshound who would rather be chasing thieves than beautiful women. Elena was most certainly beautiful, a thought he tried to remove from his mind.

His cell phone made its noise, a ringtone that seemed like a good idea when he bought it but now rattled him with its odd, Dr. Strangelove-like tones. Did anyone even know who Dr. Strangelove was anymore? he wondered, as he stared at the phone and saw that Dave was calling. "How's the ace reporter?"

"We need to talk in person." Dave sounded scared.

"What's up?"

"How fast can you get here?"

"Tell me what's up and I'll tell you."

"That's not a good idea."

Sid thought of the listening devices in the cabin and it occurred to him that Dave wanted to talk about something that he didn't want to share with Frank and the others who were involved, whoever they were and whatever they were about. "It's rush hour. Sixty-six will be backed up all the way to Gainesville. It might take me three hours."

"See you then."

It took Sid nearly four hours to get to the farm and the drive up the mountain was treacherous because the temperature had dropped and ice had formed in low spots. Frank saw the headlights coming up and was waiting when Sid pulled in. "Nice to see you again, Sid. I didn't know you were coming. Let me get you a drink and you can warm up. I'll get Dave."

"Thanks, but I'll just walk on up and bang on his door." Sid tried to sound friendly, like a man who didn't want to intrude.

"Hell, I'll go with you. Tell you what, I'll slip inside and get a fifth of something and meet you up there." Frank went inside to get the liquor as Sid headed up the drive, slipping on the ice patches.

Dave had seen Sid's car pull in and was waiting at the door. "Let's go for a walk," he said, guiding Sid around to the back of the cabin and away from the camera.

"Our friend's on his way with a bottle, so we need to make this quick. What's up?"

Dave related his conversation with Ossening, and mentioned the earlier phone call in which the agent had suggested that there may be multiple killers, leaving open the possibility that an organization or group might be behind the attacks on the priests.

"I knew it!" Sid pounded his fist into his palm. "You're a goddam goat they're using to bring this son of a bitch in. Now he knows you're here. We need to get you out of here to someplace where he can't find you and neither can Frank and O'Neil and anybody else in this mess."

The two men heard the sound of boots on dry leaves and then the beam of a flashlight coming around the corner of the cabin. "Hey there." It was Frank. "Did I interrupt something?" Dave and Sid could not see Frank's face behind the flashlight.

"We're just enjoying the night air," Sid said, a touch of sarcasm in his voice.

"It's a bit chilly, that's for sure." Frank was using his salesman's voice. "I got a little something that'll warm the heart and everything else."

Sid walked toward the front of the cabin. "That sounds good to me."

The three men went inside, stomping their feet on the mat by the door. The cabin was warm from the fire in the wood stove. The men removed their jackets and hung them on the large hooks on the wall, then they sat at the table while Frank poured three tumblers of bourbon.

"Let me see if I can guess why you're here. Dave received a call from an F.B.I. Agent named Ossening telling him that the murder of Ranger Etter may have been related to the killings of the priests in D.C. That means the killer is out here. Dave here called you. Now you think Dave ought to be kept somewhere else until all of this blows over. Am I correct in my assessment of where we are tonight?" Frank's salesman smile was gone, replaced by a face that looked very serious.

Dave sat up and took a drink of the bourbon. "I'm guessing that you fellows know every time I go to the bathroom."

"Pretty much, yes."

"And you know that this killer is sniffing around looking for me?"

"We know that he's sniffing around. Actually, we think he's looking for your girlfriend, Elena."

Dave let that sink in. "Why would he be looking for her?"

"It's complicated. He's a pretty sick guy."

"Why isn't he looking for her in D.C.?" Sid was skeptical. It didn't make sense, not as it was being laid out by Frank.

"Like I said, it's complicated."

"Do you know who he is?"

Frank was quiet for a long time. "Yes."

"Why don't you just grab him?"

"I can't get into that right now."

"Is there more than one killer?" Dave laid it out for Frank to consider.

"There's a lot happening that I can't get in to. I just want to say one thing to both of you. Dave, you are as safe here right now as you will be anywhere. Nothing can happen that we won't know about. Nothing. And I'll tell you something else. Elena will be safe here, too. If you can get her to come down to see you I think, we think, we can flush this guy out and maybe make things happen. Think about it."

"Explain to me what that makes any sense. He's here waiting for her. He knows where I am. Aren't we just playing into his hands if we bring her down here?"

"I would say he's playing into ours." Frank poured himself another drink.

"You're pretty loose with other people's safety," Sid said.

"Life ain't safe," Frank said. "Take Bob the Bear down at the piano. He thought he lived a pretty safe life, I'd wager, but now he's holding drinks for me. To the bold go the victories."

The three men sat in silence while they pondered their predicament and sipped the bourbon. Each was lost in his own thoughts. Dave was feeling the hair on his neck stand up and he imagined a knife-wielding fiend coming at him and Elena and his breath caught when he considered the implications of inviting her to come to visit him. He weighed her coming versus her remaining in Washington where her safety was not assured. Whoever was tracking him had no trouble finding either him or her, so perhaps the risk of flushing out the killer was reasonable.

Sid was feeling old and responsible. He looked at Dave and imagined him dead and he, too, thought of Elena and her safety. The question boiled down to Frank and O'Neil and the others who were working with them. Could they be trusted to keep Dave and Elena alive? Could they be trusted at all? Then the reporter in him thought about the story that would result from a successful outcome and smiled. It would make headlines all over the world.

Frank was observing the other two, trying to read their minds and the moods. Sid would be allowed to go back to D.C. but Dave must remain in place. He could not be permitted to leave. There was too much at stake.

Chapter Twenty-Two

Malone went back to Washington to keep an eye on Elena. He knew that she had the next part in the drama that was playing out in Virginia and it would not be long before she crossed the Potomac. Her apartment was dark as he gazed up from a parking spot on Columbia Road. The smells of Latin cooking came to him and he had a brief thought that he could slip into a small café and pick up a papusa stuffed with soft cheese and spicy pork. His mouth watered as he imagined the Salvadoran heat from the dish, but his discipline overrode his hunger and he put the papusa in the back of his mind. Two young men walked by, arm and arm, and laughed as they caught him looking at them. "What's up, old man?"

He caught the light coming on in Elena's apartment and glanced up to see her silhouette against the curtain. He had learned that she had an account with a quick-rental car company whose vehicles were available on a moment's notice at parking garages in the city, so he suspected that she would grab one of them if she made a trip to the farm. He knew about all of her accounts and how much she owed on her credit cards. It was easy. He had acquaintances who could hack into sophisticated and so-called secure online accounts easily and deliver a detailed report to him within minutes. That is how he knew about her LightCar account and how often she used it and where she went and for how long. He would know exactly when she made an online reservation to go to Virginia.

He stepped into a puddle of just-melted ice and felt the cold water seep into his shoe, soaking his sock, and he regretted that he had chosen the leather loafers over the water-proof hiking boots that now sat warm and dry in his room. He had chosen a businessman look for the evening and so was wearing a suit and tie under his overcoat. It occurred to him that in Adams Morgan a middle-aged man in a suit and tie might stand out more than a guy in a leather jacket and water-proof boots, but it was too late to change, so he lit a cigarette and hoped his wet foot would not become too numb to run if he had to.

Elena took a bath to calm herself. She brought candles into the bathroom and set her smart-phone to play her favorite music on an Internet station that played Latin ballads from the 60s and 70s, the big production numbers with horns and conga drums; the songs that made her move and cry. She sat in the steaming water and closed her eyes, imagining a tropical beach under the stars, dancing in bare feet on the warm sand with Dave, who was bare-chested, wearing white pants and moving seductively, whispering that he loved her. It was a dream that she replayed every evening as she sought sleep. She wept as she asked herself if it would ever come true.

The moment was shaken from her by the incoming call that broke the mood by blasting a ringtone of a Latin rock band. She sat up and saw that Dave was calling and for a moment she considered rejecting the call and sending him to her voicemail, where, she knew, he could plead for her to call him back, so she answered. "Hola."

"It's me."

"I could tell. How are you? How is life on the lamb?"

"Very funny. When can you come to see me?"

"I don't know if I want to." She felt far away from his reality and she was still tied to the fantasy on the beach where he was another Dave, a loving Dave, not the distant, hiding Dave on the phone.

"You'd like it here. It's nice. It's quiet." His voice was soft.

She considered what that meant. "Are you bored?"

"Yeah, I suppose. I miss you. I want you to come."

Their conversation dragged through the weeds and thorns that couples throw down for each other in moments when their emotions are raw and they're not sure if they want to talk to each other anymore. He was scared and lonely and he wanted to tell her the truth. She was weary of the games that they had been playing and she was feeling a moment of relief that he was locked away on a mountaintop. They looped through it all and, in the end, she agreed to visit him in two days, on her break, but she would not promise to spend the night. He begged and she relented. One night. She felt exhausted when the call ended and her Internet music resumed. She had no further interest in the fantasy that it produced, so she turned if off, dried herself, and spent the next two hours trying to find sleep.

Minutes later, Malone's phone vibrated and he pressed the "answer" button but said nothing. A voice told him that Elena would be going to Virginia in two days. He ended the call and went to his room, where he removed his wet shoe and placed it on a heating vent. He took a hot shower to warm himself and enjoyed a good night's sleep.

Captain O'Neil was not as fortunate. He was wrestling with a political problems on Indiana Avenue, where the chief and her minions were fielding calls from Justice and Interior about Ranger Etter and the link to the priest killings. The F.B.I. had not been reluctant to share the link and, in fact, had been calling everyone in their Rolodex to share the news. A source at the Washington field office had informed O'Neil that an agent named Ossening had even called Dave Haggard to share the news.

O'Neil saw this for what it was: the F.B.I. was grabbing the priest killings and its ancillary issues, Dave included, under the assumption that it was now a federal case. This presented some problems for O'Neil. No department welcomes federal intervention in its cases. Some of it is the natural tension between the locals and the feds. In O'Neil's case, there were too many tentacles wrapped around too many arms in this investigation to feel comfortable walking away. There was too much to lose.

A new detective, a woman named Angela de Angelo who had been moved up from undercover district duty, was sitting across from O'Neil's desk, waiting for him to assign her a partner and a case. She was a chubby black woman from Northeast who had recently completed required course work at the University of the District of Columbia, making her eligible to move up in the department. O'Neil looked at her. "What do you do when you have two bad choices?" he asked

She assumed "the attitude" of the black-woman-in-charge and spit out, "Pick the one that's worse and go with the other one." She offered him a steady gaze that said there were no other options.

O'Neil took a deep breath. "You're right. You'll be with Jefferson on the priest cases."

Detective de Angelo was ecstatic. The priest killings were the top-of-the-line cases in the homicide unit at the moment. She had no way of knowing at that moment that Jefferson had asked for someone to "do the shit work" of organizing reports and other paperwork, work that no one else wanted. It would keep her at a well-worn government desk while other detectives worked the streets. But for now, she was happy and felt worthwhile.

"You can go," O'Neil added, waving her to the door. He watched her leave as she closed the door. He picked up his cell phone and called Dave, who was sleeping in the cabin and having a dream that he was about to go on the air for a national broadcast and had no copy and was not prepared in any way to speak to America about anything. It was a dream he had been having for years. He always woke up breathing hard. But this time the dream did not reach its conclusion because the dobro ringtone woke him. In his dream state he believed that Elena was calling. "Hi, are you here?" he answered.

"Where?" O'Neil's voice startled Dave.

"Oh, hi, Captain. I was sleeping. What's up?"

"Well, it appears that you already know what's up, that's why I'm calling. How are you?"

"Under the circumstances, I'm okay. I hope you're calling to tell me you got the killer."

"Not quite but we've got some leads working."

"Sounds like a press release. Speaking of that, have you guys released the autopsy findings that link the priests killer to the Etter murder?"

"Indiana Avenue is working on that. Our good friends at the F.B.I. are pissing on the furniture around here, so things are touch and go, case-wise."

"In other words, they're taking over the investigation."

"Not yet, maybe later."

"Does the F.B.I. have anything to do with me being here?"

O'Neil took a moment to answer. "It's not their place, no. But I'm pretty sure they know where you are."

Dave thought about Ossening's call and knew damn well that the F.B.I. knew pretty much everything, maybe even the stuff that Frank was alluding to and probably hiding. He listened to O'Neil breathe and wondered how long he could take to say something before O'Neil jumped in on his own. The near-silence spoke volumes to O'Neil.

"You've talked to Ossening, haven't you."

"He called to say hello and how are you," Dave said.

"And to tell you about the autopsy, I'd wager."

"So, Captain, what's next?"

"We're working on it. Promise me you won't do anything stupid for at least twenty-four hours."

"And what would you consider stupid?"

"Leaving where you are or advertising your location. Stuff like that."

"Elena is coming down to see me. She'll be spending the night."

O'Neil was relieved. Elena's presence would lessen the chance that Dave would go out beyond the wire, so to speak, and get hurt. She might calm him down and give O'Neil time to work up a plan to keep things from blowing up. "Good. That's good. I'll get Frank to take you two out to dinner. You'll be safe with him."

"Sid and I had a nice little talk with Frank, by the way. He's an interesting guy."

"Frank's got some stories to tell, that's for sure, but I wouldn't take them too seriously." O'Neil would call Frank later to hear what he had told the newsman. It was critical that their stories match. "I'll let you get back to your nap. I'll let you know if anything happens."

Dave was wide awake and he jotted down notes about the conversation. It was a story that kept evolving and changing, almost as if the priests killings had become secondary to something else. How much could he share with Elena? He wished Sid were there to sift through it with him. He opened his laptop and wrote a think piece about another day in hiding, called the desk and filed it, and searched the cabin kitchen for a bottle of bourbon, which he found under the sink. He poured himself a small glass and stared at the fire in the wood stove.

Chapter Twenty-Three

Elena's rental was a Smart-Car painted the same shade of iridescent green as the vests worn by highway workers. The tiny car was splashed with the bright pink logo of LightCar, an urban vehicle rental service designed to provide quick and easy access to city dwellers who need something to drive. A toy-like car in bright colors was nothing special in downtown Washington among the vegan professionals for whom LightCar was designed. But in Rappahannock County, Virginia it stood out among the pickup trucks driven by men who raised beef cattle. Someone wishing to blend in among the hills there would do well to be driving a dirty Ford F150 with a bed full of manure. An iridescent tiny car with D.C. plates was something to be noticed by even the sleepiest bench warmer outside a gas station.

Father Darius, still bearing a Washington state driver's license identifying him as Walter Williams of Seattle, was not sleepy. He was very alert as he sat in the red MG in the parking area of a small store on Rt. 211, reading a local weekly. He scanned the stories about high school basketball, a controversy over a new football field, and announcements about who had visited whom on a recent Sunday. A gunshop's ad caught his attention because the owner, who dominated the ad, was a bearded giant who looked like a cartoon character from a hillbilly strip. The man stood proudly in front of his shop, holding a .50 caliber sniper rifle for sale for ten-thousand dollars. Father Darius was shocked that an ordinary citizen could purchase such a weapon. *Whatever happened to American values?* he wondered.

He was only a mile or so from the entrance to the farm and was happy to spend the entire day, if that's what it took, watching for her arrival, which he believed was imminent. He was not disappointed. Her arrival was announced by the bright tiny car, being slowly driven down Rt. 211 by a beautiful young woman who appeared to be very much out of her comfort zone. The little car drew the attention of other drivers who smiled and waved to her as though she were on display or in some kind of parade. Father Darius smiled and watched as she drove by, escorted by a Jeep-load of teenagers who were trying to get her to look at them so they could take a picture. Elena appeared to be ignoring them but her face revealed tension and anger.

He was about to pull onto the highway to follow the small car when he saw another vehicle trailing about a quarter-mile behind her. It was an older gray four-door sedan with plates identifying it as a rental car, probably from an airport, he thought. The driver's face was partially hidden until it was opposite Father Darius. The driver turned to look at the MG and the two men looked at each other. Malone was shocked to see the man gazing back at him and experienced a moment of panic as he believed his plan was following apart. Father Darius only smiled and waved. *The game is on*, he thought.

Elena was unaware of any of this drama. She thought she was lost and drove at an even slower, tractor-like pace as she checked her phone's GPS instructions and glanced at the written directions she had laid on the passenger seat. On the right, she saw the turnoff to the farm and pulled in under the sign and slowly drove over the creek and up the mountain, certain that a dangerous wild animal would attack the car at any moment. At last she drove into the yard of the house where Frank was waiting with his salesman's smile.

"Why, hello there. You must be Elena! We've been waiting for you." He opened his arms and gave her a welcoming hug against his heavy wool coat.

Elena was not eager to be embraced by strange men, particularly those as friendly as Frank. She half expected a roving hand to check her out but Frank was not that sort. She pulled back and stood straight and nervous. "It's very nice to meet you. Is Dave around?"

"Let me walk you to the cabin. He's waiting up there. We weren't sure what time you'd get here. Do you have a bag?"

He carried her small suitcase and led the way to the cabin, chatting about the wonders of mountain life. He pointed out areas of interest down in the valley, although she had no interest in anything in the country. Dave was waiting at the cabin door, a smile on his face, leaning against the frame, hands in his pockets.

"Your gal's here. I'll leave you two alone. Here's her bag." Frank waved and walked back to his house.

Elena stood looking at Dave, taken by his smile, which she also saw as a smirk. She felt awkward there at the cabin with the trees and the mountain breezes blowing over them. "Well, aren't you going to invite me in?"

He stood aside and watched her walk through the door. She stopped midway through the kitchen area and looked around. It was quite nice, she thought, better than his apartment. It had been professionally decorated in a sweet, country way and it reminded her of every bed and breakfast she had ever stayed in, with the same homey, high end look they all conveyed. The kitchen area was small but useful. The bed was king-sized and coordinated. The pictures on the walls were tasteful, if you liked that sort of thing. All in all, it was not Dave. It was designed to appeal to the female half of a professional couple spending a weekend in the country. "Nice," she said, taking off her coat.

Frank sat at his desk and adjusted his headset. He could clearly hear the small talk that they made and it was evident that Elena had not been told about the danger she was in. He sat back and closed his eyes, settling in for a long period of eavesdropping. As he listened, it occurred to him that wiretaps are pretty boring, typically. Most people talk about very ordinary things such as the weather, their clothes, how they feel, what they believe the other person has done wrong, and whether they're hungry.

Dave and Elena went through this dance as they became re-acquainted with each other in this new setting. The issues of their relationship flew like little butterflies around the room as they assessed one another.
"So, how are you holding up?" she asked, looking lovelier than he remembered.
"I'm doing well," he said, writing her a note that read "This place is bugged." He held a finger to his mouth in a gesture to warn her not to respond to the note. "It's a little boring. Not much to do except breathe the mountain air."
"Can we go for a walk?" Her eyes were wide with fright.
"Good idea. Get your coat. There's a nice view at the top."
Frank could hear them walking toward the door, the door open and close, then only room noise. He closed his eyes and imagined them walking up the road to the top, chatting like lovers do. Only he knew that this would be no lovers' chat and that Dave would be telling Elena things that she would rather not know.

The air was cold and the breeze on top of the mountain cut into them as they walked up the rugged old road that would take them to the top. Dave was wearing waterproof shoes that kept his feet warm and dry but Elena was shod in stylish heels that she wore to call attention to her legs. Her feet hurt as she walked over the rocks and branches that marked the road. At first they walked in silence, each lost in thoughts about the other. He was weighing what and how much to tell her and he worried that even a small amount of information would send her back to Washington and even more danger. She was her own person and she had a right to know everything, he decided.

"We're bait, you and me," he said, telling her everything he knew about the priest killer and possible police links. He spoke without interruption and she listened without comment. He was surprised that there was no hysteria, no accusation, no drama.

They stood in a clearing at the top of the mountain, a ling of cold rain bearing down on them, looking at each other. "Are we going to die?" she asked, giving him a plain stare.

"We seem to be surrounded by people who are well armed," he said. "We're not alone." He hoped his comment would have a light tone and therefore appear to be evidence that he was not concerned about their safety, but he could see from her expression that his attempt at humor was not going anywhere. It occurred to him that she was not calm at all. He remembered that her first reaction to something that would send her into hysteria was usually calmness, followed by a meltdown. She was in the calm phase, processing the new information that would bring her to the realization that her murder was a possibility, something with which she had never dealt. He put his arm around her. Her body was stiff and unwelcoming. "We're going to be okay."

She pulled back and stared at him as tears rolled down her cheeks. "How could you do this?" Her face was twisted in anger and pain. "Why didn't you tell me to run?"

"This is the safest place. There are people here who will protect us. They know how to handle something like this."

"Who would that be? Frank? He's an old man. I don't see anyone else up here. Where's your friend Captain O'Neil and his cops? Where's the army?" She was shouting and waving her arms. "You asked me to come to see you because you were lonely for me, remember? Or was that just a lie to get me down here so some crazy man could kill me?" She had balled her hands into fists and she pounded on his chest. He grabbed her arms and held them down. She struggled and then gave up, allowing herself to collapse against him. "I hate you, you know that." He nodded and held her.

The late-day light was thin and gray when they walked back to the cabin. They were huddled together like refugees; he with his arm around her, she with her face against his jacket, walking in lockstep with their feet making crunching noises on the rough road. Frank had been watching for them and was within moments of going up to find them when he heard them coming down. He saw that they were upset and suspected that Elena was close to a breakdown. He had talked to Malone and O'Neil and hoped their plan would end this mess.

Chapter Twenty-Four

Three hundred miles to the north, a plan was being set in motion. Far from the cabin where Dave and Elena were huddled together, a small group of the Warriors of Mary was preparing to move. They were all cops; although they could not be referred to as New York's finest.

The New York City Police Department is larger than some countries' armies, employing some thirty-five thousand uniformed officers. It is also one of the oldest police departments in the United States, dating back to either the Dutch in 1625, when it was New Amsterdam, or the City of New York, when the current department was created in 1845. Both dates are used, depending on the argument being made. The department has been an avenue to the middle-class for generations of families. Irish, Italians, Latin-Americans, African-Americans and other groups working their way out of the tenements have found the department to be a welcoming way to a steady paycheck.

A great number—at times a majority—of the officers, men and women, were raised in the Roman Catholic Church, which had been a part of the fabric of the culture of the countries of their ancestors who came to America looking for a better life. The exceptions mostly being the African-Americans, whose ancestors did not come here by choice.

Catholicism and the veneration of the Virgin had a long tradition within the department, at least on the surface. The Archdiocese of New York and the NYPD have a history together. At one time nearly half of the officers on the force were Irish Catholics. It is not unusual to see officers with ashes on their foreheads on Ash Wednesday at the beginning of Lent.

And so there was nothing unusual about a group of white police officers gathered in a small union hall in Queens to say the Rosary together. They had arranged their folding chairs in a circle and were being led by an elderly priest whose red face bespoke his Irish heritage and his fondness for strong drink. He wheezed as he recited the prayers, adding a slight distraction to the contemplation being sought by others. Finally, he led the group in the concluding prayer, "Hail, holy Queen, Mother of mercy, our life, our sweetness and our hope…" to its end, "Pray for us O Holy Mother of God." And the group responded "That we may be worthy of the promises of Christ." The priest kissed the crucifix on his Rosary and sat back, closing his eyes in a private prayer.

A beefy detective named James Byrne assumed control of the group. "Thank you, Father." The priest understood that his role in the evening's events was over and he excused himself, taking a sugar cookie from a small table against the wall near the door as he exited. Byrne and the others waited until the priest had left before anyone spoke. Byrne stood and raised his arms in what could have been interpreted as a benediction. "This meeting of the Posse Maria of the Warriors of Mary will come to order."

The others had the sad, serious look of Mafia soldiers on the eve of war. There were murmurs from a few of the men.

"We have a situation that must be dealt with and we don't have much time." Byrne explained what was happening in Virginia. "I need some members to do what needs to be done. We can't let this go on. We have him in the trap. All we have to do is spring it. Are we in agreement?"

All of the men nodded and looked at one another.

"We'll be getting cooperation from our friends at SWAT. We'll draw weapons in one hour."

Special Weapons and Tactical armorers were familiar with the Warriors of Mary even though there were no active members in the armory at the moment. It was no trouble to set aside weapons and gear to be logged out "for ongoing training". That is how Byrne and his men picked up their night vision equipment, an M-14 rifle for long distance shots, a Manelli M1 shotgun, 9 millimeter handguns, and an M4 combat rifle. They did not take body armor on the assumption that they would not need it.

The men climbed aboard a nine-passenger van that bore the name of a charity and, with Byrne at the wheel, headed south on I-95 for the five-hour drive to their destination. By dawn they were sleeping in two rooms at a chain motel in Warrenton, where they would spend the day preparing for what was to come. Byrne arranged to meet with Frank at a fast food joint to review the property on the farm and set fire lanes for the possibility, or likelihood, that shooting would break out. No one wanted to shoot a friend by mistake.

By sunset the sky was clear and the warmth that the winter sun had brought quickly gave way to a frosty night with a full moon. The day's melt was quickly freezing. Byrne and his men drove to the farm and positioned themselves in what they believed were the natural approaches to the cabin, spreading in an arc from high ground to low. Byrne would act in much the way a platoon leader led an infantry unit, going from position to position, checking the men and receiving reports.

Frank stationed himself between his house and the cabin, armed with a Colt 38-40 single action revolver. The gun was over a hundred years old and had been handed down in his family from father to son. The old gun had left the colt factory in the 1890s with bluing and a five and a half inch barrel but a gunsmith in Oregon had turned it into a chromed beauty with a seven and a half inch barrel, making the weapon heavier and somewhat more accurate at distance. It was no match for modern handguns but in Frank's mind it was a perfect gun to dispatch a lunatic and so he wore it proudly on a pistol belt and holster fashioned from water buffalo hide by a Vietnamese scout near Phu Bai in 1968, where it had last drawn blood.

Inside the cabin Dave and Elena were dozing, exhausted by the emotions of the day. Dave's sleep was fitful while Elena had fallen into a deep slumber after a long period of weeping onto Dave's shoulder. Dave heard muffled voices near the cabin and knew that something was taking place and that Frank's friends had arrived to protect him and Elena and to kill or capture the priest killer. He imagined doing it himself with his grandfather's 10 gauge shotgun, a monster with a barrel as round as his thumb. Loaded properly it would blow through a barn. The antique over his grandfather's fireplace would probably explode if fired, but in his fantasy the priest killer was suitably dispatched to threaten no more.

He admitted to himself that he wished he were out with the men who were setting the trap. He could imagine being in an ambush, hidden under leaves and brush, waiting for his prey, like the times of his teenage years in Tennessee, waiting for his first buck. He had come to despise the priest killer and he felt his fear of the man melting away as his desire to kill him rose inside his chest. He found that he was breathing hard and he had an urge to leave Elena and ask Frank for a weapon, but he controlled his desire to be a part of the kill team. He lay next to her and stroked her hair, acknowledging to himself that in moments like this he was more drawn to the excitement of the hunt than to a desire to be safe. It was not fair to her, he knew, but he had no idea how to separate his conflicting inner lives. The cabin drew dark and chilled so he got up from the bed to stoke the fire and add some wood. He used the poker and saw that it was sharp on the end with a thick, pointed hook about four inches up from the tip. It was built with a solid metal handle and he saw it as a potential lethal weapon, either as a spear or a club. With it in his hand he felt armed and confident. He sat by the fire and allowed his mind to rest. He had a moment of peace and watched Elena sleep, her chest rising and falling with the rhythm of a child at rest.

Chapter Twenty-Five

Father Darius was also at peace. He had eaten a fine meal at the inn and had prepared himself for his mission. He wore black waterproof outdoor clothing purchased from an outfitter at an overpriced supermall in Tyson's Corner, Virginia. He had no worries about cost. He left the MGA in its spot behind the Holly tree, tucked away unseen. He walked away from the inn on County Road 626, making a dogleg where the town ended at the base of a wooded mountain, a place where an old logging trail was hidden behind kudzu vines that had obscured a break in the tree line. Occasional weekend hikers had found the trail and had walked it on fine days when bright young professionals from D.C. were in the mood for some nature, but mostly the old road was as forgotten as the logging business that had died out years ago.

What Father Darius knew from his earlier scouting expeditions was that the trail led to Frank's property and wound up to the summit of the mountain behind Frank's house. Years earlier Frank had walked the trail on trips to the town, but summertime rattlesnakes that infested the rocky hillside had persuaded Frank to drive and the path was left to grow over. The winter darkness settled before Father Darius was ready to move, so the road was dark when he went looking for the path. He couldn't find it and used a small flashlight to see, and he wandered back and forth until a woman walking a dog along the road asked if he was lost.

"There's an old path in here somewhere that I'm trying to find," he said, not bothering to explain why he was hiking in the dark.

The woman had the look of the aging hippies who lived in the area with their beads and crystals and homegrown marijuana. She wore a down jacket over a plain wool peasant dress and was shod in something that looked like combat boots with painted flowers. Her face was red from the cold and her smile was open. "It's over by the mailboxes, right behind them. Are you going to camp overnight?" She appeared to be looking for some camping gear.

"No, just looking for the path. It's a beautiful night and the moon is bright, so I want to spend a few minutes alone in the forest." He hoped he sounded new-agey.

"Wow, that's cool. I totally understand." She nodded her head, grinning. "Yeah, over behind the mailboxes. Peace." The woman walked away, falling in behind the dog.

He moved across the road to a row of large rural mailboxes that had a weather-beaten and rusty look in the moonlight. They were in a line on an old board held up by two fence posts. Each box had a name either stenciled or hand-painted, now mostly faded. He assumed the mailman knew who owned which box. He moved behind the mailboxes and through the dry kudzu and into the tree line. The moonlight created a mysterious image like a painting of black tree trunks and light gray landscape crossed by silhouettes of branches; a disorienting and, to Father Darius, religious scene that sent him to his knees. He found himself in a copse of small maple trees that were attempting to claim a portion of the old road.

He removed his jacket and his shirt, exposing his back to the night air. He opened his pack and removed a leather whip whose ends were knotted and run through with tacks. He held the leather handle in his right hand and opened his eyes to the forest, believing that he was gazing upon an image sent to him by Her, the Virgin. She was calling out to him in a sweet, heavenly voice. "Send me home. Send me home." He saw the face of Elena in the vision and believed that Elena was the Madonna crying out for her heavenly home. She had been sent back to the filthy world of men and had accomplished whatever mysterious and glorious mission she had been given and now it was up to him to send her back to Him, Lord of Lords, Light of Light, who sitteth at the right hand of the Father. He was humbled to tears that he had been chosen.

Her face was beautiful. He had known it from the minute he saw her all those weeks ago with that reporter, who had no idea who she was. He had followed her to New York but had known immediately that the time was not at hand. The vision had told him what he had to do and he had done it. He had sent the others, the worthy others, home to be there to welcome Her. He was exhilarated and wept as the lash did its work, tearing the skin from his back in glorious and painful sacrifice. He heard his grandmother's words. Offer it up, boy.

He stared into Her face as the pain was transformed into grace, at least in his mind. He would have gladly died on the spot and gone to his reward at that moment, but he knew his work was not finished and he could not fail or he would face eternal damnation and fire with Lucifer as his mocker and tormentor. He became too weak to move the whip, so he rested to gather his strength for what was to come. Blood covered the ground where he knelt and glistened like small red globes in the moonlight. It cheered him.

After a period of recuperation he put on his shirt and his jacket, aware that his sacrifice would require him to find additional strength to move forward. He placed his pack upon his back, feeling his shirt and jacket press against his bloody body. Offer it up. He used his small flashlight to find his way, adjusting its beam to its widest display. He felt light and strong and his gait quickened as he moved up the mountain.

Malone was not far behind. He had gone into the town to search for the MG and, after an hour of wandering around the small village, found it tucked behind the holly. It had not been driven recently. The engine was cold and the side curtains were smeared with dried bird droppings, something the car's owner would never have tolerated had he driven the car. A few dried holly leaves were on the fabric top, further evidence that the car had been left for a period of time. Malone asked at the desk inside if a middle-aged man matching Father Darius's description had been seen recently and was told that the description matched almost every male who was a guest there. However, a man whose appearance was in the general range had gone out wearing outdoor clothing about an hour earlier, if that helped. Otherwise, perhaps a quick look into the dining room would turn up the man Malone was looking for. He did not think his quarry was having dinner at that moment. He would look for the man in the outdoor clothing.

Malone walked in wide circles, looking for any indication that Father Darius was about, but he knew that the man he was hunting had begun his move toward the cabin. His gut told him that the man in the outdoor clothing was moving up the mountain. He spotted the tree line on County Road 626 and crossed it, shining a flashlight into the dry kudzu, looking for a way in or a sign that someone had gone into the woods. A dog barked behind him, startling him and causing him to turn around. A woman had the dog on a leash.

"It's busy around here tonight," she said.

"Excuse me?"

"Is something happening in there? You're the second guy tonight who's rooting around here."

"Who was the first?"

"There was a man here not long ago looking for the old logging road that goes up the mountain. He was decked out for hiking. You look like you'd be more comfortable at home." She had an easy laugh and Malone wondered if she was stoned.

"What'd he look like?"

"Hard to say. He looked like most of the guys around here. Not young, not old, white, not fat. Kind of a generic guy."

"Which way did he go?"

"I guess he went in behind those mailboxes over there. That's where the old road is. Like I said, is something happening up there tonight? You guys on some kind of adventure?" She had the tone of a child in her voice.

"No, nothing like that. We're just looking around." He smiled but she couldn't see it in the darkness along the road. She would only make out a silhouette of a middle aged man who looked like he was dressed for yard work. "I'd better go see if I can find him. Thanks for the information. Have a good evening." He turned and walked behind the mailboxes, shining his flashlight into the underbrush until he found signs that someone had gone through the kudzu.

"Say hi to that other fellow for me," the woman said. "Don't get lost."

Malone looked back to wave and saw the woman walking away, lighting what appeared to be a small pipe. *To each his own*, he thought. He had never been attracted to drugs other than tobacco and alcohol.

He had no trouble finding the old logging road once he had cleared the tree line near the road and he soon came upon a bloody patch in a copse of small trees. He shone his flashlight on the scene, noting that the blood was still wet. The whip was where Father Darius had left it, evidently believing that he would not need it anymore. Malone reached into his jacket pocket and took out his cell phone, pressing a number for Frank, who picked up after one ring. "He's on the move. He's coming up the logging road from town. I think he's in one of his trances. He'll be hard to bring down. It's worse than PCP for this guy. I'll try to catch him." PCP was a drug that gave its users extraordinary strength and stamina, often requiring several beefy police officers to bring them under control.

Frank sent a text message to Byrne. "He's on the move. Be alert."

Byrne went to check on his men and to alert them. He used his night vision gear to get around in the woods, struggling on the sloping terrain to keep his footing on the re-frozen ice patches that had formed in the small pools that had formed during the day's sunshine. The moonlight caused the image he saw to appear ghostly as he pushed on through the trees and over the slick rocks on the hillside. He was looking for a recently-retired precinct sergeant named Joe, whom he had placed on a rocky ledge overlooking the cabin. Joe was overweight and out of shape and would never pass for a crack SWAT officer, but he was an experienced cop and a committed member of the Warriors of Mary and its enforcement unit, Posse Maria, so he had been brought along to solve the problem presented by Father Darius.

"Joe! Joe!" Byrne whispered, his boots crunching on the dry leaves and twigs near the ledge. There was no sound. "Joe! It's me. Answer me." Silence. Shit, Byrne thought, he's asleep. He tromped the last few yards not caring whether he made any noise, hoping to wake up Joe before he chewed him out. He found the ledge and saw that one of the M4's spare magazines had been left out, but there was no sign of Joe. Byrne assumed that the man had gone to take a leak and had abandoned his post and he decided to take his position on the ledge and wait for the sound of Joe's footsteps and perhaps scare him, then chew him out. He sat on the cold stone, feeling the chill numb his backside, recalling his younger days when finding a way to sit comfortably on a rock was not a problem. He looked around, hoping to find another spot that would be easier on his aging body. Maybe that is what Joe did. He needed a more comfortable place to position himself.

Byrne moved to the far side of the ledge and looked down, hoping to see a soft patch of ground or even moss. What he saw was Joe lying on his back, eyes open, his chest a mass of wet liquid that looked gray in the strange night vision light that came to Byrne. He moved down to the body and saw that Joe's chest had been cut open to reveal his heart, which had been chopped to pieces. Joe was still warm. At first, Byrne just stared. He had seen many dead bodies, some in very disturbing states, but he had never seen anything like this. He looked up and scanned the trees, knowing that Father Darius was nearby. He grabbed his cell phone and called Frank, who picked up after one ring. "He's here. He killed Joe. It's on." He then sent a text message to the others, warning them to be vigilant. "Lock and load."

Byrne's men had their phones set on vibrate to prevent their ringtones from calling out their positions when they received the text messages he had told them to expect regarding the operation that was underway that night. What neither Byrne nor his men understood is the quiet of the forest on a still winter night. The sound of vibrating phones was like a chorus of frogs wafting through the trees and up and down the hillsides, telling Father Darius where his enemies were hiding, not that he didn't have a pretty good idea, at least in a theoretical sense. The vibrating phones gave him a mental picture of a clear zone through which he could reach his goal, although he had to move fast now that the others were alerted. It would not be as easy as it was with the man on the ledge who was half asleep and preoccupied with his discomfort in the cold.

He moved quietly in his black clothing, a black ski mask covering his face, among the trees to the cabin. He went to the side that was closest to the woods and peered into a small window where he could see a portion of the bed and the area near the wood stove. He saw a woman's feet moving on the bed, crossing and uncrossing as though the woman was nervous. The man, Dave, was sitting by the stove holding a poker and speaking without looking at the woman on the bed. He felt sorry for Dave. He had no idea what was happening or why. *It's a pity,* thought Father Darius. *Soon, very soon, all will be known.*

There was a small utility room at the back of the cabin where Frank had installed a hot water heater and a heat pump. The electrical breaker box was also there, along with spare furnace filters. The tiny room had two doors. One allowed access from the outside in the event that something needed servicing or replacing. The other, located in a corner near a closet, was to allow convenient access from inside the cabin for such things as filter replacement or addressing breakers that had been thrown by power surges or electrical shorts. Frank had not bothered to install deadbolts or sophisticated locks on the doors, choosing instead cheap locks from a big box store in Warrenton. Those who had checked the security of the cabin did not notice the oversight and, in any event, assumed that under the current circumstances the locks on the utility room would not be an issue.

Father Darius was clever. He had, in fact, been here before on a scouting mission and knew that the locks were easily picked, which he did with the aid of a small kit purchased at a police supply store in Baltimore. His main concern was that the lock was rarely used and would make noise when its mechanics were disturbed. The outside lock made a weak metallic sound that did not travel far. The inside lock was warmer and made no sound at all. Father Darius removed items from his backpack and stepped into the cabin.

Chapter Twenty-Six

Elena was nervous and looking for something to take her mind off the danger she was facing. She had woken with a start after a dream that she could no longer recall. It had left her breathing hard and she could feel her heart beating in her chest. "Isn't there something to do around here? We can't just stay cooped up in this place."

Dave was poking the fire and thinking the same thing. "O'Neil said Frank will take us to dinner someplace nice. It's getting late. I'll go see if I can find him. There are some really great restaurants out here."

"Don't go just yet. Talk to me. Are we going to be okay?" Her voice had a pleading note that broke his heart.

"I told you, Frank and O'Neil have this covered. All we have to do is sit here until it's over. Then we're okay and we've got a hell of a story."

"Is that all this is to you, a story? Are we doing this because you want to be a big man on the street?"

"You know that's not true. I didn't have anything to do with this."

"Really? It seems to me that this all began with your story idea about Father Phil and his homeless shelter."

"I had no way of knowing what would happen, Elena." He tried to put a soft tone to his voice but it came out as a weary whine.

"It's never your fault, is it? Your problem is you don't think. You don't think about consequences and you don't think about anything outside yourself. You have a reputation for recklessness. Did you know that?"

"I don't want to talk about this right now. I just want to get past what's happening and we can talk about other stuff later."

"Other stuff? Do you mean like us? Do you mean about feelings and other people? Is that what you say we can talk about later?" She got up from the bed and glared at him. "Because of you I'm here in this fucking cabin in the middle of nowhere with you telling me it's okay that a psychotic killer is looking for me. Can we talk about that or do you want to talk about that later, too?"

Dave felt helpless as usual under these circumstances and had no idea how to respond. "I'll see if I can find Frank and we can maybe go to dinner."

"I have to use the bathroom. Wait for me." It was only steps to the bathroom door and he heard it close, which gave him a moment's feeling of peace before what he knew was coming, the emotional fireworks that were the hallmark of their relationship. The more he thought about it, the dumber the whole thing seemed to him. He leaned back in the chair and looked at the fire. He never saw the shadow behind him and he saw only a momentary flash in his brain when the blackjack hit the base of his skull. He fell forward onto the floor where he was left unconscious, the poker still in his hand.

Elena splashed cold water onto her face, hoping it would revive her after her sleep. She felt groggy and scared and was worried that she was not alert for whatever might take place. It was unreal to her, this experience, and she had no way to measure it against the rest of her life. She was smart and accomplished. She was a graduate of the best journalism school in the country. She was beautiful and men wanted her, powerful, rich men. Why was she wasting her time with Dave, who was not rich and not available in the sense that a woman needs a man to be there for her. Why did she fall for a man who was unable to commit? She liked his swashbuckling attitude about life but it was no way to choose a mate. She was not ready to throw him overboard but it was becoming clear that there was no long term with him. She wanted a few more romantic weekends and more of his newsroom war stories before she looked around for someone else. Her hands were shaking and her eyes were red. She felt the first tremors of hysteria coming on and hoped she could get through dinner with Frank.

She dried her face and brushed her hair, leaving aside any idea of makeup. It would not be that kind of evening. She thought of the little black dress she had brought to tempt him but rejected it in favor of jeans and a sweater. She took a last look at herself in the mirror and opened the door to face the evening. Instead, she faced a man wearing black. Before she could scream he pressed a cloth saturated with ether and chloroform against her face and held the back of her head, forcing her to breath. She blacked out and was quickly wrapped in a blanket and taken out through the utility room.

For a man who was weak from blood loss, Father Darius was surprisingly vigorous as he retraced his steps away from the cabin. Elena weighed less than one hundred pounds and a man in good shape would have no trouble carrying her on his shoulder, but he was light-headed and was forced to stop to catch his breath before he reached the top of the hill. He did not put her down. He sank to one knee and allowed his heart rate to slow before pressing on. He reached the top and took a moment to orient himself toward the old logging road. He was using the moonlight to find his way, fearing that his flashlight would tell his enemies where he was. His night vision was keen after his time in the woods and he knew he could get himself back to the MG and away before he was detected, assuming all went well. He saw a flashlight coming up from old trail and moved to the side of the hilltop and placed Elena on the ledge of the cliff. He moved back into the shadows and waited.

Malone was walking slowly, tracking his man and looking for tracks to follow. He was like a hunting dog with his nose to the ground, unaware of what was happening only inches above his line of sight. He broke through the brush at the clearing on the summit and looked around for the rough road that led down to Frank's house. He scanned the clearing and something caught his eye. At first he thought it was just something a day camper had left, a pack or a picnic blanket. But it was bigger than that and it occurred to him that it was a person wrapped in a blanket. He shone the flashlight in a wide circle to see if someone else was there and saw nothing. He slowly walked to the cliff edge and bent down to look at the blanket and saw that the person wrapped in it was breathing. He was reaching to open it when the blackjack struck the base of his skull and the last thing he saw in this life was a brief flash as his brain slammed against the inside of his skull. Father Darius sent him over the cliff before he could fully collapse onto the stony surface high above the valley. Malone's body would not be discovered for two days.

Father Darius struggled to get Elena back onto his shoulders and he resumed his journey to the small red car behind the holly tree. It was nearly an hour before the MG was on Rt. 211, bound for Washington, D.C. and the Shrine of the Immaculate Conception. It had been a difficult hike for Father Darius, who stopped often to rest. Elena was unaware of any of it. Father Darius drove slightly below the speed limit, smiling and waving at the few older men who came upon the classic roadster and issued a thumbs-up to their youth, or what they remembered of it. His bloody back was dried to his shirt and the sharp pains reminded him of the holy mission he was on. He pulled his butterfly knife from a coat pocket and used it to say a Rosary and ended, as usual, with sexual release. In his tormented and demented state, he experienced a kind of mystic hysteria that caused him to laugh out loud. He told himself that he had never been happier.

He was past Warrenton and headed for Interstate 66 before Dave came around. He first thought that he must have passed out and fallen to the floor and he wondered why Elena had not come to help him. He moaned for a few minutes, thinking it would bring her, kind of like a child acting out for attention from its mother, but there was no response. "Elena! Elena! Help me!" Still nothing. He sat up, holding the back of his head, still groggy and experiencing double vision. He felt nauseous and briefly wondered if maybe he was suffering from food poisoning. "Elena! I need help!" There was no response. He managed to get to his knees and then back into the chair, where he saw that the fire had burned down. He was unsteady when he stood but braced himself against the wall and turned to look at the bed, which was empty. The bathroom door was open and he staggered to it and looked inside. She was not there. He began to worry. Had she gone for help? Was she outside? Had she left the mountain to return to D.C.? She was not in the cabin so she must be somewhere nearby.

Dave went to the front door and opened it, looking for her. Frank saw him standing in the bright light of the door and yelled for him to get back inside. "You and Elena need to stay put right now. We think he's around here and it's better that you don't show yourself."

"She's gone. Elena's not here," Dave said.

"She's got to be in there. I've haven't seen anyone come out and I've been right here since dark."

"She's not here. Come in a look for yourself."

Frank bounded into the cabin and searched the rooms and the closets. His face told his mood. He pulled his cell phone from his coat pocket and called Malone. There was no answer. He tried again and went to voicemail. He called Byrne. "We've got a problem. Come up to the cabin."

Within minutes the Posse Maria was aware that Father Darius had managed to get past them all, murder one of them, knock out Dave, and get away with Elena. And Malone was not answering his phone. Dave began to throw things around the cabin. "Goddam you! She'll be safe here, you said. Get her up here and we'll spring a trap and we'll have this guy. You're a bunch of Keystone cops who couldn't find a cat in a birdcage. Now she's gone and that deranged lunatic has her doing God-knows-what!" Frank and the others were silent as Dave vented his rage. His head ached and he was dizzy but he could not stand another minute in the cabin.

Frank agreed with Dave's assessment of how it had gone. They had been made fools of. All of their planning and computer-based gizmos had not been enough to stop a crazed and determined madman. Joe was dead and Malone was missing and Elena was on the altar of whatever Father Darius had in mind for her. "We know what he's driving, Dave. We'll catch him."

Dave looked at Frank with disgust. "What is he driving?"

"A red MGA. Black top. Wire wheels."

"How do you know that?" Dave could barely contain his rage.

"We've known it all along. We thought we had a trap set. He slipped it, but he won't slip it again, I guarantee it."

"You can't guarantee anything, Frank. You and your stupid gang that can't shoot straight should have made sure this guy was picked up before he got this far. How hard can it be to find a red MG out here?"

"We had to wait until he came to us." Frank tried to soften his voice but he was feeling some intense frustration of his own and his tone was angry. The others in the cabin looked ashamed of themselves.

Elena had left the keys to the rental car on a table by the door and Dave grabbed them and ran to the vehicle, not bothering to grab his jacket. He sped down the mountain and slammed into a oak tree when he hit a patch of ice, but the little car bounced off the tree trunk and kept moving. He didn't know it, but he was one hour behind the red MG, which was stuck in traffic near the beltway.

Chapter Twenty-Seven

The Washington area is one of the most traffic-congested regions of the United States, rivaling even Southern California. The public officials who are charged with trying to do something about the traffic backups are usually years behind any meaningful policy and, in any event, the states of Maryland and Virginia are not always on the same page, traffic-wise, and commuters are the worse for it. The traffic is so bad that off-hour traffic backups are common. The state of Virginia decided that its portion of the Capital Beltway should be expanded to include HOT lanes, "high occupancy toll" lanes on the most-travelled portion of the beltway. The idea is that flexible tolls, rising with traffic volume, will allow a few well-heeled motorists to drive faster than the peasants who can't afford the exorbitant tolls the swells can pay. The accomplish this, the state ripped up miles of the Beltway for years and, in the process, also began a major expansion of the Metro System through the same area at the same time, creating a monumental mess for drivers at all hours.

The worst of it was where Interstate 66 crossed the Beltway near a suburban center called Tyson's Corner, once known only as the site of a shopping mall, now a jumble of outdated roads that were nearly impossible to navigate at peak hours. The nighttime hours were the peak construction periods in this project. Into this drove Father Darius and his prize, now beginning to come around in the small trunk of the MG. Traffic was backed up to Route 123 and the electronic sign over the roadway informed drivers that all exits to the Beltway were closed. Since nearly all of the motorists wanted access to the beltway, they were forced to remain on I-66 until they could find a suitable exit somewhere in Arlington and a road that would take them where they wanted to go. That meant that Father Darius would be travelling at five miles per hour for a very long time.

Adding to his problems was the car itself, a standout on a road littered with gray sedans and dark SUVs driven by suburbanites obsessed with safety and room for their bikes. The men who were trapped in their vehicles, idly pondering the option of chucking it all for points west and a life in the Rockies, glanced at the small red car and smiled. Overheated anxiety in traffic jams can cause heart attacks and all sorts of horrible physical reactions as stress chemicals flood the brain, which explains why some people go berserk and open fire on others or simply get out of their cars and start walking anywhere. A brief fantasy about another life can relieve some of that anxiety and a small classic roadster was an ideal outlet for such fantasies. Which is to say that the car was noticed.

The backup eased at Glebe Road, but by then Father Darius was in no condition to carry on with his mission that night, so he drove to a small house in North Arlington, a post-war bungalow that he had rented furnished and used as an occasional safe house. He was weak and light headed and nearly passed out while he was driving down the residential street and up the driveway to the back of the house, to a small, free-standing garage which he opened with great difficulty, straining under the old, wooden door that rotated outward from the bottom. He managed to park the car in the garage, lift Elena from the trunk, close the garage door, and stagger into the small kitchen, where he placed Elena on the floor.

She was moaning and moving against the rope that tied the blanket around her but she was far from alert. He sat on a chair and watched her struggle to come around, feeling a great love for her. She is the physical manifestation of the

Virgin, he thought, smiling down at the form on the floor, and she must be returned to her eternal home. His head fell back and thought he was losing consciousness. His back was wet and he knew he was bleeding and it worried him because he would be delayed in his work. He got up and poured himself a large glass of orange juice, thinking it would fortify him. He needed rest. He would deal with her later.

He struggled to drag Elena into the living room where he tightened the ropes around the blanket and tied her to a radiator. He pulled a portion of the blanket away from her face and pressed the ether and chloroform to her nose and mouth to send her into unconsciousness, and collapsed onto the sofa, allowing himself to sink into welcome oblivion.

Dave was emerging from the traffic backup still in a rage, but he had set the wheels in motion to find Elena. He had left the mountain with no clear plan but by the time he got to Warrenton he had his thoughts together. He called Sid and briefed him on what had happened.

"What a bunch of dingdongs," Sid said. "All bets are off with these guys. I'll call the desk and tell them you'll be filing on this. Don't bother to write it up, we'll just do a Q and A. Don't leave anything out and mention the red MG as often as you can get it in. We'll run a special every hour in morning drive and you can bet your ass that the networks will be all over this. I want you to make yourself available to every news outlet that wants you, which will be all of them. Take a minute to get your thoughts together and call the desk. They'll be ready. We'll get this up on the website as soon as possible and alert some other reporters to check it. This thing will be headlines for every swinging dick that gets up in the morning. Goddam it!" Sid hung up.

Dave tried to get his thoughts in order but he needed to talk to O'Neil, who no doubt would be in bed or at least having a last nightcap. He called his number and it rang several times and Dave thought he was going to voicemail when O'Neil answered. "I know what you're calling about. All I can say is I'm sorry."

"What the hell happened, Captain?"

"It got away from us. We'll find her. We're doing all we can."

"Who's 'we'?"

"All of us, Dave."

"Are you talking about the police department or the dumbasses out at the farm?"

"It's not easy to explain, Dave."

"Why don't you give it a try? I'm going with this all over the country in a few hours and I'm not leaving anything out, so now's the time to contribute your end of it."

"I wouldn't do that, Dave. There are some things you don't know."

"There are some things I do know, Captain, and one of them is that Elena was kidnapped by this mad dog killer under the noses of the guys you sent to protect her. Who are those guys, anyway? Are they cops or some freelance lunatics you and Frank happen to know?"

"Look, we're working with the F.B.I. on a press release. It will say that pretty much what you know and we have an APB out for the MG, which should not be hard to find. We don't want to drive him underground. Let us handle this and work with us on what you put on the air."

"Fuck yourself, Captain. Your way isn't working out."

"You might want to rethink that position. You and I have a relationship that works for both of us right now but there are no guarantees it will be like that in the future."

"Thanks for the threat. Now go to hell." Dave hung up and called the desk at Now News. The pasty news assistant named Megan answered and put him through to a production manager who was ready to record. He recited everything that had happened, working backward from the most recent event, beginning with Elena's kidnapping. He outlined all he knew, including the monitoring equipment in the silo, the mysterious men who had failed to protect him and Elena, and O'Neil's attempt to censor his report. When he was finished, he did it again using different phrasing. This would allow the production manager to have two versions and could cut them up into smaller bites to use on newscasts, special reports, and feeds to the stations. A printed version would be posted on the Now News website, along with sound bites and a full version. The production manager was very good at what she did. By four o'clock, just as the morning drive news producers were having coffee and checking the news menu, Now News was in full bloom on all of its outlets and the network morning shows were calling and requesting live interviews with Dave.

He went to his apartment to shower and change into television-friendly clothes, clean Levis, a nice sweater, and a preppy jacket. He looked every inch the swashbuckling journalist as he walked into the Now News newsroom to the astonished looks of the morning crew. A desk assistant went to a printer and handed Dave a story from the AP. Headlined *"Washington Journalist Kidnapped."* It outlined the information contained in Dave's Q and A and attributed most of the details to him, with confirmation from the F.B.I. that authorities were looking for a red 1959 MGA and the driver was thought to be the man responsible for the murders of priests, a park service ranger, and possibly others. The F.B.I. had no comment on what Dave claimed to have happened in Rappahannock County nor did it have any comment on his report that a group of men there were engaged in electronic and communications monitoring of unknown persons. D.C. police were said to be preparing a statement on the alleged link between the kidnapping in Virginia and the priest killings and possibly to other murders cited by Dave Haggard, a journalist employed by Now News.

Sid arrived and walked into the newsroom with his hands in the air. "Attention! I want your attention! As you all know by now, one of our own has been kidnapped. Until she is returned to us we are a one-story organization. Am I clear? We are a one-story newsroom. It is our story and I do not, I repeat do not, want to us to be scooped by another other news organization about any aspect of this story. Am I clear?" There was a round of murmuring as the staff looked at each other. "Dave Haggard is our lead on this. He will get whatever he needs. He has given us the lead story for the entire country this morning. He will be appearing on most if not all of the morning shows. You will all work your sources even if they don't seem to have any connection to this story. They might have heard something or know something that no one has asked them about, so call them and work the phones. Pass along to Dave anything you get. Do not sit on it. Let him decide if it's important and relevant. I don't know if any of you pray. Such things are not a normal part of the journalism experience, I know. But right now we will take a moment of silence to talk to whatever higher powers we believe in to send our best to Elena. God bless her. Now let's get to work!"

Dave's first interview was with the Now News affiliate in Chicago, the station that had, in effect, stolen his clandestine interview with Captain O'Neil about the priest killings, and possible ties to Warriors of Mary and police officers. It was a quick Q and A version of what Now News was putting out all over the country. Next was Boston, then New York. He had decided that the lead was the kidnapping of Elena and the man in the red car. His secondary points were the activities at the farm. He let the anchors who were talking to him use the priests killings in the introduction. He knew the value of bullet points on the air and the need to stay within easily understood boundaries. It was a given that people who listened to the radio or watched television in the morning were doing something else at the time, like brushing their teeth or toasting frozen pastries, and could only absorb a limited amount of detail. He wanted to hammer the point that Elena had been taken by a man in a red MGA. Find the MG and we find Elena. He said it as often as he could.

By seven he was on the network shows from a small studio on M Street that was available for such things and was often used by guests on the Sunday morning "game shows", the network news-a-thons that were created to provide something to report on Sundays, normally a slow news day. Government officials and members of Congress would sometimes appear on all of them and had no time to race from one to another, so they sat in one studio and were plugged into a series of shows.

Dave ran through the facts as he knew them and mentioned the red MGA. Find the car and find Elena. The priest killings, the Warriors of Mary, the farm, the police connections, all were relegated to the later stages of the interviews, not that they were considered unimportant, but these aspects of the story were considered less perishable, if not less sensational.

By eight o'clock Virginia State Police were fielding dozens of calls about the MG. Fairfax County and Arlington police were also getting calls from men and women who claim to have seen the car. So were cops in Illinois and California. Every red MGA that had recently been on any road or highway was suspect and was reported. The only ones that mattered were ones that might have been travelling between Rappahannock County and D.C. the previous night. As it happened, there was only one. A man reported that he had been stuck in a traffic jam next to such a car and had even memorized its license plate number as a way to pass the time. He passed it along to an operator in Arlington. The car had a Massachusetts plate. It was registered to a priest who was listed as deceased, dead in an accident in Dracut, Massachusetts, on Pelham Road near the New Hampshire line the previous month, following a report that the MG had been stolen. The accident had produced a fire that had left nothing much to identify.

Around the time Arlington was running the plate number phoned in by the motorist a D.C. cop was watching television and, like everyone else, was caught up in the details about the kidnapping of Elena and its connection to the priest killings. Dave Haggard, now showing his fatigue, was mentioning the red MG, saying yet again that anyone with any knowledge should contact the authorities immediately. The officer recalled such a car days earlier travelling in the snow down Constitution Avenue in the middle of the night. Could it be the same car? He decided to call his supervisor.

O'Neil was fielding calls from all of his superiors, federal agents, and leaders of the Warriors of Mary. He was holed up in a coffee shop off Pennsylvania Avenue not far from the Justice Department, where meetings were underway about how to proceed with a situation that was fast spinning out of control. A section head was sitting at a conference table asking others in the room how something like this could happen under their very noses. Television trucks were lined up outside, waiting for the Attorney General to say something. She was waiting for more information.

O'Neil's phone buzzed and he saw that it was the chief's office. She was calm, which he knew was a bad sign. "How fast can you get here?"

Indiana Avenue was nearby but he had no desire to go anywhere near headquarters any time soon. He also knew he had no choice. "Ten minutes."

"Make it five." The line went dead.

The phone buzzed again and it was Ossening at the F.B.I. "How soon can you get here? I'm at the D.C. field office." While the J. Edgar Hoover Building, the F.B.I.'s national headquarters, was within sight of the Justice Department, it's nominal master, the D.C. field office was a few blocks away on 4th Street Northwest, not far off the tourist paths, although tourists were not encouraged to drop by.

"I'm booked," O'Neil said.

"I don't doubt that, but we have a few things we'd like to talk about."

"I'm off to see the chief. We'll have to see how that goes." O'Neil was feeling weary.

"She's going to advise you to cooperate with us."

"Did she say that?"

"It was implied."

"Like I said, let's see how it goes. I have a busy day."

"Don't we all." Ossening hung up.

The chief was standing when he walked into her office. "So," she said, "let's start at the beginning. We'll be recording this."

Chapter Twenty-Eight

Elena was trying to breathe but the blanket that was tied around her made her feel as though she were suffocating. Her mind was foggy and she thought she might be in a dream, a nightmare, and wondered when she would wake up. Her left side was numb. It was the part of her body that had been against the wooden floor for hours. Rope was wrapped around her head, neck, chest, waist, thighs and ankles, making it impossible for her move her limbs. But air was her chief concern. The more she told herself to be calm the more hysterical she became until she began to suck great quantities of air and blanket into her mouth, causing her to thrash about against the radiator where she was tied.

Father Darius was in a state of delirium caused by loss of blood and exhaustion and his breathing was shallow. He was only a few feet from Elena but he did not hear her moans and cries for almost half an hour, not until her shrieks and bangs against the radiator brought him around to the point where he was aware that something was happening in the room. He opened his eyes and stared at the ceiling, which was cracked from the weight of the old plaster over decades. For a moment he just stared at the outdated light fixture, a yellowed globe put up in the fifties when people spent their evenings under overhead lights. The globe occupied his thoughts, mingling with the sounds of the hysterical young woman. The globe turned into the Virgin, who smiled down at him, beckoning to him, "Come. Come to me." He held up his arms and expected to rise up to the ceiling and beyond to his heavenly reward, but he remained where he was, crying like a child.

The lassitude lingered as he began to glance around the room, not really taking in the physical aspects of the place. He saw it as a kind of waiting room for Heaven, a place where She had come to get him. His back ached with a fierceness he had not felt before and he was feverish. It was several minutes before he realized that the shrieks he was hearing were not coming from him but were rising from the moving form on the floor and it took him even longer to understand that there was another person in the room. He tried to sit up and cried out when his movement pulled his shirt from his back, where much of the blood had dried against his wounds. There was a half-filled glass of water on the table near the sofa and he drank it, feeling a welcome wetness in his mouth, which had gone dry during his sleep.

He shook his head, trying to clear it, but the effort made him dizzy, so he held it with his hands and tried to focus. The form in the floor was moving and making animal noises. He watched it and slowly it came to him. He was confused about what to do. Part of him knew that the woman named Elena was wrapped in the blanket and that he had taken her. Another part of him saw her as the Virgin, a holy being who was crying out to be returned to her heavenly home and that he had been chosen as the vehicle for this saintly task. *Maybe she would like some water?* He thought.

He tried to stand but the effort forced him back to the sofa, where he caught his breath. He tried again and was successful enough to stagger into the kitchen where he grabbed a glass and filled it with water. He walked to the form on the floor and watched it writhe and make its noises. "Are you thirsty? Would you like a drink of water?" The form stopped moving.

Elena heard his voice and knew for the first time that she was not alone. Her hysteria had helped bring her out of a stupor and she recalled the man in black who had drugged her. She wondered if Dave was still alive. She thought she must still be in the cabin.

"Would you like some water" the voice asked again.

She stopped moving her body and nodded her head, not knowing what would happen next. She paused, and nodded again.

"Okay," said the voice.

She heard a moan as the man knelt beside her and felt the rope around her head being untied. It took him awhile and he seemed to be having trouble with the knot. She saw daylight in front of her and felt a hand pulling the blanket away. She saw a face peering down at her and at first she thought the man was dead. His hair was plastered to his head in tangles. His eyes were swollen and red. Tears rolled down his cheeks. His face drooped as though it had melted in great heat. He seemed to be in pain. He placed the glass on the floor and set himself in a posture of prayer. He felt an obligation to speak in the ancient language of the Church.

"Mater Dei," he said. *Mother of God.* "Dominus mihi ignoscat." *Lord, forgive me.*

"Da, quaesumus Dominus, ut in hora mortis nostrae Sacramentis refecti et culpis omnibus expiati, in sinum misericordiae tuae laeti suscipi mereamur. Per Christum Dominum nostrum. Amen."

Grant, we beseech Thee, O Lord, that in the hour of our death we may be refreshed by Thy holy Sacraments and delivered from all guilt, and so deserve to be received with joy into the arms of Thy mercy. Through Christ our Lord. Amen.

With that he picked up the glass and helped her drink. She was wide-eyed with fear but the water was welcome and she stared into his face looking for signs of kindness. What she saw as madness.

Father Darius leaned over and looked into her eyes. Elena could smell his foul breath as he spoke. "I know who you are. I will help you."

"Thank you," she whispered, assuming he would untie her.

"I must rest before I can send you home," he said, pressing his lips against her forehead. "I am not well."

"Just let me go. I can get home by myself. Just untie me."

"No, that will not do. I know what must be done. I will bring you to the Shrine but only after I have rested. Then I will send you home." His mind was losing focus and he again saw the Virgin in Elena's face and he began to weep over her. "Thank you. Thank you for coming to me in this way. I am not worthy."

Elena's mind was clearing just as his was clouding and it came to her that he was mad and it caused her hysteria to return. "Let me go!" she shouted. "I haven't done anything to you."

Her voice startled him and she took on the form of Satan in his eyes, forcing the Virgin from his vision. He reasoned that this was the central term of his mission, to destroy the Satan that had come to soil the Virgin. He stared at Elena and it came back to him. He had been following her for months, ever since he saw her on the street and knew that she was the one. He had been waiting for a sign and it came to him in a snap, just like that.

He had first seen her outside Dave's apartment building and had plotted and planned and prayed and waited. Even as the Virgin was giving him instructions about the priests who had earned their right to Heaven, as he studied those he knew would try to destroy his mission, even as he developed a deep loathing for Dave Haggard, he had tracked her and brought his mind to focus on the task of returning Her to Heaven in this physical form. He had even presented holy relics to Dave in the belief that he would see them as a sign, a proof, that something truly acta sanctorum had been ordained, a holy act. *Why didn't he listen? Why didn't he honor the sacrifice? Why did he withhold her?*

Now, he was forced to separate Satan from the Madonna. It was a supreme act of exorcism and he must be strong for this final act of his life on earth. He applied chloroform and ether to a small towel and pressed it to Elena's face, holding it there until she was still, then he tied the blanket around her head and went to rest.

At that moment Dave was at a work station at Now News, trying to write a special report, but it was not coming easily. The events of the past hours were overwhelming him and he needed sleep but his mind and his body were at odds over the issue. His mind was sparking like a shorted-out radio but his body was failing him. He closed his eyes and leaned back, hoping that a short rest would give him the boost he needed to get through the next hour, then the hour after that. He had been saying the same things about the same events over and over all morning and, like someone who has said the same word over and over, nothing had any meaning anymore and he had no idea where to even begin. He had the image of Frank's cattle feeding on hay near the silo-cum-communications center and wondered why he was thinking of that. He drifted off and was startled when Sid shook his shoulder.

"Hey, Ace, how are you doing?" Sid's voice was soft. "I hate to wake you but there's a guy on the phone who won't talk to anyone else. He says he has information you'll want to know about."

"How long have I been sleeping?"

"Half hour, give or take. The guy's on line three."

Dave picked up a handset and pressed the blinking light for line three. "Dave Haggard," he said, still drowsy.

"Mr. Haggard, my name is William Lowry. I live in North Arlington a couple of blocks off Glebe Road. I saw you on television this morning, a couple of times, actually, and I heard you talking about what happened. I'm very sorry about your girlfriend and what you had to go through."

"Thank you. What can I do for you?"

"Well, I called this in to Arlington Police but I haven't seen anyone come around yet, so I'm calling you. There's a man living in a house on our block. He's renting it. It's a rental place that the guy who owns it rents furnished and on short-term leases. It's been a sore issue in the neighborhood and that's why people notice who's living there. Short term rentals don't bring in the best people, if you know what I mean."

"Okay," Dave said, wondering where this was going and wishing he had been allowed to sleep a little longer.

"Well, the man drives the kind of car you were talking about, a red MGA. It has a black top and wire wheels. I don't have the license plate number but it's out of state. There's a garage behind the house and he keeps it in there when he's around. He's been gone lately and when he's here he's out at odd hours."

Dave thought the caller must be a busy-body to spend time observing the habits of the other people on his block and keeping track of their activities. "Do you know if he's there now?"

"He is. He pulled in very early this morning and put his little red car in the garage. It's there now, I believe."

"Did he have anyone with him?"

"I couldn't tell that. The garage is around back. I want to tell you that I think this guy is a little strange. I'm surprised the police haven't been here already."

"Why do you say that?"

"It's just his manner. He doesn't seem right."

"Has he done anything, you know, that's suspicious or illegal?"

"I don't know what to say about that. He's odd, is all, and I don't want to be one of those neighbors who wait until something happens to speak up."

"What's your address?"

The man gave Dave his address and the address of the suspicious neighbor. He promised to look into it and thanked Mr. Lowry for his information. He called O'Neil, who was sitting in his car wondering if he should talk to the F.B.I. He saw that Dave was calling and picked up.

"You gonna beat me up again? If so, get in line."

"I'm sure you have new and dramatic details of about your investigation that you would love to share." Dave's voice was dripping with sarcasm.

"Yes, actually, I do. The chief and everybody else around here has been beating the shit out of me all morning."

"To any effect?"

"Not that I'm aware of. What can I do for you, Dave?"

"We're getting lots of calls about the red MGA. Most of them are people who already called the cops. How do you guys handle stuff like that?"

"Like how to we separate the wheat from the chaff?"

"Yeah, like that."

"Well, first you weed out the ones you know are from well-meaning tipsters who just want to be part of what's in the news, you know the kind. The old lady who says her brother-in-law used to have a car like that and maybe he got another one and he is the killer, that kind of thing. Then you look for the ones that might be the real deal and go from there. If I were you, I'd let the pros work this out. My guess is they're running down every lead that's being phoned in. Let's face it, Dave, there's ain't no bigger story around here right now than Elena and this priest killer."

"I got a call from a guy in Arlington who says a red MG belongs to a creepy neighbor who's renting a furnished house on his block. He says the guy pulled in early this morning and left the car in a garage in back of the house. He didn't see anyone with him."

"And I'd guess that every police dispatcher in the Washington area has fifty calls just like that." O'Neil decided he would talk to Ossening and wanted Dave to get off the phone. "Listen, I'd love to talk all day but I have a date with the F.B.I. to talk about this very case."

"Can I come along?"

O'Neil laughed out loud. "Jesus, Dave! Ossening would love that."

"Ossening? What's he got to do with this?"

"You might recall that he's with the D.C. field office. They're crawling up our ass now. Gotta go. I'm real sorry about what's happened."

Chapter Twenty-Nine

Dave was restless and exhausted and his nerves were jangled from too much caffeine. He paced around Now News and bothered all of the other staffers who were working on angles to the story. He listened as interviews were conducted. He recorded video excerpts for the website, he drank even more coffee, and worked the phones, calling all of his sources, even members of Congress who were as shocked by events as he was. By mid-afternoon he couldn't stand the newsroom and most of the staffers were eager to have him out of their hair. He picked up the address Mr. Lowry had given him and drove Elena's LightCar to Arlington, crossing Key Bridge from Georgetown and taking Wilson Boulevard up to Glebe Road and winding through a neighborhood using his phone's GPS system until he found Mr. Lowry's address.

The house was a modest brick bungalow built after World War Two in a neighborhood that housed federal employees who would raise baby boomer children who would take to the streets in the sixties to denounce their parents. Now, decades later, older people lived side-by-side with young professionals who paid kings' ransoms for the homes, which they doubled in size with additions furnished with high-end kitchen appliances. It was not unusual to see hundred-thousand-dollar European cars in the driveways of the homes of the newer residents, something that shocked and amazed the white-haired neighbors who had moved in when it was just a middle class neighborhood of government workers.

William Lowry was one of the old timers, a retired GS-14 who had worked for the Navy Department for thirty-one years following his own military service. He was the type of retiree who wore dress pants, a starched white shirt, and a good wool sweater, even though he had nowhere to go during his day. His hair was short and combed, his posture erect, and his face was shiny from his shave. He wore gold-rimmed glasses. He had a smile from a fifties sitcom when he greeted Dave, bright and showing lots of teeth.

"Welcome, Mr. Haggard. It's good to see you. I've made a fresh pot of coffee. Please come in." It was the welcome of someone who doesn't meet many strangers.

The living room was a period piece. Vaguely Scandinavian furniture, a New England oval rug on the blond oak floors, photographs of a much younger Lowry and a woman who looked a little like Donna Reed, the wholesome actress from sixties family shows, and a photo of two sleepy-looking boys under a Christmas tree next to a Big Wheel. There was slight odor of mold and bleach.

Dave sat on the sofa while Lowry went into the kitchen for coffee. He returned a few minutes later with a porcelain pot that looked to Dave like it had come from a little girl's tea party. It was white with small flowers in a springtime pattern, or so he thought. There were matching cream and sugar containers. The cups were good china and the spoons were silver. "May I?" Lowry asked, holding the pot over a cup.

"Please," Dave replied, wondering if he had somehow slipped into a children's story.

Lowry poured the coffee and sat back in an easy chair with a look of deep concern. "You've come about the man and the red MG. I'll show you the house."

Dave took a sip of his coffee and wondered if it had been percolated. It had a slightly burned tasted. "First, tell me about this guy. How long has he been here and what does he do that you're aware of?"

"He's been here about a month or so. He's gone a lot. Comes and goes at odd hours and sometimes he's gone for days at a time. It's hard to miss the car, especially in cold weather. We have a few other men in the neighborhood who have classic roadsters but they only take them out on warm and sunny days. This man has only this car that I know of."

"What do you think he does for a living?"

"I have no idea if he does anything. If he has a job it's not something with normal hours. I don't know of anyone who's had a conversation with him, neighborly or otherwise. Of course, these new people don't have much to do with anyone else. It used to be that we all knew each other and our kids all played together. Now, people don't even wave. They just double the size of their houses and stick to themselves and take their kids to play dates, whatever they are."

Lowry spoke in the manner of someone who had said the same thing over and over to anyone who would listen. Dave thought he probably said it at family holiday dinners while his sons and their families rolled their eyes.

"Where's the house?"

"Finish your coffee and we'll take a walk." Lowry raised a pinky when he sipped from the cup.

"I'm ready now. I've had a lot of coffee today."

Lowry looked disappointed but he put down his coffee and stood up, stretching his back and forcing his paunch out in front like a pregnant woman. He went to a closet near the front door and took his time selecting a coat, finally choosing a wool overcoat. It was five more minutes before he was ready to go out, wrapped in a scarf and wearing a Russian fur hat and leather gloves. Dave assumed that men who have nothing to do all day take their time at everything just to make the clock move.

"Let's go," Lowry said, as though he had been waiting for Dave.

The sidewalks were uneven from the tree roots that had grown in the decades since the neighborhood was new and Lowry walked in the street, where the going was easier.

The houses represented an era when Americans were frugal and got by with smaller kitchens and bedrooms. The homes where older people lived contrasted with the multi-story mansions that had been erected by the younger, affluent residents who had installed koi ponds, Japanese gardens, and stone terraces. It was as though the fifties were being slowly eaten by the new century.

"There, that's it," Lowry said, nodding in a conspiratorial way in the direction of a small house with a small yard that appeared to be neglected. There was a driveway next to the house that was two cement paths, car-width, cracked and crumbling. "The fellow who owns it doesn't keep it up. That's another irritation. The car's in the garage around back."

Dave walked up the driveway and peered into the back yard where a single-car clapboard garage appeared to be leaning slightly to the left. It had been painted many times but never scrapped, so the boards appeared to be scaly. The garage door was the type that swung open from bottom up and there was a row of dirty windows in the middle of the door. Dave had been a street reporter for a long time and had long ago lost his reticence about intruding onto someone else's space, so he walked up the driveway and peered into the garage. If someone yelled at him he would say he was looking for someone else and was at the wrong address. He would apologize and leave. It was dark in the garage and the windows were grimy, so it took him a minute to make out what was inside. He wiped the glass with his glove and saw the rear of the red MGA. It's small trunk was open. There was no spare tire. Dave could see that the trunk compartment protruded into the rear of the passenger compartment but it was still very small. Would there be room for a person? Elena was tiny. The car had a Massachusetts plate. It appeared to have a normal amount of road grime but no mud or anything to suggest that it had been on an unpaved road or path. He wrote down the plate number and walked to the back door of the house, planning to ask for someone he knew in another city.

The back door was located over a set of three concrete stairs that led to a small stoop. An old rusty pipe served as a banister. The screen door needed a coat of paint and the screen was torn and hanging against the frame. Dave reached through the screen and knocked on the windowless door. There was no response, so he knocked again. Still no response. This time he banged on the door with the side of his fist, pounding it.

Inside, Elena was barely consciousness and was struggling to breathe. Father Darius was on the floor next to her, delirious from loss of blood and from his proximity to the towel which he had soaked with ether and chloroform. He did not lie close to it by plan but by accident, having fallen there after losing his balance after a trip to the bathroom. If he heard the pounding, it did not register.

After a few minutes, Dave gave up. "He must have gone out or he's sleeping."

"Maybe he's up to something sinister," Lowry said, a light in his eye.

"I'll make some calls about the car and the license plate and let you know. Thank you for the tip." Dave felt very tired. He shook hands with Lowry and drove back to Now News, where the phones were ringing and producers were producing and reporters were reporting, but Elena was nowhere to be found.

Chapter Thirty

O'Neil needed a drink but it was too early in the day and he had many more interviews ahead of him. It had not gone well with the chief and Ossening had been downright hostile. It never went well if a plan failed. It always went well if a plan succeeded. This one had failed in a spectacular way and there was a stampede to get away from it. Stampede was a good word, O'Neil thought, given that both the chief and Ossening had called him a cowboy, a "rodeo rider", and a fool.

"See, here's where the shit hit the fan," Ossening had said. "You work with contractors and they didn't know what they were doing. You bring down some of your friends from NYPD and look what happened. You didn't bring down New York's finest. You got involved with some guys in a prayer group who go to the range once a year and spend their rest of their duty hours eating donuts. What the hell were you thinking?"

The chief was more direct. "You fucked this up. Tell me why I should keep you around. This is a very high profile case and you decide to play amateur hour. Go clean this up or clean out your desk."

He wished it was that simple. There were things he couldn't say to either Ossening or the chief or to anyone else they wanted to throw at him. He wanted to call Frank but assumed his calls were being monitored. He wanted to hear the details. Maybe Frank had some ideas. Ossening had told him that the Bureau was already examining, "performing an autopsy", on the monitoring operation at the silo on the farm. "See what happens when you use contractors?" he had said. "You go outside the tribe and it all falls apart."

Whose tribe? O'Neil wondered. The police tribe? Law enforcement in general? He had known Frank for years, even back when they both were rookies, O'Neil on the Metropolitan Police, the formal name for the D.C. department, and Frank at D.E.A., working the crack trade back in the 80s, when kid gangs were perfecting the drive-by shooting and leaving bodies all over the city. And Andrew. Poor Andrew Krieger. He went so far undercover they never really got him back. He was a good man in his day, though. He still he still had some value working the streets using the name Peppers, but you never really knew what was going on inside. He went over to the dark side in a psychotic, dysfunctional way. Damn shame. O'Neil had his suspicions about who had killed him but that would wait until the current crop of fires was out.

And Malone. What about Peter Malone? A prudent man would have behaved differently. O'Neil was against bringing Malone into the effort to find Father Darius. Malone was a sociopath and, for all O'Neil knew, Malone had been involved in a few of the priest killings himself, if only to expand the outrage against Father Darius. The key question that had yet to be answered was at what point does devotion become fanaticism that leads to horror? And when does going along become complicity? He knew that under the law he was as guilty as anyone else in this mess, but he was not satisfied that he had met the moral standard of the Warriors of Mary, which, to him, was the real test. And what about this woman Elena? Was she still alive? What happens if she's found? How much can Dave figure out? Or Sid? O'Neil knew that Sid was another old lion like himself and probably had better instincts than Dave and all it would take is one good sniff for Sid to get an idea of what the big picture looked like. Another problem to be dealt with.

All of this was on his mind as he walked into the Justice Department building for a meeting with an Assistant Attorney General who was Grand Vizier of the Warriors of Mary and a man who held the power to issue edicts in absolution. The title Grand Vizier originated in the Ottoman Empire as a chief officer who wielded power and influence for weak Turkish sultans. How the Warriors of Mary came to use the title was subject to the whims of whomever was telling the story, but it appears to have originated during a round of drinking following the funeral of a long-ago leader.

This particular Grand Vizier of the Warriors of Mary was known to be a severe rule follower who had no qualms about issuing "final orders" to dispatch errant members. Members such as Father Darius. O'Neil assumed that such an order would have been issued for Peter Malone once the Father Darius issue had been sufficiently dealt with.

The Justice Department building had been the laughingstock of Washington during the second Bush administration, when Attorney General Ashcroft ordered that statues known as the Spirit of Justice and the Majesty of Law be covered by a curtain. Spirit of Justice, a dozen feet tall, is a woman holding her arms up. One of her breasts is exposed. Majesty of Law is a scantily clad man. Both were installed during the administration of Franklin Roosevelt, a period more repressed than now, but the sensitivities of the day were not upset by the statues. Ashcroft found them objectionable and covered them up. The modesty left the building with Ashcroft, but the silliness of it lingered on and visitors to the Grand Hall routinely recounted the episode.

O'Neil was not concerned with such matters as he walked past the statues. He had other things on his mind. The fifth floor office of the A.A.G. was set midway down a long, government-standard hallway. The man was ensconced in a suite that held a small conference room, space for staff, and his own, somewhat grand and officious office where he spent his days doling out grants to fight youth gangs across the country, among other duties. The man would, by any standard, be described as severe. His thin face was never known to smile. His dark eyes were a shadow behind black, horn rimmed glasses. His hair was cut in a military style, high and tight. He wore dark gray suits, white shirts, and blue ties. He stood erect. His lone human hero was J. Edgar Hoover, who, as he saw it, knew right from wrong and had no reticence about wielding power for the good. And, like Hoover, he kept files on everyone he knew. His sources, his minions, at the F.B.I. were his eyes and ears and they fed the files that were buried in locked portions of his external hard drive, the one in his home safe.

He was sitting behind an antique mahogany desk when his secretary informed him that O'Neil had arrived. He had been reflecting with the tips of his fingers touching, staring at the ceiling, and pondering his options. There were no good options, in his opinion, only some that were less bad. Final orders were out of the question. There had been too much of that already, not all of it his doing, but people had been killed and that brought attention where none was welcome. On the whole, things had been botched. That was it. It needed to be cleaned up. Too much was a stake. He looked up to see O'Neil standing in the doorway looking every inch the big city cop who's seen and done it all.

"Hello, Captain. Come in. Have a seat."

O'Neil took chair in front of the desk and waited.

"Well, I hear you've been making the rounds. What conclusions have been reached, may I ask?"

"We're in a shit storm," O'Neil said, looking the man in the eye.

"We?"

"All for one and one for all, as they say."

"That's not how I see it, Captain. I see it as a mess you need to clean up. So, my question to you is, what do you plan to do about it?"

"Just what part of this are you talking about?"

"Let's start with the woman, this Elena. Where does that stand?"

"We're working on some leads."

"Spare me the press release. Do you know where she is or not?"

"Not yet but we'll find her, one way or the other. Father Darius's weakness for the red MG will be his downfall. Half of Northern Virginia saw him in it last night because of the traffic jam on 66. We were up to our eyeballs in phone calls this morning and one guy had the plate. It won't take long. We don't know how long he keeps them before he kills them. The priests at the shelter and at Catholic University were killed on the spot. The monsignor was kept alive for awhile."

"What about Chicago and San Francisco?"

"Maybe it was him, maybe not."

"I've heard that theory. Do you think it was Malone?"

"Hard to say. He was an odd one. He's missing and I'd bet that Father Darius took care of him. We don't have a body yet, so Malone could be sunning himself in Miami, but I doubt it."

"Okay, so you find the woman and take care of the good father. That's problem number one. The bigger issue is the mess you made out of this business with the reporter, Dave Haggard, and the unbelievable foulup at the farm. What in God's name were you thinking?"

"That's been the number one question all day," O'Neil said. "I thought Frank could handle it. He couldn't. I thought Byrne and the guys from New York were better than they were. We went outside for this and it didn't work out."

"Thank you for your analysis of the obvious. I won't be able to keep this from going up the pole, you know that.

The organization must come first. You may be the lamb, if you get my drift. The boys at the Bureau are all over this and there are forces over there that are not sympathetic to our cause. Do you see how this is spinning away from us?"

O'Neil had been on the other side of many such conversations and they always ended with the strong side convincing the weak side to concede and accept punishment. "Let me take care of this."

"I suppose if I didn't believe in miracles my faith would be weak, so I'll give you until the end of the day."

"Twenty-four hours. That gets me to midday tomorrow."

"I'll be having lunch at the Willard in the Occidental Grill. See me there."

So that was it. One day. Well, he reasoned, by then Elena would either be dead or alive. If he could bring in Father Darius, or at least kill him, the priest killings could be proclaimed "solved". Dave was another matter. He liked the reporter and he didn't rule out something non-lethal by way of a resolution. His phone rang and he saw that it was Dave. What are the odds? he wondered. "I was just thinking of you. How are you, Dave?"

"How do you think I am? I'm out of my mind. I might have something for you. Didn't I hear that some guy on I-66 last night got a plate number for the MG?"

"Yeah, that's what I heard too."

"I went to see that guy in Arlington, a nosy neighbor type, who took me to a house where another guy has been parking a red MG. I went to take a look and I got a plate number. Do you have the one that was phoned in?"

"Not with me, no, and I'm in transit now. I'll call you when I get back to the office. I'll be half an hour or so. Listen, we need to talk in person. How about I buy you dinner tonight?"

Dave was in no mood to spend personal time with O'Neil but he was aware of his need to maintain contact with him until Elena could be found and rescued. "Yeah, sure. Call me when you get the plate number. We can make plans."

Dave was at his apartment when he made the call to O'Neil and he felt empty. He ended the call and laid down on his bed and quickly fell into a dreamless sleep, the sort that takes the sleeper down into a near-coma where the world is shut out to all but the most insistent intrusions. An hour later the dobro ringtone was not enough. He slept through it. Five minutes later it rang again and he was immune to the noise, even though the phone was inches from his head. O'Neil gave up and left a message on Dave's voicemail that contained the license plate number and the name of a South American restaurant just off Dupont Circle where he would meet Dave for dinner at seven.

Chapter Thirty-One

The winter sun had set by the time Dave stirred with a need to relieve himself from the effects of all the coffee he had consumed earlier in the day. He staggered to the bathroom barely conscious, keeping his eyes closed in an attempt to do his business and remain asleep. He had trouble finding the sink to wash his hands so he turned on the light and that brought back the reality of the day. He slumped against the sink and thought of Elena and wondered where she was and if she was still alive. His knees gave way and he slumped to the floor and sat there for several minutes trying to gather his thoughts. He could not remember whether he had filed lately and decided to check his phone to see if Sid had called. If he was needed at Now News Sid would have been calling him in. There was no message from Sid but there was a message from O'Neil with a license plate number and the name of a restaurant. In his confused state, the plate meant nothing to Dave but he remembered he wanted to talk to the cop so he checked the time and saw that it was almost seven. The restaurant was within walking distance. Dave splashed water on his face and dressed in jeans and a sweater. He grabbed a University of Tennessee baseball hat, his jacket, and quickly walked to the restaurant, where O'Neil was waiting at the bar, drink in hand.

"You just wake up?" O'Neil had the cheery look of someone who had been at the bar for awhile.

"Yeah, I kind of passed out. I need some coffee."

They were taken to a table near the window to Connecticut Avenue and watched a parade of street fashion go by. "Not quite New York but I like the feel of this place better than the downtown area with its business suits and everybody walking around like they have sticks up their butts," offered O'Neil, nodding to a young woman sporting a bright red Mohawk and a face tattoo.

"I'm not big on tattoos on the ladies," Dave said. "It's kind of a turnoff."

"Well, that depends where it is," O'Neil made a small chuckle.

"So, how's your day been?"

"Interesting. I'm getting a lot of pressure to get this wrapped up."

"I'll second that. How's it going?"

"You know, a lead here, a lead there. Everybody and their mother is on this and the biggest problem is sorting out who's running the investigation. The F.B.I. is all over it, chasing down everybody they can think of. They've got Frank, Byrne and the other New York cops buttoned up someplace and they're swarming all over the farm. They're acting like they didn't know about the monitoring station. Hell, they paid for it."

"The F.B.I. paid for it? This was an F.B.I. operation?"

"Either that or somebody else in the Homeland Security world. It was federal money. Frank's a contractor."

"So, you're not sure who's been running all of this."

"I know it was not just Frank. He didn't set it up to entertain himself."

"Who was being monitored?"

O'Neil took a pull on his scotch and looked at Dave. "Like I said, it wasn't just Frank entertaining himself."

"And that means...?"

"He was told who to monitor."

"By...?"

"Look, this isn't an easy thing to pin down."

"I'll try to make it easier, then. He told me, or strongly suggested, that you guys know who's been killing the priests and that this whole thing at the farm was just a way to flush him out, to get him down there, with Elena and me as bait, so you could nab him. But there's more to it than that, isn't there."

"He was right to tell you that."

"But was he right in what he said?"

"Mostly. Like I said, it's complicated. I need you to lay low on this and not go around reporting things of a sensitive nature. That could complicate our efforts to get Elena back."

"When you say 'sensitive', what does that mean?"

"You reporters don't know when to stop asking questions, Dave. Let us handle this and understand that some things need to remain confidential."

"Or what?" Dave was ready to pound the table.

"Or more people get hurt." O'Neil offered Dave his cop face, the stony stare that all cops develop as a way to tell ordinary citizens to step aside.

"I have my job and you have yours. Enjoy your dinner."

Dave stormed out of the restaurant and walked to Now News as a cold drizzle settled in. The cold helped him calm down and it shook off the last of the lethargy from his sleep and he felt energized. He used his electronic pass to get into the building and walked into the newsroom, where Sid was haranguing an intern about something that had not been done to his satisfaction. He looked up when Dave walked in.

"Dave, come over here. This is Jennifer. Jennifer is attending the University of Maryland where she is studying journalism. Based upon a recommendation from an old colleague who teaches there, I brought Jennifer on as an intern this semester. But apparently the University of Maryland no longer teaches its journalism students that no one cares what they think, so she assumes that her opinions are suitable material for news reports." Jennifer was near tears and looked to Dave like she had been all but whipped.

"So, edit it out," Dave said.

"That's not the point. What if we had her on live? We couldn't cut her copy. It's important that everyone who reports the news knows the difference between a fact and a rumor, for one. For two, it's important that said reporter knows the difference between what she can prove and what she can opine."

Dave felt sorry for the young woman, who was shaking. "Don't worry about him, Jennifer. He's an old lion. I need you to help me with something. Excuse us, Sid." Dave led Jennifer away to a work station. Sid stormed into his office. He stopped at his desk and turned, walking to Dave.

"Anything new?" he asked.

"Not that I'm aware of," Dave said.

Sid went back to his office while Dave tried to calm the young woman in front of him. "So, what happened?"

"He asked me to write an update about, you know, what's happening. I did but he didn't like it."

"What did you say?"

"I laid it all out like we've been reporting all day and I used the word 'horrific' to describe what happened to Elena. He told me that was an opinion word and it has no place in a news report. He just went off on me."

"What happened to Elena was horrific, Jennifer. I think he's just showing the strain. We all are. I'd let it go if I were you. We all think you're doing a terrific job." That seemed to calm her and she smiled. "How long have you been here?"

"Since six this morning."

"Go home. It's okay. You need some rest."

The young woman looked at her hands. "I'd rather stay." Her eyes teared up. "I don't know what I would do at home just thinking about it. I need to be here."

Dave looked around and saw that the newsroom was packed with staffers who could not go home because they wanted to be where the story of Elena was being worked. They wanted to know the latest as it happened. They wanted to see her walk through the door again.

Chapter Thirty-Two

The pain woke Elena. She had been on the floor for too many hours and the numbness had become an ache and she tried to roll over onto her back to relive it, but the radiator prevented much movement. She had wet herself while she was out and it was cold down there against her body, where her underwear stuck to her. She was horrified at the thought of soiling herself which she knew would happen unless she used a toilet soon. She was strangely lucid and understood that she had been kidnapped by the man who gave her water and that he was insane. She did not know where she was nor did she know the time of day, or even what day it was. She knew that she must remain calm and not cause him to drug her again. She had a headache and assumed it was from the drugs. She concentrated on her breathing, slowing her breaths and taking in as much air as possible through the blanket, then slowly exhaling, trying to control her heartbeat. It was easier to breathe because she was not fighting for the air. She had taken a yoga class in New York and applied the breathing technique she had learned. Slowly, breathe in. Slowly, breathe out. Focus the mind.

Father Darius was on the floor next to her, studying her breathing in the weak light offered by the lone lamp that was on in the living room. He felt stronger as he watched her, believing her to be the Virgin, allowing a wave of love to wash over him. He was groggy and his back ached, but his mission had become clear again. He must deliver Her to her rightful place in Heaven, and so must gather his strength. He would wait until he felt strong enough to do what must be done. In the meantime, he would do what he could for Her.

"Do you need anything?" His hand lightly brushed against the blanket covering her face.

She nodded but kept silent. "Would you like me to open the blanket?" Again, she nodded and tried to keep her breathing under control, but her heart was racing. "Okay. That will be okay. We can talk then." He again had difficulty untying the rope around her head and she thought she would panic as she waited to see again. He was sitting up looking at her face when he pulled the blanket back and she blinked as she looked into his teary eyes. He had the look of a man who was seeing a vision. "Mater Dei." *Mother of God.* He believed that Latin was a holy language and was the only way to truly speak the divine. He got up on his knees and wrapped a Rosary around his fingers. "Credo in Deum Patrem omnipotentem..." *I believe in God, the Father Almighty...*

She watched him pray and it occurred to her that he was praying to her. He believed her to be holy in some way. He called her Mater Dei, Mother of God. Mary? Did he think she was Mary? If so, what did he have in mind for her? She had no doubt that this was the man who had been murdering priests in a grisly, bloody manner, but what did the Virgin Mary have to do with it? Was he acting on her behalf? Was he just crazy? She watched him pray, working his way around the beads on the Rosary. At some point he began to touch himself and weep in anguished wails, bashing his fist against his forehead. His release came as he ended his prayers and she had trouble controlling her building hysteria. What sort of monster is he? she wondered. He collapsed against her and begged for forgiveness. "I'm so sorry, Mother. I am not worthy to be your servant."

"You must untie me," she whispered.

He sat up and composed himself. His face was hard. "Are you Catholic?" He again saw her as Elena, not the Virgin.

"Why do you ask?"

"Are you familiar with the Holy Trinity; the Father, the Son, and the Holy Spirit?"

"Of course." She wondered where this was going.

"Not that I am comparing you to the Holy Trinity, but my point is that it is possible to be more than one being at the same time. You, for instance, are two beings at this moment but soon you shall be only one." He took on the attitude of the priests she had feared as a girl, the attitude of righteousness and absolute knowledge. "Inside you is the spirit of the Mother of God, the Virgin Mary, She who contains no sin, no taint of human weakness, no degrading desires. Her spirit is trapped in the body I see before me, the consort of the reporter Dave Haggard, with whom I know you have soiled your soul in desires of the flesh. Your body is no longer a holy temple, it has become a repository of filth from which She, the Virgin, must be freed. Do you understand?" His face was severe and his tears had dried. His weak, mad appearance had been replaced by something else, something stronger.

"No, I don't understand. Tell me." She was trembling and her breathing was quick.

"You and She must be separated. Her spirit must be allowed to return to its heavenly home."

"Why doesn't she just leave me?"

He looked at her with pity. "That is the task for which I have been chosen. It is the culmination of my work on earth. It is I who was given the honor of preparing Her way, of sending before her those whose holiness was sufficient to welcome her home. I was given the honor of freeing the souls of the special priests who were worthy to sit at her side. They are there now, waiting. You should feel blessed and eternally grateful that you are the chosen vessel of her spirit, if only for this brief moment."

"You must untie me. I need to go to the bathroom. I will soil myself if you do not do as I say." She took a severe tone with him, more like a mother than a hostage. "Do it now!"

He was taken aback by her order and sat in silence as he pondered her words. He stood up with some difficulty and looked down at her. "If you try to escape I will kill you right here and you will not have the benefit of the blessings of the Shrine. For that you will pay for all eternity."

She had no idea what he was talking about but she agreed by nodding her head as she watched his face. The knife appeared in a flash, as though it was part of a magic trick, and the ropes were cut. He helped her out of the blanket and stood back as she struggled to her feet, which were numb and unresponsive. Her clothes reeked of urine and were still wet in places and her private area was chafed and sore. "I will need some privacy."

"I will not leave you alone under any circumstances but rest assured that I have no interest in your physical self. Do what you must do but only under my eyes."

She suffered the humiliation of his presence as she relieved herself, avoiding his stares by looking at the floor. Once finished, she cleaned herself and stood up, removing all of her clothing. "I need clean clothes. You cannot believe that the Mother of God finds it acceptable to occupy a body wrapped in filthy clothing. Bring me clean garments." She stood naked, glaring at him.

He could not help himself. He stared at her in horror and shame. He ran from the bathroom and stood in the small hallway, breathing hard and banging his head against the wall. "No! No!" He rushed into his bedroom and rummaged through his small suitcase for a pair of pants and a shirt, which he threw at her. "Here. Put these on now." He stood near the door until she came out in the clothes, leaving her soiled items on the floor.

"Now what?" she asked. She was much shorter than he and her head only reached his shoulder, but to him she seemed larger and more powerful. He struggled to remain in control.

"We have to go somewhere."

"Where?"

"I must take you to the Shrine."

"Is that where you will do it?"

"Yes, it is where my mission will be accomplished."

"Will you die there?"

"I will go with her, yes." That seemed to strengthen him.

Elena walked to the sofa and sat down. "Let's talk." She wanted to slow down any plans he had. Father Darius complied like a schoolboy, coming over to her and sitting next to her on the sofa, a meek expression on his face. The only troubling aspect to this moment was the butterfly knife he kept open in his left hand, the hand farthest from Elena. She glanced at it and then at his face, which was having a neutral moment. "Tell me about yourself," she said in the manner of a school teacher interviewing a new pupil.

He displayed a shy smile. "I'm a priest. I was a parish priest for awhile in a place where most of the people were wealthy, or at least financially comfortable. I didn't like it very much. The parishioners were not faithful to the church nor were they faithful to Our Lady. I prayed for them. I really did. But the Father had decided that they were too far gone and he had other plans for me." He looked at her with pride.

"How long have been on your mission?"

"For about a year, in one way or another. It was not easy, I can tell you that. I was first led to others like myself, those who venerated Her, then one thing followed another and I am nearly at the moment of my salvation." He looked concerned. "Are you hungry?"

"Yes, I am very hungry. Do you have food here?"

"No, but we can order something and have it delivered." He looked like a child who had come up with a great idea. "There are all kinds of really good places around here. Do you like sushi?"

She laughed out loud at the idea that this madman would order a sushi delivery before he drove her to the Shrine and killed her in what he believed to be an act of faith. He was upset at her laughter so she stifled it. "Sushi sounds wonderful. Do you have a menu?"

He opened a drawer on an end table and removed a stack of door hanger menus that had been left by canvassers. There was pizza, Chinese, Thai, Salvadoran, Mexican, subs, and, near the bottom, menus for two sushi places that offered delivery. "Here we are," he said. "Sushi Hot and Cold."

"I thought all sushi was cold," Elena said, catching herself in what was fast becoming a normal conversation.

"They're talking about spicy." He seemed almost charming and normal and she knew that this was a sign of a sociopath and that he could turn on her with a murderous intent in an instant.

"I'd like the spicy tuna and crispy chips," she said, glancing at him. "What will you have?"

He face turned dark and the smile was gone. "I won't be eating. I have no further need of nourishment." He stood up, opened his cellphone, and placed the order for Elena's food. "Twenty minutes," he said, closing the phone. "They always say that."

Chapter Thirty-Three

Sid was a little drunk. He kept a bottle in his desk and it was no secret that if he was working after six in the evening his breath had a bite to it. It was well after six and Sid had downed a good amount of the bourbon, along with several cups of strong coffee. The combination had rekindled his desire to light up thin, black cigars, the type favored by gangsters in dinner jackets in old movies. He walked to a cigar shop nearby and bought a dozen of them, lighting one as he strolled back to his office. He had always liked the way a blend of drink and smoke could bring him a sense of peace and contentment, which he sought on this cold winter night. But it was not a night for such things and found he himself chewing on the cigar as he thought about Elena, Dave, and the murders of the priests. It occurred to him that he had been covering stories about mad killers for decades and had even seen some of their work firsthand, but never had he had to breathe their foul air as he was doing now with this mess.

Sid had come to believe that Captain O'Neil was either corrupt or incompetent or on somebody's payroll. This business at the farm was a farce of the first order and not the work of professional, in Sid's opinion. How on earth one man could find and capture Elena, who, presumably, was in a safe place protected by cops was beyond him. He approached the lobby to the building where Now News was headquartered and threw the cigar into the street, causing a young woman to yell something about the environment as she pointed to the cigar rolling in the gutter. Jesus, he thought. It never ends.

Dave was waiting in his office, sipping some of the bourbon from a plastic cup. "Can I borrow your car?"

"Nobody borrows my car. My insurance won't allow it. Why?"

"I'm feeling trapped here. What if I need to go somewhere if something comes up?"

"Maybe you should have a car of your own." Sid was glad to be having a normal conversation.

"I had one but I never drove it."

"Then sticking to renting. Right now, it's late. Go home. Get some rest. The cops are going to issue an update in the morning and I'll need you there."

"Are you sure you want me to cover this stuff? I'm part of the story."

"I'm not sure what I need, Dave. I got a call from the U.S. Attorney's office saying they're considering declaring you a material witness and shutting you up. I've got our lawyers working on it."

"What would that do?"

"It would keep you from reporting on what you know. There's nothing they can do about what you already reported but I gather they'd rather you just went home and locked the door. You'll probably be called before a grand jury at some point. You and all of the other guys down at the farm. They've got everybody else buttoned up. I've been trying to get hold of Frank to get something from him about his little surveillance operation but I got nowhere."

"O'Neil told me they had them somewhere for questioning."

"What do you think they're asking?"

"My guess is it's something along the lines of 'what the hell happened?'"

"Do you have any theories?"

"I don't, not right now. I wonder what O'Neil's role in this is. How much did he know? How much did the F.B.I. know? Who else knows what? These guys know who killed the priests and they just waited for him to come to them. Is that good police work? Are they working another agenda? Makes you wonder, you know."

"I think O'Neil's got some secrets that he's not sharing with anyone. I think he's ass deep in this Warriors of Mary group and he's protecting them. These cops from New York, the ones who botched the security at the farm, they're in it too. Frank, a so-called federal contractor, has to have some connection. This killer is also in it and my bet is O'Neil is playing both sides. I'd also guess he's not alone and there are other law enforcement types protecting the home front. I have no proof of anything but that's the angle I'd work if I were on the street." Sid leaned back and lit another cigar in clear violation of the laws of the District of Columbia against smoking in office buildings and against the express policies of Now News, which Sid himself had written. At this moment, he could not care less.

"I had dinner with O'Neil tonight. Well, kind of. I got pissed off when he tried to get me to close down my reporting on this and I left him."

"Did he have anything new? How about the car, that MG? Have they found it yet?"

"Shit! I got something about that. A guy in Arlington took me to a house where some renter is driving a red MG. I took a peek and wrote down the plate number. O'Neil left me the plate number that a guy got on I-66 last night." Dave took a small piece of paper out of his pocket and placed it on the desk. He called his voicemail and checked his messages, replaying the one from O'Neil. He stared at the paper as he listened to O'Neil and Dave's fell pale. "Give me your keys. Now! Goddam it, she's in Arlington."

Sid stood up. "Let the cops handle this."

"Yeah, like who should I call? O'Neil? I need your keys."

Like Father Darius, Sid's vanity was his car. He was not fond of classic roadsters. He was drawn to Detroit's biggest, referred to as "boats" by critics. Sid drove a Lincoln Town Car, the longest car built in the Western Hemisphere, at over eighteen feet. He saw the size of his ride as equal to the size of his life and he thought he was living a large life as the chief of a Washington news service. He associated size with comfort and his car was like a rolling living room with a premium sound system that blasted Motown Classics, Dave Brubeck, and Frank Sinatra's Capitol Records hits. It was true that he never allowed anyone else to drive it, not because his insurance company wouldn't allow it, but rather he couldn't stand the idea that someone else would be behind the wheel of the big machine. He paused for only a moment and handed his keys to Dave. He wanted to say "be careful" but he knew it would sound trite under the circumstances, so he remained silent as Dave ran out the door to the basement garage where Sid's pride and joy was parked.

The rush hour was over and the streets were clear of heavy traffic as Dave raced the big car down to K Street and over to the Whitehurst Freeway for the access to Key Bridge, avoiding the Georgetown traffic on M Street. The bridge was busy, as usual, but traffic was moving as he made his way to Ft. Meyer Drive and up the hill to Wilson Boulevard and south to Glebe Road. An Arlington cop was sitting at a light near the courthouse and Dave slowed to avoid attracting unwanted attention. He briefly considered waving down the cop and telling him that Elena was being held in a nearby house but he was suffering from a lack of trust in all law enforcement, so he kept going. He had no trouble finding the neighborhood and he drove by the house where the MG was parked in the garage and saw that a light was on in a front room. He pulled to the curb and briefly wondered which way the MG would go if the man who held Elena made a run for it. He would later lament that he did not block the driveway.

An age-darkened concrete walkway led past overgrown evergreen bushes to a set of concrete stairs that time had separated from the small stoop at the front door. The stairs listed to the left and there was a gap of a few inches where they had pulled away. Dave saw it as evidence that no one cared about the house and probably had no concerns about what happened inside. It was the ideal rental for someone up to no good. There were leaves piled up against a rusting railing where the wind had gathered them in the fall and where they had been left without anyone bothering to clear them away. A porch light was dark but Dave could see that its glass cover was missing and a bare bulb was hanging at an angle and he assumed that it was burnt out.

He stood at the front door and it occurred to him that he had no plan. Should he knock or try to break down the door? Could he do it if he tried or would he just injure himself? Did he have any idea what he was doing? He recalled his rough days as a boy in the Tennessee mountains and the scrapping and fighting that was part of growing up there and his confidence began to rise. He pulled open the aluminum screen door and noted that there was no screen, only the metal frame. The front door was wood and had three small diamond-shaped windows placed diagonally high up, making it impossible for someone standing outside to see what was happening in the house unless they were standing on something. Dave looked around and saw nothing he could use as a platform to see into the house, but the stoop was small and the railing was only a couple of feet from the door, so he climbed up on it and placed his hands against the rough brick face of the house and leaned forward, hoping he wouldn't slip off and fall on his face. He had trouble getting an angle into the front room. The window that was closest to him was also the highest on the door and only allowed him a view of the ceiling. The middle window was lower down but farther away and he had to press his hands against the door frame and lean far forward to see inside but could only glimpse a closet door and a small section of the room. The lowest window was his best chance of looking inside but it was on the opposite side of the door and he strained to lean far enough to see and nearly fell. He could see only a section of the room and he pressed his face closer to the glass to get a better view.

Elena was sitting on a sofa wearing a man's clothing, eating something out of a Styrofoam container, looking disheveled and frightened. He caught a glimpse of a man sitting in a chair, watching her and smiling. The man was holding a knife. Dave nearly called out her name before he caught himself and then nearly fell off the railing before he could climb down and approach the door. His plan was simple. He would knock on the door and shout to Elena that he had come for her. This, in Dave's mind, would confuse the man holding her by dividing his attention between the man at the door and his hostage, possibly giving her time to run out the back while he came through the front door. Dave was not experienced in this sort of thing and the pros and cons of his plan were not apparent to him, other than he thought it would be better to do something than nothing. The idea of calling the police was lost on him.

He stood in front of the door and took a deep breath, then he pounded on it with the side of his fist. "Elena! It's me, Dave. I'm here for you! You, the guy holding her, open this door right now!" He hoped his pounding would rouse the neighbors. He pounded on the door for a full five minutes without reaction from inside. He shouted at it. He threatened. He pounded some more. All the while he stood directly in front of it, ready to attack when it opened. He was so occupied with the door that he did not notice the man stepping up behind him with a towel soaked with ether and chloroform until the cloth was pressed against his face. Dave was much bigger than Elena and it would take more time for the chemical to work, so he had nearly a minute before he blacked out. He had taken martial arts classes for several years when he was younger and although he was out of shape and out of practice, some of it came back to him. He raised his left foot and raked the back of his heel against the Father Darius's shin, causing him to yell out in pain, but it was not enough to force the man to release Dave. He tried to get his foot behind the man's leg to trip him, but Father Darius was too fast and pulled back.

    Dave could feel his attention fading and he was breathing hard from the struggle, so his time was running out. He remembered a move that one of his instructors had told him would always work against a man. He moved his right hand down and behind him, grabbing Father Darius's testicles and squeezing as hard as he was able. The priest cried out and moved back, tripping and falling down the short flight of stairs into the yard, where he lay in pain for a few seconds. Dave wanted to jump down and overpower him but he was too woozy from the ether and chloroform and exhausted from the struggle, so he leaned forward with his hands on his knees, breathing in the clean air and waiting for his senses to return, and that was enough time for Father Darius to gather himself and run to the garage. Dave went after him, but was slow in his movements and confused about what to do. The MG raced down the driveway and into the street. Dave could hear the engine screaming as it headed north in the direction of D.C.

Chapter Thirty-Four

He could not kick in the door, despite several attempts. He briefly wondered how soldiers in war did it and made it look easy. He made it down the stairs and walked around to the back of the house. His head had cleared by the time he found the backdoor open and went inside. The container of food was still on a small coffee table but there was no sign of Elena. He ran into the other rooms and the only sign of her was a pile of her clothes in a bathroom. He ran to the Town Car and went after the MG, racing toward Glebe Road and the route back to the District. The Town Car was fast and had a big engine; despite its styling, the MG had only a 1500 cc, 72 horsepower engine and could not keep up with modern vehicles, even small ones. The MG tended to sound faster than it really was, although under ideal conditions it would top ninety miles per hour.

These were not ideal conditions. Wilson Boulevard to Key Bridge had a stop light on every corner and at this hour they were timed outbound to help the Georgetown crowd get home. The road went past the Arlington County Courthouse, where dozens of police cars were coming and going. Rosslyn, the high-rise district across the Potomac from Georgetown, was built along old Colonial and Indian trails that followed no discernible pattern and crossed at odd angles and became one-way in-or-outbound in what for first-timers seemed willy-nilly. Only someone who travelled the area every day for years could make it down Wilson Boulevard, through Rosslyn, and into Georgetown at a high rate of speed. Everyone else would be satisfied remain among the not-lost.

Father Darius had studied the area and thought he had a good route that would get him into the city even with someone pursuing him. He had to make a choice whether to race through the area and risk being pulled over for running the lights or go with traffic and hope he made it. His decision was made for him when he saw two police cars near a red light. He stopped and waited for it to turn red and he felt the MG swaying from Elena's attempts to break out of the trunk. He had not had time to drug her into unconsciousness after he tied her hands and feet with duct tape and jammed a sock into her mouth to keep her quiet. The sock was held in place by a strip of tape and he idly wondered if she would smother or managed to scrape the tape off to cry out. Either event would be a disaster, in his mind. He could not worry about that now.

He hit nearly every red light on Wilson Boulevard and thought the game was up when a half-dozen Arlington sheriff's deputies walked up to the car at a light near the courthouse and began asking questions about it, admiring the paint and wire wheels. One of them remarked, "A car like that was in the news." The light turned green and he waved and said goodbye. He glanced in his rearview mirror to see if they were following him but they returned to what they were doing and walked away. It would be ten minutes before one of deputies remembered the details of the search for a red MGA and another thirty minutes before the sighting was reported on the police radio system which, even after 9/11, was not automatically connected to other departments in the Washington area. By that time, the MG was headed down Pennsylvania Avenue.

Dave was not far behind and knew Arlington well enough to take parallel streets when he could. These streets were part of a confusing, ancient grid that no sober urban planner would consider, but such planning was not part of Colonial Arlington and the streets ended or looped in other directions, but they got Dave past many of the lights on Wilson Boulevard. He was roaring north on Oak Street having looped left from what had been 16th Road when he saw the MG pulling away from the light. Father Darius could either go left on North Lynn Street to Key Bridge and Georgetown, or turn right into a warren of streets that would eventually take him to the Roosevelt Bridge and Constitution Avenue. Dave did not know how much Father Darius knew about the streets of Arlington but he guessed he would head for Georgetown because it was the easier route. He got stuck behind a delivery truck that blocked two lanes on North Lynn and pounded his horn while the driver gave him the finger and opened the back to make a delivery. By the time he got around the truck the MG was across the bridge and making a right turn onto M Street. Traffic, for once, was light and he knew the little car would make good time past the shops and clubs.

The western end of Pennsylvania Avenue begins at M Street and angles south and east past George Washington University, the White House, where it is blocked for security and where it doglegs, and then down to the U.S. Capitol. The section between the White House and the Capitol has been called America's Main Street and is on display every four years when the just-sworn-in President rides or strolls down the new pavement, waving to the crowds. On most days and nights the avenue is just another city street with cars and trucks moving or stopped at lights.

On this night the traffic was light but the D.C. and U.S. Park police were out in their usual force, watching for trouble. The D.C. Police Department's newer cars had low level red LCD lights that blinked constantly. The idea was to help citizens who were looking for a police car to find one. The red MG pulled up next to such a police car at 12th Street. Father Darius was breathing hard and trying not to act in a suspicious manner. The officer at the wheel, a duty sergeant, was having an argument with his wife, who was berating him on his cell phone. The sergeant was only dimly away of the other vehicles at the light and was trying to calm her down and so he failed to notice the small red car, which slowly pulled away when the light turned green. The sergeant did, however, notice the Town Car that sped past him and up to the bumper of the smaller car, honking his horn. The MG pulled away and the two cars more or less stayed within an acceptable speed, so the sergeant decided that whatever was going on probably involved two friends who had been clubbing and were horsing around on their way home. On most nights he would have pulled them over and administered a breath test, but tonight he was fending off an accusation that he had slept with a neighbor, which was true. So he let the two cars go.

Dave stayed on the MG's bumper and panicked himself when he tried to come up with a plan for when the driver of the car stopped, however long that might take. Would he fight him man to man? What if the man attacked him with the knife? He tried to remember what he had been told about knife fighting. He should wrap his coat around his arm to protect it. That much he remembered. He did not have a knife of his own, so he was at a severe disadvantage there. He called Sid in his panic and told him what was happening.

"I'm calling the cops. You can't handle this on your own," Sid said in a soothing voice, hoping to calm Dave down.

"No! Don't. We can't trust them." To Sid, Dave sounded hysterical.

"How do you plan to handle this?"

"I'll figure something out."

"The guy you're chasing is nuts, you know that. He's killed people. He'll kill you if he gets a chance. You're lucky he hasn't killed you already."

Dave was surprised at how calm Sid sounded and wondered if he was drunk. "He has Elena. If I can get her away from him then we can let the cops take care of the rest."

To Sid it sounded like a plan a ten year old would come up. "Where are you now?"

"We're coming up to Constitution. Wait, he's heading up Louisiana to Union Station. I think I know where he's going. He's taking her to the Shrine of the Immaculate Conception. That's where he killed a priest. I'll call you back." Dave ended the call so he could concentrate on following the red MG.

Captain O'Neil had been enduring another tail-chewing session at headquarters on Indiana Avenue, this one attended by not only the chief and her minions, but also the F.B.I. and some suits from Homeland Security, who wanted to know more about the monitoring operation at the farm. O'Neil had seen the signs during the meeting; the glances, the feigned interest in his future, the soft way in which the chief addressed him. It all added up to one thing: he was going to be thrown under the bus. He guessed that the only question to be answered was whether he would be charged with a crime. He sat in his big car and lit a cigar, something strictly forbidden in the new, non-smoking world. The department had decreed that normal people, meaning those who did not smoke, should not ever be subjected to the offensive aromas left by those who do. There would be no smoking in department vehicles, offices, or other facilities and property. To hell with them, he thought, as the smoke filled the car. He was stopped at the light at 3rd and Constitution, working up a grand sense of outrage, when the red MG sped by with a Town Car hot on its tale. There, at the wheel, sat Dave Haggard, talking on his cell phone. It took O'Neil less than a second to assess the situation.

He turned left on Constitution and saw that the two cars were heading for Union Station, but the red car turned onto North Capitol Street and made the light at the Main Post Office with Dave in the Town Car right behind him, on his bumper. A D.C. cop at the wheel of a patrol car was hassling a prostitute and was telling her to move along when he saw the two cars speed by. He turned on his lights and siren and went after them, thinking they were a couple of drunks.

O'Neil turned on his own flashing lights and siren and pulled up next to the patrol officer and tried to wave him off, but the officer, who was black, felt he was being disrespected and gave O'Neil the finger. O'Neil tried to pull ahead of the patrol car but a Metro bus was blocking the lane, so he settled for fourth place in the caravan that was moving north.

Father Darius had come to the conclusion that the drama he had been sent to perform was in its final moments and that he no longer had anything to lose, so he began to run the red lights, swerving to avoid cars that were proceeding across his direction, sending Dave in his big sedan careening around busses and cars that were proceeding on green lights at the cross streets. The patrolman and O'Neil were blaring sirens and emergency lights as onlookers wondered what was going on.

Elena had managed to scrape off the tape that held the sock in her mouth and was screaming for him to stop the car. She was also chewing the tape that bound her wrists. Father Darius began to pray out loud to drown out the screams coming from the back.

Dave was sandwiched between the red MG and two D.C. police cars, one of which he recognized as O'Neil's. He assumed that Sid had called O'Neil and he vowed to punch Sid in the nose when he had a chance.

By the time the caravan had reached New York Avenue they were travelling at close to sixty miles per hour, a speed that would doom them all if maintained through the lights up ahead. North Capitol crossed under New York, so that was not a problem, but the letter streets had lights. They caught the light at P Street and got past Florida Avenue but there was a small backup at the red light at R Street. Father Darius swung the small car to the left, where the turn lane was clear, and squeaked between a bus and an SUV to cross the intersection. Dave swung to the right and sped through the clear right turn lane but sideswiped a carpet company van that was slow to move through the intersection, wiping off the driver's side mirror and caving in a section of Sid's door. The driver of the van, an illegal Nicaraguan, sped away, hoping that no one got his plate number.

The patrolman was on his radio asking for backup and O'Neil was on his cancelling the backup, saying he was a Captain and had the situation under control. He switched to another frequency and alerted his available units to meet him at the Shrine. Just past Prospect Hill Cemetery, in front of the row houses that lined North Capitol, a man heading to work at the Government Printing Office pulled away from the curb and into the path of the MG, which swerved to the center lane. Dave, following close behind, slammed into the man's Toyota Corolla, glancing off the driver's side, sending the smaller car up and over the curb and through a chain link fence that enclosed his small front yard. The man suffered a broken shoulder but was otherwise unhurt. Sid's Town Car suffered another blow to its perfection, this time a deep, open gash along the right front fender and both doors. But the car kept moving at a high rate of speed.

The next major intersection was Michigan Avenue and a right turn to the Shrine. The four cars wove through the light traffic and the MG skidded into the left turn lane of traffic moving in the opposite direction but missed two cars that swerved away in a chorus of squealing tires and shouting drivers. Other drivers were honking their horns as the four cars sped by.

Dave kept his eye on the car in front of him and assumed that Elena was in the trunk and that thought kept him from ramming the MG. He knew that O'Neil was behind him and didn't know what the cop had in mind once the caravan came to a stop, which he believed was soon. The Shrine was just up ahead on the left, its blue dome glowing in the light that shone upon it. Father Darius made a sharp, high-speed turn into the circular drive that wound around to the front of the structure. He caught site of a handicap ramp along the curb and pressed the accelerator to jump the MG into a landscaped area next to the stairs that led into the upper church. The MG came to a stop against a tree and some bushes that were bare of leaves. Dave lost control of the Town Car and skidded over the curb in front of the stairs, blowing out two tires. Father Darius jumped out and pulled Elena from the trunk before Dave, O'Neil, or the patrolman could reach him. He appeared very calm. She was screaming. He held the butterfly knife to her throat. "She must be free to return to her heavenly home," he said, smiling. "I am a priest and I have come to this holy place to perform a holy act. You will not stop me."

Chapter Thirty-Five

Captain O'Neil knew that Father Darius would act and his plan was to get off a clean shot at the priest's head without harming Elena, but the priest knew about clean shots to the head and kept his head low and Elena in front of him. He did not want to die without accomplishing his mission.

Dave ran up to Father Darius and was about to grab Elena when O'Neil pulled him back. "He'll kill her, Dave. Let me handle this."

"Like you handled everything else? Get the hell out of here. Elena, are you okay?"

She was whimpering and struggling against her captor. "Help me, Dave."

Father Darius began to drag Elena up the stairs into the upper church, a seventy-six thousand square foot religious center that can welcome six thousand worshipers to a single service. The upper church is a massive testament to faith and the power of architecture to lift the human spirit to the realm of the divine. The nave lifts the eye upward to the massive dome, some one-hundred-fifty feet above the floor. The Romanesque and Byzantine art lift the senses with a majestic example of the pleasures of spiritual pursuit. Small chapels to the Madonna line the sides of the upper church and offered solace and prayer to the faithful who come in reverence or to seek relief from suffering. It has the power to overwhelm the senses of even the most jaded skeptic.

Like a monastery, the Shrine is other-worldly and calls to mind a time long lost when mankind was concerned with more than gadgets and the price of things. For most people, even non-Catholics, the Shrine is a place of worship, prayer, contemplation and adoration. So it was obscene that a young woman was being dragged up the stairs by a madman with a knife. Should that madman perform his murderous act upon the altar in a consecrated holy place, the consecration would be in jeopardy, and, in the eyes of some, the place would be returned to the realm of Satan and a re-consecration would be required, an act that can only be performed by someone of the status of bishop or higher. And so it was that a priest, a monsignor, rushed to the Shrine.

Father Darius found the door to the Shrine locked, as it was most nights during the winter. The Church had learned through bitter experience that leaving the doors open could lead to temptation for those of weak disposition in the presence of valuable art. In the winter, the Shrine closes at six in the evening unless services are scheduled for seasonal or other reasons. Father Darius had his back to the door and was holding Elena as a shield.

"Aperi portam!" He shouted in Latin. *Open the door.*

The monsignor had arrived from his residence on the grounds and rushed up the stairs. "Inclusum est in nocturnis." *It is locked for the night.*

"Sacrum munus mihi," Father Darius said. *I have a holy mission.*

"Let us speak English, Father," the monsignor responded, "for the benefit of the others."

"Alii non cadit." *The others do not matter.*

"We all matter in the eyes of God. Please, release the woman. Do not profane this place."

'I decus huc venimus ad missionem et meam impleat Madonna," Father Darius replied. *I have come to honor this place and to fulfill my mission to the Madonna.*

"The Holy Virgin Mary wishes no violence upon anyone. She is love. She is the mother of our Lord. She must be honored in love and peace. She commands you to release the woman." The monsignor was pleading and slowly approaching Father Darius and Elena, who was moaning and crying.

"Et mulier illa liberata est, unus et spiritus redeat ad caelum." *She and the woman are one and Her spirit must be freed to return to heaven."*

"Quæ est in cælo. Captus fueris satanas. Oportet eum id." *She is in heaven. You have been captured by Satan. You must cast him off.*

"No! You are wrong! I am with Her. I am doing Her work. Open the door."

A squad of O'Neil's homicide detectives had arrived and were deployed around the stairs, handguns drawn, watching the scene unfold. Dave had been moving slowly up the stairs as Father Darius's attention was focused on the monsignor. He moved to a point near the door and stood in shadow as the drama played out, waiting for a chance to grab Elena. He had no knowledge of Latin and was lost in the conversation that was taking place. So was O'Neil, whose only exposure to Latin had been as an altar boy serving the rare Latin mass. An observer might have thought he had stumbled upon a movie being shot or a Shakespearean scene played by actors: A crazed man holding a small, frightened woman against wall the of a great church while another holy man attempts to reason with him in a dead language and all while armed men watch and wait for an opportunity to kill the man with the knife.

"Let her go!" Dave shouted, rushing at Elena in an attempt to pull her away. The blade flashed and a bright scarlet line appeared across her face. She screamed as blood ran down her cheek and onto her clothes.

Dave was enraged and ran at Father Darius with such force that he could not stop and he grabbed Elena around her waist and pulled her away while the priest frantically waved the knife, shouting "Mater, mane apud me." *Mother, stay with me.*

O'Neil and his men were on him as the monsignor watched. "Do not harm him! He is not in control of his thoughts. Do not harm him!"

O'Neil's first thought was to grab the knife and use it on Father Darius, but there were too many witnesses and his men were subduing the priest to arrest him. O'Neil wondered if his personal situation had just got worse. Depending on his mental faculties, Father Darius might have a very interesting story to tell to those who already had their suspicions about O'Neil. The priest was on the stones near the door, weeping, but handcuffed.

Dave was holding Elena and trying to calm her, but she was too shaken to be comforted. Her cheek had been sliced open from her mouth to her hairline but it was a shallow, clean cut and would heal without a dramatic scar. But her ordeal would not heal for a long time. She was shaking and whimpering, looking at Dave like he was from another world. "I'm cold," she said.

Dave wrapped his coat over her shoulders and held her close. He glared at Father Darius, who was shouting apologies to the Virgin and begging the homicide detectives to shoot him. He seemed small and frail and not at all the hardened killer. To O'Neil he looked like just another parish priest, pasty and soft. Only this one was mad. He went over his options for damage control and decided to take Father Darius to 4D and where he could isolate him until he thought up a plan to make the problem go away. He knew he would have at least twelve-hours before Indiana Avenue would come calling, given the late hour. That would give him precious time.

"Get him up," he ordered. "We'll take him to the squad and process him there. Then we can call the chief and get the PR ball rolling." He wanted to signal his men that homicide would get credit for the arrest of the mass murderer. Dave's rescue of Elena would be all over the news but the actual police work would go to O'Neil and his men. Father Darius was helped to his feet and was being escorted to the stairs when two black SUVs pulled into the circle. Both had U.S. Government tags. They stopped at the foot of the stairs and a rear door open. Out stepped a thin middle-aged man in a dark suit and rimless eyeglasses. He wore close-cut hair and an expression of disgust.

"Captain O'Neil, I'm Special Agent Ossening and these men are with me. We are assuming custody of that man." He pointed to Father Darius. "We have a warrant charging him with federal crimes. I've already spoken with your chief."

O'Neil was furious. "How did you know we had him? We just took him into custody."

"We have radios too, Captain. He's ours." Ossening's team moved to Father Darius, placed another set of handcuffs on him, removed the cuffs that O'Neil's people had used and gave them to O'Neil. "Here, these are yours."

"Where are you taking him?" O'Neil asked, stepping in front of Ossening.

"We need to get him checked out and ask him a few questions. You know the drill. Oh, and by the way, we're assuming custody of those two." He pointed to Dave and Elena. "She looks like she needs medical attention. We'll take good care of her." A female F.B.I. agent placed an arm around Elena and led her to the second SUV, while a male agent pointed to Dave and then the vehicle.

Within minutes Ossening and his team, Father Darius, Dave and Elena were gone and the entrance to the Shrine was swarming with D.C. cops, federal agents, and soon, the news media. It was too late to make the 11 o'clock news on the Washington stations but the cable news outlets were going wall-to-wall with the big "get" being the monsignor, who was quick to point out that the Church did not have anything to do with the insane and bloody acts committed by Father Darius, who was clearly out of his mind.

O'Neil watched while his men and others went over the MG and took statements from everyone who was there about what had happened. The D.C. patrol sergeant who had chased Dave and Father Darius up North Capitol Street was telling everyone who would listen that he could have handled it if Captain O'Neil had not interfered with the chase. His comments were duly noted to be part of the file that would go to the chief, who would smile and ignore them.

Chapter Thirty-Six

The D.C. field office of the F.B.I. was busy, even at that late hour. Men and women were at desks and in offices, staring into computer screens and chatting in small groups. The first floor cafeteria was open and agents were sitting at the picnic-style tables, drinking coffee and laughing. Some of them looked up when Ossening brought Dave and Elena up to the counter and got a coffee for Dave and tea for Elena, who was wearing a white bandage on her face, which had been stitched up by an F.B.I. contract physician who had appeared as soon as the SUVs pulled up to the front door.

"Get what you want and we'll go upstairs," Ossening said in his most neutral F.B.I.-trained manner. "How are you feeling?" He offered Elena a look of deep concern.

She looked back at him with an expression of exhausted contempt. "I want to go home, take a shower, and sleep for three days."

"You can rest soon. I know you've been through quite a lot."

"How long will this take?" Dave asked. His hands were shaking. He looked down at them. "I think I'm coming down from all of this."

"Let's go upstairs where we can talk." Ossening led them to a small lobby where an elevator was waiting. They rode up in silence. Dave wondered if the silence was part of the treatment, a way to make him and Elena uncomfortable. He leaned against the elevator wall and closed his eyes. He felt the floor slowdown and the door opened to a government-issue hallway that reeked of the lowest bidder. The tile floor was shiny and showed new buffer marks. A cleaning woman was pushing a cart loaded with paper towels and plastic garbage bags and she stopped and stepped aside as the three walked past, not looking at anyone's face. Ossening stopped at a small conference room. "Dave, you can sit in here. I'll be back shortly. I'll be taking Elena to another room where someone will take care of her." His voice was less friendly and his eyes were hard.

Dave entered the room and saw a round table with four chairs, all padded in neutral colors. Two additional chairs were against the wall on opposite ends of a small credenza upon which was a multi-line telephone and triangular device that was used for conference calls. The credenza was locked and a printed sign that said "secure" was taped over the space between the doors that opened to the shelves inside. There were no pictures on the walls. There was nothing in the room of interest to someone who was passing the time. He took his cell phone out of his pocket and saw that the battery was nearly dead. He called Sid but the line went dead before Sid could pick up. An agent stood in the door. "I'll have to ask you to turn that off or we'll take custody of it." The man had no smile and his voice betrayed no human warmth. Dave wondered if he was under arrest.

It was nearly an hour before Ossening returned. Dave was in a semi-sleep and his head was on the table when he heard the door open. "Knock, knock." The agent was attempting a smile but his eyes were glaring at Dave. "We have Elena settled. She seems to be bearing up well under the circumstances. How are you doing?" Ossening sat at the table in a chair opposite Dave. He was carrying a small, hand-held recorder and a leather-bound legal pad. "Why don't we get underway?"

Dave sat up and rubbed his face. "What can I do for you?" he asked in what he hoped was a friendly, service-desk voice.

"Why don't we start at the beginning? How do you know Captain O'Neil?"

"I thought this was about the priest killer, Father Darius."

"We'll get to that. When did you first meet Captain O'Neil?"

The sun was up before Ossening announced that they were finished "for now". He had questioned Dave about O'Neil, everything that had happened at the farm, the priest murders, how he found Elena in Arlington, the chase, and, finally, the events at the Shrine. He asked the same questions over and over and picked at Dave's answers if they were not consistent to even the smallest details. At one point Dave asked Ossening if he was under arrest and he was told that, no, he was not but that he was considered a material witness to criminal activity. Dave knew that he could be detained, probably indefinitely, under the prevailing statutes and chose not to ask whether he was in custody. He would find out soon enough.

"May I see Elena?"

"She's resting. She's been through an ordeal. She's being very helpful. Listen, I know you would like to go home and maybe go back to work but I'm afraid that won't be possible right now. As I said, you're a material witness, so under the law we can hold you. I'm sure you know all that. We do have a problem with what you can report because it has a direct bearing on a criminal case in which you are involved. We have some issues to resolve along those lines. An assistant U.S. Attorney will be here shortly to explain the situation. After that you may telephone your boss and we'll see where we go from there."

"It sounds like I'm under arrest."

"At the moment you're being held as a material witness. You've committed no crime that we know of. If there's something you would like to tell us, we would be glad to listen."

"Can I get something to eat?"

"By all means. What would you like?"

"Some fruit and coffee would be nice."

"I'll have to ask you to remain here. You can use the men's room if you like. You'll have to be escorted, of course."

Elena was resting on the sofa in an office belonging to a supervisor who was not due for another hour or so. She was in a half-sleep and worked to keep her mind off the nightmare she had been through. She wanted to go home and make it all go away but, like Dave, she was being held as a material witness and was being watched by a female agent who, to Elena's judgment, had no personality whatsoever.

Father Darius was in a basement interrogation room where he was handcuffed to the floor. He was only vaguely aware of his surroundings and paid no attention to the men who were trying to ask him questions. He was looking up, seeking a vision of Her, which eluded him. He took that to mean that she had abandoned him due to his failure to fulfill his mission, which was to return Her to Her rightful place in Heaven. He believed that such a failure doomed him to an eternity of fire and damnation. Under the circumstances the demands of these men around him were of no consequence.

"Mater doleo. Ignosces." *Mother I am sorry. Please forgive me.* He repeated it over and over.

"What's he saying?" one of the agents asked.

"He's saying he's a shitbag," another responded.

"Father Darius. Can you hear me?"

"Mater doleo. Ignosces." The priest was sweating and the wounds on his back were beginning to bleed.

"This guy needs a medic," an agent said.

"He needs more than that. He's either nuts or he's playing us. How long are we gonna do this?"

"I'll call Ossening, see what he says."

Father Darius was allowed uninterrupted access to his delusions while the agent placed a call to his boss. "It looks like he's going to St. E's," the agent said, closing his cell phone. St. Elizabeth's Hospital on Alabama Avenue Southeast is the District's public psychiatric facility and a convenient drop-off for federal prisoners and others in need of quick and intense mental health services. It has been home to high profile Americans, including the poet Ezra Pound, who was found to be too crazy to commit treason during World War Two, for which he had been charged, and John Hinkley, who shot President Ronald Reagan. The hospital was founded in 1852 by act of Congress and has held the great and near great of the psychiatric world's delusional beings for decades. It was about to get one more. "They're sending somebody over," the agent said. "Who wants to babysit until they get here?" No one raised a hand, so an agent was assigned to sit and listen to the priest's demented ranting until the men in the white coats arrived.

Dave was pacing in the small conference room when a thirty-something woman in a dark, skirted business suit knocked on the door and entered. She was dark complexioned and Dave could not determine whether she was Hispanic, Italian or Arab. She wore her hair to her shoulder. She wore fashionable glasses. She wore a plain gold wedding ring. She wore no smile nor did she attempt to be friendly.

"I'm Patricia Stanford and I am an assistant U.S. Attorney here in the District of Columbia. I'm here to ask you a few questions and to discuss a number of issues. Is there anything you need? Water? The restroom?"

"I'm fine." Dave was dizzy from lack of sleep and stress and he told himself all he had to do was listen and try to understand.

"You are not being charged with a crime. Has Agent Ossening told you that?"

"Yes."

"You are a material witness to several serious crimes, as I understand it. Is that your understanding?"

"I've been told I'm a material witness, yes."

"Then you understand that we can, under the law, detain you?"

"Is that what you're doing?"

"We do not believe it would be wise for you to go home just yet. We have made arrangements for you to be housed at a location near here. Your friend will also be in administrative custody for a few days. You will be well looked after." She paused to see the effect of her words on him.

"So I'm under arrest."

"No, if you were under arrest you would be in a cell." She gave him a look that was intended to whither opposing witnesses in court.

"I'm a reporter. As far as I'm concerned, this is a story. I need to report it. For that to happen, I must be free to do my work."

"We are seeking to enjoin you from releasing certain details of these cases. We are not attempting to block your First Amendment rights, only to protect the legal aspects of the cases we are or will bring against certain perpetrators. In this case, you are not an ordinary journalist."

"I suppose we can hash that out in court."

"If you choose, but for now we are acting in what we believe to be the best interests of justice. Have I made myself clear." She had the tone of a kindergarten teacher addressing a boy who had just thrown a mud-ball.

"May I call my boss?"

"Soon. We'll make arrangements in a little while and you can make the call before you are moved. It's important that your employer understand your status." She reached into a soft leather briefcase and removed some papers. She looked them over and pushed them across the table. "This will explain everything. You should read these thoroughly before you sign them and if you have any questions please ask for clarification."

Dave picked up the papers and scanned them. It was clear that he needed to discuss them with a lawyer before he signed anything. His first reading was that he was agreeing to anything the government wanted and waiving his right to speak publicly about what he had seen and done regarding the events of the past few days. "I'll have to talk to an attorney about this."

"I need you to sign these before we can move forward," she said in her best clipped prosecutor tone.

"Not going to happen," he said, pushing the papers back across the table.

"Take a moment to think about it. We have you and we can keep you."

"As I recall, the Supreme Court ruled that you guys can lie and mislead anyone, all, presumably, in the interest of justice. I, on the other hand, face criminal charges if I lie to you. Is that right?"

"If what you're saying is true, why would you care how I responded?"

Dave laughed. "Excellent point. So let me get to my point. I want a lawyer. Now."

"You're not under arrest."

"I am in custody."

"True. But so what?"

"I have nothing more to say."

"Have it your way." She got up, stacked the papers into a neat pile, and pushed them back to Dave. "Think about it. And think about your friend, Elena." She walked to the door, glanced at Dave, and closed the door. He could hear her shoes clacking on the tile as she walked away.

Chapter Thirty-Eight

While Dave was cooling his heels at the D.C. field office of the F.B.I., O'Neil was undergoing an ordeal of his own at the Justice Department, where the Assistant Attorney General and Grand Visier of the Warriors of Mary was holding forth about the mess at hand. "Here are our options," he began. "We can come clean about everything and take our lumps. I think we agree that that is not the best course of action. We can begin a process of denial of everything which, again, is a poor option, given that these things always blow up in this town. That leaves us with what I believe is our best course of action. We put Father Darius on ice, so to speak, which is already in motion. If we have him at St. E's, locked away under sedation, he won't be showing up in a courtroom to testify about anything. And, as we know all too well, he's as crazy as a bedbug." The man offered a tight smile of satisfaction.

"Okay, that's one down," O'Neil said, showing his cop face.

"We've already taken care of your friend Frank. He's a team player and he's willing to accept a contract to do some security work in Iraq or some other hellhole for a year or two, at a high rate of pay, I might add. He's not a worry. Byrne and the other N.Y.P.D. guys will keep their mouths shut for two reasons. One, because they're embarrassed at how amateurish their operation was, and two, because we told them to. Malone is dead, so that's off the table. I say good riddance, by the way. He was a loose cannon and probably as bad an apple as Father Darius."

"So that leaves Dave Haggard and Elena, along with Dave's boss and any other snoopy reporters who happen to be sniffing around." O'Neil was playing along.

"Just so, yes. And something dramatic will not be productive." The words "something dramatic" had a weight that disturbed O'Neil.

"So, what are you thinking?"

"At the end of the Vietnam War the ones who fought on our side were sent to so-called re-education camps. There they were told that what they had witnessed and what they believed was not what really happened at all. In fact, they were told, everything they had seen and been told was a lie. The strangest part of all of this was that most of the former South Vietnamese soldiers either accepted what they were told or acted like they did, which is the same thing. Do you see where I'm going with this?"

"Are you planning to put them on ice in some kind of camp?"

"I am suggesting that they be offered a detailed and highly edited explanation of what happened. For instance, the monitoring station in the silo at the farm. It's my understanding that Dave Haggard never actually heard or saw any monitoring of anyone. He was told by Frank that such monitoring was underway but Frank might have been playing a prank or simply lying about it. My point is Dave doesn't really know much of anything that can hurt us. He has suspicions. He's been told certain things that, as he will come to understand, were not accurate. This Elena woman doesn't really know anything and all she's been told she got from Dave. Are you following?"

"Misinformation, in other words." O'Neil was already tired of the game.

"Information, my friend, not misinformation. Besides, he's a material witness, so we can keep him for awhile. Ossening says he won't sign our little shut-up agreement until he talks to a lawyer. No lawyer in this city will let him sign it, so we won't get far with it, but the issue gets us a little time. He's over at the D.C. field office and so is she. She's a scared little mouse right now and I doubt if she'll be a problem."

"So what would you like from me?"

"Go talk to him. Soften him up. Tell him there are things you couldn't reveal before but now you can and explain that Frank liked to brag about things that weren't true and so on. Apologize for what happened and say it will never happen again and that those responsible will be held accountable and, well, you know the drill."

"What about the woman?"

"Let him talk her down."

"Dave's boss, this guy Sid, is pretty sharp."

"Have a talk with him. Play the national security game if you have to. Offer him something. Tell him you'll be the best source he has and hand him a good story."

"Like?"

"Give him some background on Father Darius and tell him we're shipping him off to St. E's. No one has that story yet."

"They've got everything else. I don't think there's any other news today. They're all screaming for details and wondering where the hell Dave and Elena are. The U.S. Attorney hasn't said a damn thing. How long do you think you can keep the lid on this?" O'Neil himself was getting dozens of calls from media types who wanted to know what was happening. "The Washington Post guy said there's a rumor going around that Dave and Elena are dead."

"He's fishing. Don't worry about it. We have a few hours. We're moving Dave to Greenbelt. I'd like you to go out there in a few hours to have a little talk with him to see if you can get him on board about this. I'll have Ossening call this Sid guy and have a meeting. We'll try to get this buttoned up by the end of the day."

The federal courthouse in Greenbelt, Maryland is an ugly turned-in-on-itself edifice that was designed to make it difficult for a terrorist bomber to blow it up. Its façade is set back from the nearest vehicle access point, like a man lying in the fetal position. Anyone approaching the building must first gaze at its back, which is also set away from the road and the parking lot. Federal courthouses of an earlier era were positioned in downtown areas and were designed to express the majesty of the justice system and the government that enforced it, and so these structures are stone and columns and statues. The structure in Greenbelt expresses the government's fear of bad guys.

The lobby is a multi-story opening that resembles hotel lobbies, only this one is minus the plants and graciousness. Federal marshals man the metal detectors that all visitors and staff must pass through. A visitor looking up will see balconies that lead to courtrooms, the U.S. Attorney's office, offices of local members of Congress, conference rooms, and the clerk of the court. There is no sign or any indicator of the holding cells or the law enforcement presence in the building. That is all behind plain locked doors. There are ways to access these areas without members of the public observing the procedures.

Special Agent Ossening and Assistant U.S. Attorney Stanford were sitting in the back seat of a black SUV as it pulled into an underground garage at the courthouse. Sitting between them was Dave Haggard. Elena was in another vehicle that was five minutes behind. Ossening was in a jovial mood. "See, Dave, we do cooperate with each other. Ms. Stanford and I work in D.C. offices and the good people here in Greenbelt are more than happy to welcome us and help in any way they can." He seemed to take delight in that.

"What are we doing here? Nobody was killed in Maryland." Dave was feeling the pressure that the F.B.I. and Justice Department wanted him to feel.

"It's a nice neutral place. Don't worry." Ossening looked at Stanford, who remained silent. She had only come along because a phone call from the Justice Department told her to.

The SUV pulled into a parking spot near a door marked "Security". "Here we are," said Ossening. "I need to use the head." He got out and motioned for Dave to follow. He knocked on the door and it was opened by a large black man wearing a small ear bud attached to a wire. The man did not speak. Ossening led Dave down a hallway into a large room that looked like the government version of a bank lobby. There was an open area with chairs that Dave took to be a waiting room. Two sides of the room were lined with security glass, behind which sat men and women at work stations. There were small openings between the work stations and the waiting area where those being dealt with could pass documents and other items.

"Processing," Ossening said.

He led Dave to another steel door and knocked on it. Again, it was quickly opened by a large, silent man. The door led to an area that contained two large holding cells and an open shower. "The shower is to wash off the tear gas if we use it. Some of the guys get a little rowdy. We only have the showers because the law makes us, otherwise we'd let them cry it out."

They were met by a pleasant-faced, middle-aged man who could have been the corner druggist. "This is Mr. Smith. He'll process you."

"What do you mean 'process'?"

"We're going to put you into the system for a little while. We'll get your prints, take your picture, things like that." Ossening had a smug look on his face.

"I'm under arrest?"

"How many times do we have to tell you you're just a material witness. Nothing to worry about."

Mr. Smith took mug shots, got Dave's prints, and noted scars and the lack of tattoos. Dave was left to sit and wait within a few feet of the holding cells where several dangerous-looking men stared at him with a look that said we'd like to get our hands on you. Or that is what Dave assumed they were thinking. In fact, they were F.B.I. agents playing a part.

Ossening took Dave to a small interrogation room down the hall from the holding cells. It was painted government yellow, walls and ceiling, and was furnished with a small, square metal table and two steel stools. The stools and the table were bolted to the floor. There were rings on the floor and table where handcuffed prisoners could be restrained. There were two surveillance cameras mounted on the walls. To Dave, it looked like something out of a bad cop movie. "Wait in here," Ossening said, closing the door. There was no interior door handle, only a key slot.

Dave sat on one of the stools and looked around. There was nothing to look at, only the cement block walls and the floor. He glanced up at the cameras and stared at them, then he smiled and waved, mouthing "hello". The wall near the table was marred by scuff marks and he wondered how they got there. The table was scratched and gouged and he allowed his imagination to flow over the various scenarios that could have produced the marks. Most likely prisoners on drugs had gone berserk against the restraints. There may have been more sinister reasons but his daydream was cut short by the sound of a key in the door. When it opened, Captain O'Neil was standing there with a serious look on his face.

"Hi. Dave," he said, offering his hand.

"What are you doing here?" Dave was wary. O'Neil was a D.C. cop. What was he doing in a federal courthouse in Maryland?

"I've come to have a little conversation, that's all. This is neutral territory and we can talk without any pressure, that sort of thing." He sat down on the stool opposite Dave and removed his coat, which he laid on the floor. "So, I hear an offer is on the table."

"Maybe you can explain it to me."

"I've just a little chat with Sid Slackey about all of this. He's on board, so to speak. I explained things to him and he understands."

"Understands what, exactly?"

"Sometimes things aren't what they seem, Dave. What you've seen in the past few days seems to be one thing when, in fact, it's something else."

"Could you be a little more vague?" Dave thought his sarcasm was amusing.

O'Neil thought it was childish. "I understand that you and Elena have been through a lot and you went through things that would make some folks have nervous breakdowns. I get all that. But when you went on the air and reported all those things, well, it was wrong. It was not correct."

"Just what was not correct?"

"The telephone monitoring. Frank showed you some computer screens and told you he was listening to some phone calls but he never played one of those calls for you, did he? Did you ever actually witness anything? No. Why? Because he was blowing smoke. He was playing a game with you. Anybody can put some computers in a barn, turn them on, and say anything they want about why they were there. It doesn't mean it's true."

"What else?"

"Here's the story. This guy, this Father Darius, went nuts and killed a lot of people. We did have a line on his, that's true, and we did suspect that he was tracking you and Elena, but there's not much more to it than that."

"How did you know that?"

"Some of it was obvious. He was sending you souvenirs of his crimes. That meant he was watching you and knew where you lived."

"And Elena?"

"We had some intelligence about that and I can't go into it. We had federal help, that's all I can say."

"And what do you want me to do?"

"I can't make you do anything, Dave. I think you should take some time to calm down. What the government is asking is not out of bounds. You are a material witness. You will be asked to testify in court. On this particular story you are the story, not the reporter, and some of what you know can be used by Father Darius and against our case. Agree to what the government is offering, that's all." O'Neil had a sad, world-weary look and Dave almost bought his argument.

"So what did Sid say?"

"Sid agrees that you never actually saw or heard Frank or anyone else monitor telephone calls, so it's really an unconfirmed claim. He also agrees that you've been through a lot and you and Elena need some time off."

"When can I talk to him?"

"Soon."

"When can I see Elena?"

"Soon."

Dave looked up at the security camera. "Did you hear that? He said I can see her soon!"

"Just do it," O'Neil said, standing up. He offered Dave his hand. "Take some time." Dave ignored him.

Chapter Thirty-Nine

Sid was furious. Seven thousand. That's what the body shop guy offered as his "best guess" to repair the Town Car, although he added, "I can't give you a solid estimate until we go over it." Sid took that to mean the real cost would be double the seven grand. Goddam it! The guy also said it would never "drive the same", meaning his beloved car was now junk. He felt stupid. He had never allowed anyone to drive it and he had never had an accident. The one time he gave the keys to Dave turned the luxury behemoth into a pile of dents and twisted metal. He would sell it the minute he got it back from the body shop.

His rage had been tempered by healthy doses of bourbon in his coffee and he had a warm, buzzing feeling as the anger slipped into something else a little more accommodating. O'Neil's deal had his mood improving. O'Neil was showing a weak hand and Sid had gone along with it. What was the old joke? You can't un-blow the horn. Dave had already blown the horn about the farm but O'Neil and the people he was speaking for wanted him to un-blow it and say it was all just a misunderstanding. What a laugh! Sid took another drink from his cup. Dave knew what he had been told and what he had seen and, in fact, O'Neil had confirmed it days ago. So that meant that whoever was trying to manage this mess was hoping to make it go away by shutting Dave up. *Well*, Sid thought, *it might work, given the short attention span of the news business and the news-consuming public.*

He had taken the deal with his fingers crossed. O'Neil had offered a trade. The details of the monitoring station at the farm would come out in due time. The lead right now was Father Darius and O'Neil had put a steak upon the news table, so to speak. The larger story as Sid saw it was the capture of Father Darius and the solid link to the Warriors of Mary, whoever they were. O'Neil hadn't asked him to back away from that. *Curious.* And the deal had included the exclusive news that Father Darius was at St. Elizabeth's for "evaluation", meaning he would not be seen or heard from for months or even years. A mass murderer caught. End of story. By the time Father Darius's status as a mental patient was determined the public would have forgotten about the story and reporters and editors will be shouting about something else.

Dave was effectively muzzled by his status as a material witness and Elena was a basket case. Sid called a friend, a literary agent who handled the famous journalists based in Washington.

"Have you been watching the news?" he asked with a playful tone in his voice.

"No, anything happening?" The agent went along with the gag.

"Do you think you can sell Dave's story?"

"I can get him a hundred thousand today, "she replied. "Is he there?"

"Not yet. He's on ice. The government has him in custody as a witness. I'll have him call you. He'll need to take a leave from this place until everything blows over so he'll have time to crank out a book."

"I'll make some calls. I'll see if I can get a bidding war going. Good talking to you, Sid."

She owes me, he thought, hanging up. There was a wrap on his door and he looked up to see Gabriel standing at the window. He motioned him to come in. "What's up?"

"Dave's on the line and he wants to talk to you."

Sid took a healthy gulp of his coffee and picked up the phone. "How and where are you?"

"I'm in the lockup in Greenbelt at the federal courthouse. Have you talked to O'Neil?"

"Yeah, he gave us a good story. Father Darius is at St. E's."

"They want me to shut up about some things, Sid."

"They have a right to limit what you can say about what happened, Dave. I checked with our legal people. You're a witness."

"What about the equipment in the silo? Don't you want to chase that angle?"

"You didn't actually see anything but some computer screens. You didn't listen and you didn't hear anything. I'm not saying I don't believe you but I'm not sure I believe this Frank guy. He sounds like a nutcase to me. Let it go, Dave. There's a hell of a story here without that and we have all we can handle just reporting about you and Elena and now Father Darius. Chicago and San Francisco are chasing some solid leads there about this Warriors of Mary group. Take a breath, settle down, and get some rest."

"They won't let me see Elena. I don't know where she is."

"Captain O'Neil says she's fine and in good hands. When are they going to let you go?"

"Undetermined, if you can believe that. They want me to agree to their deal and we can talk about me going home after that."

"Here's something to brighten your day. Do you know Karen Henderson? She's a book agent in Alexandria for the Huffman Group. She wants to talk to you. She thinks she can get six figures for a book about your experience. You'll need to take a leave from here anyway, so it will give you something to do. Life is good, Dave."

"Screw you, Sid." Dave was laughing. The money would be nice. Maybe he could buy a car? "Do you think I'll need to clear what I write with O'Neil or Ossening?"

"Talk it over with your publisher. Oh, by the way, don't spend it all. You owe me for the car." Sid paused and he could hear Dave breathing on the other end. "Don't sign anything until we can get it past our legal people. Tell them anything they want to hear and mean it. Come to see me as soon as you can. We have a lot to talk about."

Special Agent Ossening and Assistant U.S. Attorney Stanford listened and nodded. Ossening looked at her. "Let him go with the usual warning about statements and testimony. It's not like we won't know what he's up to."

Stanford was tired of the game with Dave and wondered what Ossening's real motives were. She was not comfortable with the marching orders she had been given and her instincts told her that things were not what they appeared to be. She was a note-taker with an excellent memory and if anything were amiss she would have no trouble producing a detailed account of what had transpired around her. "I'll advise him to get his legal people with us as soon as possible. I assume this Sid character has already put that in motion."

"Downtown is putting out a press release and there'll be a media pony show to spin this our way. We'll call Dave some kind of hero, credit the D.C. cops, and push ahead with our case. We've got a lot of work to do."

"What are you going to do about O'Neil and the guys at the farm?"

"O'Neil? Right now, nothing. The guys who were out at the farm, especially Byrne, are singing like canaries. They thought the Warriors of Mary and the Posse Maria thing was some kind of social club with guns. The problem is, they don't know very much."

"And Frank?"

"Frank's a tougher nut but he's cutting himself a nice little deal. O'Neil's the key right now. He's the one we need to track. He's got some interesting numbers on his phone. One of them is DOJ." DOJ is shorthand for Department of Justice.

Stanford stared at the agent. "I assume I'll be briefed at the appropriate moment."

"That you will."

"First things first. Let's get Haggard out of here."

Dave was sitting on the metal table when a U.S. Marshal opened the door to the small room. The marshal motioned for Dave to follow him and led Dave to the processing area, where Stanford was waiting.

"Just a couple of things and you're out of here," she said. "We'll forget the other stuff for now and schedule a meeting with your attorney to go over your status. Right now you'll need to acknowledge that you are a material witness and agree to withhold public comments that may be relevant to your testimony before the grand jury and other proceedings. We're not trying to harass you here, we're protecting our case. I'm sure you would agree that this is the most important priority at the moment." She was in her schoolmarm character, looking at him over her glasses with her mouth pressed into a tight line.

"How is Elena?"

"She's been taken to George Washington Hospital where a good plastic surgeon is repairing her face. That's my understanding. She's also being given a thorough physical and psychological examination. I have been told that she will be there for a day or two and will not be receiving visitors until she's evaluated. I'm sure she will be happy to see you when she's able." Stanford handed Dave some papers. "These are pro forma. They'll get you out of here. Don't be surprised if D.C. police, maybe your friend O'Neil, come by your place for a little talk later today. I'd get with your legal people as soon as possible if I were you."

Dave signed the papers and handed them to Stanford. "I need a ride home."

Two hours later Dave walked into his apartment and collapsed on his bed. He closed his eyes and allowed himself to drift into a state of lethargy and heaving the random thoughts that precede sleep when his phone rang. He considered ignoring it but he considered the possibility that it was Elena, so he answered it. It was Sid.

"We need to chat," Sid said by way of introduction.

"I'm passing into unconsciousness at the moment," Dave replied. "Have you heard from Elena?"

"She's okay. We sent Megan to be with her. She doesn't want to see you right now. They're fixing up her face."

"Yeah, I heard. We need to set something up with the Now News lawyers. The U.S. Attorney's office wants to go over my status, whatever that means."

"We're on it. We've got a meeting with them tomorrow morning. Don't say anything to anyone until then. We've got our angle covered here and we're saying you're not making any statements at the moment. Our Chicago station is digging up some good stuff. We can talk about it. When can we meet?"

"I need some sleep. How about dinner?"

"I'll pick you up. Get some rest."

Five minutes later the phone rang again and this time it was O'Neil. "I'm on my way over."

"Not now. I'll call you later. I'm passing out." Dave ended the call and sank into a deep and dreamless sleep.

He was still groggy over dinner with Sid at a sandwich place on Connecticut Avenue and stared at his meal while Sid stared at him. "I have to hand it to you. This may be the greatest story I've ever been a part of. This one has it all."

"Yeah? Like what?" Dave moved a French fry though a puddle of ketchup and shoved it into his mouth.

"Murder, intrigue, religion, insanity, a car chase, even if it was my car that got wacked. It will make a hell of a book."

"So, what's next for me at New News?"

"You're on leave to write a book. That's your status. We can't have you working the street stories as famous as you are and we've got this witness stuff to worry about. I wanted to get with you in person and away from the phones because we have to assume that all the phones are bugged. This business of trying to shut you up about the monitoring station at the farm is so much crap. I went along with it to get O'Neil off my back and I'm surprised he thinks it worked. Potentially, this is the biggest angle of the whole mess. These guys are running what amount to wiretaps from some farm in Virginia. If this was legitimate they wouldn't be set up in a silo. What's going on here? You need to get that into your book. Who are these people? What's O'Neil's angle? Is the F.B.I. a part of this?"

"I can't think right now, Sid, so I don't have any answers. O'Neil is coming by later to have a little chat. Again. We've got the legal meeting in the morning when the government will try to shut me up. There's too much to process right now."

"I understand. Just do me one favor. Don't say anything about the book to anyone. Don't have sensitive conversations on the phone. Let's agree to meet for lunch every day until further notice so we can have private chats. Agreed?"

"Sure. Thanks for your support, Sid."

O'Neil was waiting when Dave arrived back at the Philadelphia House. He had pulled his unmarked car into the circle in front of the door, where it blocked access to everyone else who wanted to drop off or pick up a resident of the building. He left a police notice on his dashboard and jumped out to greet Dave.

"I thought I had missed you." O'Neil seemed nervous and was not his usual arrogant self.

"I'm pretty shot, Captain. How long will this take?"

"I need some of your time, that's all." The cop was very subdued. Dave thought O'Neil was being too nice.

The two men sat at Dave's table and sipped espresso. O'Neil was quiet and it took him a few minutes to gather his thoughts. "I'm in trouble, Dave. I need you to agree to something for me."

"What kind of trouble?"

"Can you give me a guarantee that this goes no further?"

"Are we making a confidentiality deal between reporter and source?"

"Something like that. I need to tell you something and it can't go further."

Dave thought it over. He had an idea that this was not about a story but rather was about O'Neil, so it fell outside the bounds of a normal journalism agreement. "Okay, sure."

"If this gets out I'll know where to look." O'Neil was displaying his cop face.

"Maybe you should keep it to yourself, Captain. I don't want to be under any kind of threat right now. I've got other things going on, as you know."

O'Neil seemed to think it over. "What the hell." He reached into his shirt pocket and took out a flash drive, which he turned in his fingers like it was an object to be studied. He looked over at Dave and pushed it across the table. "That's everything there is to know about the Warriors of Mary and even the Posse Maria."

Dave looked at the flash drive and picked it up. "What's your involvement?"

"Look, the whole thing started out years ago when some cops up in New York got together for a Rosary group and thought it sounded like a good name. It spread from there to other places. One thing led to another and it kind of became a vigilante group, but things got out of hand so we formed the Posse Maria to handle the vigilantes. When it got to that point we had to protect ourselves and we became a secret organization dedicated to preserving our secrets. You know how these things go."

"No, actually, I don't. What happened with the priests killings?"

"This guy, this priest named Darius Welsh, got into a group in Connecticut as a kind of chaplain, the guy who led the Rosary. He was pretty strange but he seemed harmless. He was out there and found a few other guys who were strange and they went crazy."

"What do you mean by strange?"

"They believed that certain people needed to die, to go to Heaven, for one reason or another. If another priest called them out for being too radical he would disappear. If somebody found out about it, that person would disappear. Meantime, the members moved up wherever they were and now some are in pretty high positions."

"Like you..." Dave let it hang in the air.

"I'm nobody compared to some of these guys."

"Are they here?" Dave held up the flash drive.

"Yup."

"Why are you talking to me?"

"They're coming for me. Ossening and the F.B.I. have been snooping around on this. There's an Assistant Attorney General at Justice who put him up to it, but Ossening doesn't know the guy is our Grand Vizier, the national enforcer. He's the one who put the hit out on Father Darius. Only the guy who was supposed to do the hit was as strange as the priest. This guy, whose name was Malone, did some priest killing of his own. I may be on the list myself, that's why I want you to have the flash drive. Use what's on it only if I disappear."

"Why did you try to get me to go along with the deal that the government wants me to sign?"

"What choice did I have?"

"Who's being monitored at the farm?"

O'Neil smiled. "Who isn't?"

There was a pounding on the door. O'Neil looked at Dave and his face sank. "I believe that's for me. Hide the flash drive."

Dave opened the door and Ossening and four agents pushed their way past him and grabbed O'Neil. "We have a warrant for your arrest."

O'Neil leaned his face close to Ossening. "You have no idea what's going on."

"We have you. That's a start."

The agents handcuffed O'Neil and took him out of the apartment. Ossening remained behind.

"If you have any information that would be important to this investigation I strongly suggest that you come forth with it. What did he tell you?"

"He told me you were coming for him. How did you know he was here?"

"We're the F.B.I. We're already at his house in Maryland. What else did he say?"

"He said he may never be seen again."

Ossening looked down at the floor. "We're cleaning up a mess here. I would stay out of it if I were you."

"I'm already in it."

"Watch yourself. We've got your girl." He smiled. "Oh, by the way, good luck with the book. I can't wait to read it."

~~~~~~~~~~

Coming soon from author Larry Matthews and A-Argus Better Book Publishers:

Brass Knuckles
The next Dave Haggard thriller

~*~

Federal Judge Alexander Beechum was a man of habit and routine. He believed that spontaneous acts were a sign of a cluttered life that had no meaning or order. His day was precise. Each day was planned in accordance with its needs, meaning, of course, his needs. His office in the federal courthouse in Washington was a tribute to his ordered mind, with a place for every thing and every thing in its place, including his well-groomed clerks and minions. "Let justice not be ill served by a misplaced fact or file," was one of his frequently issued slogans. And so it was that Judge Beechum went to lunch each day at precisely 12:30PM, walking through the front doors of the courthouse after a brief wave to the marshals who staffed the security point.

The courthouse is officially on Constitution Avenue at Third Street Northwest, within sight of the United States Capitol building. In fact, it is on Pennsylvania Avenue in a clot of intersections which, in high-tourist seasons, are packed with out-of-towners gawking at the Capitol, the Mall, the Newseum, or the Embassy of Canada, which is arguably the most impressive embassy in Washington and is next door to the courthouse.

It was early April and the cherry blossoms were at peak bloom. The blossoms bring hundreds of thousands of tourists to the city to gaze upon the fragile flowers and spend money in local hotels and restaurants. Most years the blossoms are at peak for only a few days before a front blows through with wind and rain, sending the petals into the Tidal Basin and leaving the tourists with the taste of disappointment. Not so on this day.

Judge Beechum noted that the Mall area was crowded with smiling families, all of them taking pictures of each other with the Capitol building in the background. It was Wednesday, so the judge was having lunch at Sammy's, a sandwich shop on 4th Street. He would order, as on each Wednesday, a turkey and swiss on French bread with a light smear of mayo and a handful of sprouts. The sprouts were a nod to the health concerns of his wife, to whom he had been married for thirty-four years. He had eaten the same lunch every Wednesday for eleven years. Thursdays were soup and salad.

He stood in the sunshine and enjoyed the warmth it offered after a cold, wet and rainy March. He looked up at the monument to General George Meade, the Union general credited with defeating Robert E. Lee at Gettysburg. Meade's monument is on the plaza at the courthouse complex and it comforted the judge to see such a tribute to victory. As he stood facing west with a smile on his face a loud crack bounced off the stone skins of the buildings, making it sound as though several shots had been fired, but it was only one. The 7.62 millimeter round hit Judge Beechum just above his right eye. It exited behind his left ear, leaving a wound as large as an orange, sending much of the brain that had so impressed legal scholars spewing onto the stone image of General Meade.

A lawyer who was stuffing papers into her leather briefcase nearly tripped over him before she saw the body and the carnage around it. She screamed for help but it was several minutes before the scene was secured and U.S. Marshals from the courthouse began to assess the situation. By then the gunman was gone and so was the M14 that had killed the man known as Maximum Alex. It was a nickname given to him by defense lawyers in recognition of Judge Beechum's belief that public officials who are convicted of crimes against the people be locked up for as long as the law allows. The judge had sent a good many such officials away after a subjecting them to his infamous tongue lashings about the responsibilities of those elected to serve the people. Former members of Congress were sitting in their cells at that very moment, along with a few Cabinet officers and lobbyists, unaware, of course, that the man who had sent them to long stretches at Allenwood or Cumberland or Petersburg was facing his own eternity.

One man, a sitting Representative from Tennessee, was aware. He was facing his own legal challenges and his friends had taken action in an attempt to slow the wheels of justice. He was waiting by the phone for word that the problem had been solved. As he would learn, it wasn't as simple as a quick assassination.

Radio reporter Dave Haggard was sitting at his desk in his new office in a high rise building overlooking the Potomac River in Rosslyn, a section of Arlington across the river from Georgetown. "High rise" is a relative term. In Chicago or New York it means skyscraper. In the Washington area it's anything over ten stories. The D.C. region is a decidedly "low rise" area because the Washington Monument, at 555 feet, is as high as it gets. Rosslyn, with its steel and glass modernity, was a contrast to Georgetown, with its 17th and 18th Centuries store fronts and townhouses. Dave was happy to be looking back in time. He thought Rosslyn was hideous.

His employer, a Washington-based news service called Now News, had recently moved from smaller offices near

Dupont Circle in the city to the high rise on the strength of its increased visibility and wealth created by the publicity of its involvement in the story known as The Priest Killings, a string of grisly murders of Catholic Priests. Dave had been at the center of the story and had, in fact, been part of the capture of the killer and the rescue of his then-girlfriend. The publicity had brought a rush of clients and funds to Now News, thus the new digs.

Dave was restless and bored. The tourist season had begun and it was difficult to get around the city. He was stuck covering the Justice Department and its boring leader, the aptly named Attorney General Jubal Gray, who spoke in sentences designed to suck the energy out of every moment. But Dave had to admit to himself that he liked the view. He could see the Kennedy Center, Roosevelt Island and its semi-wildness, the Georgetown waterfront, and, in the distance, the Washington Monument and the Capitol Building.

Two high school rowing teams were on the river, the four-man teams were racing each other in the long, thin boats in practice runs for the spring season. The boats went under Key Bridge and emerged heading north to Three Sisters Islands, a group of rocky protrusions in the middle of the river. The young men were powerful and the boats moved with amazing speed. Dave watched and had a moment of admiration for the boys who were on the river in the middle of a school day. The idyllic scene was interrupted by a scull being rowed by one man who pulled past the high schoolers and sped up the river by the rocky islands and disappeared behind the trees along the Virginia shore.

Dave saw powerful shoulders and arms and a white man's head under a Washington Nationals baseball hat. Later, when he was asked to describe the man, that is all he could recall. The moment was nothing more than an interruption in an otherwise idle day. He was killing time before yet another of the AG's news conferences about a legal issue relating to land rights in the West. Even the folks in Montana wouldn't be interested in this story. He wanted to press Sid for some street assignments around the city but that was not possible at the moment because Now News was still reeling from the priest killing story and Sid had made a deal with the F.B.I. to keep Dave out of harm's way. I'm a house cat, he thought, gazing down at the traffic on Key Bridge.

His phone rang. "Yeah," was his usual answer.

It was Sid, his boss, an old news lion who liked to keep the cubs in line. Dave was no cub but Sid still growled at him from time to time. "Get your ass down to the District Court. Somebody just shot Judge Beechum."

"Where?"

"Right in front of the statue of General Meade. All hell's breaking loose."

"I'm on it." Dave had his coat on and was out the door before Sid could change his mind. The taxi situation was always dicey in Arlington. Most of the cabbies wanted to drive in D.C. where there was more business. Arlington cabs mostly went to Reagan National Airport and the drivers spent a lot of time in line waiting for fares, unlike the city drivers who dropped off and picked up anywhere. Dave went out the lobby door and saw a cab dropping off a fare at the door and he raced to grab it. The driver was a Somali who had perfected the art of having no facial expression whatsoever. The man nodded when Dave told him he wanted to go to the federal courthouse at 3rd and Constitution and proceeded to head for Key Bridge.

"No, don't go that way. Loop over to Roosevelt Bridge and go down Constitution. It will be faster."

The driver kept going. "Are you aware of the Cherry Blossom Festival?" he asked in a formal, British public school manner. "There are many, many tourists here for that. It will take an hour that way." So he drove to Georgetown and headed down M Street to Pennsylvania and made it to the courthouse in twenty minutes. Dave felt foolish but he was grateful that the driver knew the city and its ways.

Pennsylvania Avenue was blocked by police cars with their lights flashing. The area was closed for blocks as federal agents searched for evidence and clues. A press pen had been established near the courthouse and Dave could see reporters frantically calling out to every cop and agent they knew, pleading for some crumb to report. Television reporters were the most intense because their bosses were yelling at them through the small earphones they had embedded in their heads. Newspaper and other print reporters were the most serene and detail-oriented because their deadlines were longer. Online bloggers tweeted out morsels of information that had no context and no one seemed to care. Press pens are areas where cops and other officials herd reporters during breaking stories to keep them from running around like a bunch of cats out of control. Loose reporters can be risky to people who are trying to control a narrative.

Dave saw a reporter from the Associated Press with whom he had shared information in the past and walked over to him. The man's name was Peter Deutch and he was a solid but conventional journalist. He could gather facts as fast as anyone but he was conservative in the conclusions he drew from those facts, unlike the cable television types who drew conclusions first and then went in search of facts to back them up.

"What are they saying?" Dave asked.

"That's him under the tarp. One to the head. I hate to say it, but this is good news for Congressman Prewitt." Deutch looked sad.

~*~

Available from better book stores, amazon.com, barnesandnoble.com or www.a-argusbooks.com
November 2012

Meet our Author

Larry Matthews

Larry Matthews is an award-winning broadcast journalist whose thirty-plus years as a reporter provide the background material for his books. Matthews was a street reporter, anchor, news director, producer and editor for major radio stations, ABC Radio, and National Public Radio. He was a producer, host and reporter for Maryland Public Television. As a reporter he covered some of the major events of the late Twentieth Century in Washington, D.C. and other cities. He is the recipient of the George Foster Peabody Award for Excellence in Broadcasting, The DuPont/Columbia Citation, The National Headliner Award, and national and regional awards from The Society of Professional Journalists, The Associated Press, United Press International, and other professional organizations and universities.

His memoir, ***I Used To Be In Radio***, was hailed as "a must-read in journalism schools, especially for those who aspire to be investigative reporters" and as "a funny and moving page-turner".

Two of his novels, ***Healing Charles*** and ***Saving Charles,*** were praised as "outstanding works of fiction." The novels are about the life of one man, set thirty years apart.

Matthews is also co-author of ***Street Business***, with Ernie Lijoi Sr., a police/crime novel based on real events in the career of retired Detective Lijoi.

Matthews's experience as an investigative reporter provides much of the background material for his Dave Haggard thriller series about a radio reporter in Washington, D.C. who finds himself at the dangerous center of major criminal investigations. The first in the series, ***Butterfly Knife***, involves the hunt for a serial killer of priests. The second, ***Brass Knuckles***, finds Dave chasing down leads in a murder/kickback scheme involving a member of Congress. The third, ***Detonator***, is about the betrayal of national trust and high-level treason.

Matthews lives and writes in Gaithersburg, Maryland.

His website is www.larrymatthews.net.

Twitter @lawrencematthew

Facebook is larrymatthewsauthor

Made in the USA
Charleston, SC
22 August 2012